Coffee Klatch

a novel by
LORRIE McCABE

Coffee Klatch

A Novel

ISBN: 979-8-35095-023-6

*For Steve, who finds a way to make everything possible,
and for my mom, Ro, an original coffee klatch member*

PROLOGUE
1997

I am the last one remaining. Strong emotions surged, and Ella Schmidt found herself holding her breath. Forty-seven years flashed through her mind in an instant.

She exhaled a deep sigh. She then pushed open the passenger door of her daughter Nan's car and proceeded to extract her diminutive frame. She closed the door softly and turned to survey her neighborhood from this vantage point.

Next door, she observed Jane's former property. Past that, on the same side of the road, she could see a portion of what used to be Anna's house. And diagonally across the street, she considered Norma and Betty's previous homes. The dwellings had endured the decades, but the original occupants were long gone. Ella teared up as she gazed upon the five houses that formed Strong Lane, the Levittown neighborhood where she'd lived since 1950.

It was a seasonably cool October Sunday on Long Island. Nan joined her mother where the older woman stood transfixed on the home's driveway.

"I guess it's very sentimental for you, Mom. This will be your last time here."

"I was just thinking," began Ella, quickly wiping her right eye with the back of her hand before tucking a short stray piece of grayish blonde hair behind her ear, as was her habit. "It has been a long time since the other first homeowners have all lived on this street with me."

Five wives with very different personalities, reflected Ella. *We found a way, though, at least in the beginning, to coexist and help each other. The five of us who were, at times, as close as sisters. But when that old secret got out…*

A competent and intelligent woman of sixty-eight, Ella was usually not one to waste time dwelling on the past. She tried to live in the present with the goal of moving forward and looking to the future, despite what life threw her way. However, she'd recently realized that since John had passed on, nostalgia and old memories popped into her head constantly.

She brought herself back from her thoughts when she heard only the last word of a question from Nan.

"I'm sorry, dear, what did you say?"

"Didn't someone else live in your house before you and Dad?" repeated Nan.

"Yes, a veteran and his wife rented this house for just about two years before we purchased it. But your father and I were the first and only ones to own it, until now."

"Well, the young couple who bought it seem very sweet, Mom. I'm sure they'll be happy here. I know I was happy growing up on this block."

"It was a very special place to raise our family. It's hard to believe I came here almost fifty years ago. Back then, the houses were so different from how they look now, with all these renovations and extensions. Remember those early photographs I have of when the houses were so small, and looked identical? There were no garages nor driveways. And all the yards were open to each other without fencing separating the plots," reminisced Ella. She continued to study the neighborhood, reimagining it as it had looked in the past. "And as neighbors in this brand-new remote development, we had to do a lot for each other."

"You'll see a few of the original ones at the town's parade today, right Mom?"

"Yes, we agreed to meet in front of the library at the conclusion of it. I wish it were all five of us…" Ella trailed off wistfully. She wondered, *Will Betty come to our little reunion, as she had promised?* Ella truly hoped so. However, Betty had previously broken her past promises to visit. The last time Ella had spoken with Betty in person was over twenty years ago at the funeral for one of their beloved neighbors.

Concentrating again on Nan, Ella said, "And thank you so much for coming with me today, dear. I really appreciate having a daughter accompany me."

"Not a problem. I'm looking forward to the celebration, too. I read in the newspaper that the parade's grand marshals will be residents who were the first to move into Levittown in 1947. Will any of your friends be part of that group?"

"No, this section of homes was built in 1948. My friends on this street were the original renters and then the subsequent owners, but they weren't the true pioneers."

"Pioneers? You make it sound so ancient, Mom."

"We were like pioneers in some ways. We settled into new homes built on a barren area of former farmland and witnessed the start of one of the first suburban communities."

"A community now celebrating its fiftieth anniversary with a big parade and festivities." Nan hesitated before sadly concluding, "I just wish Dad was here. You two should be experiencing this day together."

"He will be in my heart today, as he always is," Ella quietly responded. She took a deep breath and then said in a stronger voice, "Let's go inside and get the last of my items. I want to get the car packed and arrive at the parade early."

They walked up the front path, and as Ella unlocked the door, Nan observed, "I'm so glad you chose that cute little garden apartment out east near me. It'll be a good place for you to live until you decide what you want to do with the proceeds from the sale of the house. And don't forget that Ben and I still want you to consider moving in with us and the kids. We definitely have the room now that Jeremy is away at college."

"And Jeremy will come home for visits from college. I don't want to take his room from him. I appreciate your offer, but I don't think I can live under someone else's roof. I must decide what I want to do for this next chapter in my life," stated Ella firmly, pushing open the door with more force than necessary to make her point.

"Okay, Mom. I get it! I'm just glad you'll be living closer to me, at least for now."

Over the next thirty minutes, the two women worked efficiently side by side. The few fragile items remaining in the house had previously been packed by Ella, and Nan only needed to carry the small boxes to the car. Most of Ella's belongings had been transported to her new apartment by a moving company three days earlier. Ella hadn't wanted the delicate items handled by the movers and knew she would have time to retrieve them before the parade today. With the house closing scheduled for the next day, this was Ella's final time in her home before handing over its keys to the new owners.

"Okay, Mom. That's everything. I'll go start the car so you can take one last look before locking up."

"Thank you. I'll be out shortly, dear."

Alone with her memories, Ella thought, *it still seems impossible that it's been almost five decades since I moved into this house.* She smiled when she looked at the now empty living room and pictured its original brand-new coordinating furniture filling the space: the brown tweed armless sofa and two club chairs, with their small square scatter pillows in the then fashionable colors of turquoise and cocoa. She had been so proud of that matched set, now long gone as other more modern pieces had taken their place over the passing years. She amusedly remembered her lively next-door neighbor standing on her own front lawn, blatantly watching Ella's first furniture being delivered in that spring of 1950.

"Hey, that's some nifty new furniture you've got there," she'd enthusiastically called over as Ella directed the moving men. Ella had shyly smiled at her and gave a small wave. Then the pony-tailed woman wearing dungarees and saddle shoes (Ella recalled being a little shocked at her attire) bounded across the lawn and held out her hand to Ella.

"I'm Jane," she had gushed. "So glad to meet ya! I know you're just getting settled and all, but there's a gathering at my house on Friday at two o'clock. The other wives on the block are coming. We'd all love to get to know you. Please say you'll come…"

PART I

1950 – 1953

CHAPTER 1

Ella - 1950

At two o'clock, there was only a scant breeze carrying the muggy May air. Ella felt a trickle of sweat beginning to roll down between her shoulder blades as she nervously joined the women in her neighbor's side yard. Immediately, she realized she should not have worn her best day dress with its cinched waist and crinolines, her newest pair of nylons and sling-back pumps. The hostess, Jane Flynn, was wearing pedal pushers, a sleeveless blouse and ballerina flats. The other three were equally casual with loose-fitting dresses and bare legs. Besides being physically uncomfortable, Ella felt uneasy and very much an outsider among these four women with their confident, fast-talking New York accents.

The group represented all the families who were Ella's new neighbors, and she knew it was kind of Jane to include her at this gathering of homemakers. Their street, Strong Lane, with its five cookie-cutter, Cape Cod-style homes, was a short block connecting two longer roads. Located south of the major thoroughfare of Hempstead Turnpike, all their homes had been erected in 1948 as part of a huge assembly line system established the previous year by Levitt and Sons.

William Levitt was president of Levitt and Sons, a residential construction company that had been started by his father. William, a returning World War II veteran, had keenly observed the need for affordable housing for returning GIs. He bought tracts of Long Island farmland that had failing potato crops in an area known as Island Trees, and he began constructing small, mass-produced homes. These first Cape Cods were rented to veterans with an option to buy the home after the first year. Ella and her husband, John Schmidt, had recently bought their corner home on Strong Lane when the original GI renter opted not to purchase it.

Ella had learned previously from Jane that she, her husband, Danny Flynn, and the other three families on the block were all the original renters who had moved in as the first tenants in 1948 and subsequently bought their homes after the first year. Anna and Sal Marino lived on the other side of the Flynns, two houses down from Ella and John. Norma Lewis and her husband Gordon were located directly across the street from Jane. And the Carters, Betty and Bob, lived opposite the Marino house and next to the Lewises. Adjacent to the Lewises' house and directly across the street from Ella's home was a fenced-enclosed neighborhood sump, a deep pit designed to collect storm water through absorbent soils into the groundwater. Each of the women's homes was located on 6,000 square feet of land. Although the houses were identical on the inside with four rooms and an unfinished attic, the exteriors of the five Cape Cods were slightly different. The size, number and placement of the front windows varied as well as the colors of the synthetic shingles and shutters. There were no garages and no basements. The homes were built on concrete slabs containing radiant heating coils.

As Betty, Jane, Anna, and Norma chatted, Ella noted the four were quite comfortable with each other, having lived together on Strong Lane for almost two years. Next, Ella observed all five of them appeared to be of a similar age: early twenties. She noticed that only Betty was her own diminutive height of five feet, but that was where their physical similarities ended. Betty was as stout as Ella was petite, and her brunette hair was tightly permed whereas Ella's own straight fair hair was arranged in a small chignon. Ella also thought Betty had the loveliest peaches and cream complexion she had ever seen.

Ella guessed Anna and Jane to be about the same height, a few inches taller than her and Betty. Anna, full-figured and olive-skinned with naturally curly dark hair cut into a short style, was a sharp contrast to slender Jane, who had longer, reddish-blonde tresses and a fair complexion with a smattering of light freckles across the bridge of her nose. Anna, who upon introduction gave Ella a warm hug, seemed serene and kind; *a woman*, Ella theorized, *I can truly connect with*. Jane was bouncy and energetic; *more spirited than me*, Ella surmised.

The tallest and most glamorous of the group was willowy Norma. When everyone moved inside to Jane's kitchen, a confident Norma scooted past Betty and sat down next to Ella at the chrome and Formica table. Timidly perched on a modern dinette chair with a turquoise vinyl seat pad, which only made her sweat even more, Ella quietly observed her seatmate. She admired Norma's even-toned, flawless skin, stylishly cut chestnut hair and slightly hooded green eyes. Her five-and-a-half-foot frame boasted the best figure of all the women, and even though she was wearing a casual shift dress, it fit her perfectly. Her bare legs were shapely, and, after Norma slipped off her shoes, Ella noticed the same blood-red nail polish that had been expertly painted on her fingernails was applied on her toenails as well. Norma was the only one who stuck out her pinky finger when she picked up her coffee cup delicately to sip the hot brew.

Listening to the din of conversation, Ella soon realized that these women all had quite different personalities as well. Betty, it appeared, was the gossip of the group and was earnestly talking about the couple who had recently moved out of Ella's house.

"I don't care what you say, I always thought Ted and Alice Martin were a bit hoity-toity. Of course, they couldn't buy the little cape cod like we all did. They had to have a brand-new Levitt ranch with a fireplace and carport. Those homes cost more money, too. And they still have the same four rooms. Now I ask you ladies, is that worth the extra pounds?"

"Dollars, darling," interjected Norma dryly while inspecting one of her lacquered nails. "You are not in England anymore. And from what I hear, the new models are being sold for around eight thousand." She lifted her gaze, shrugged her shoulders, and added, "It's not that huge of a difference from what we paid for our homes. And in addition to the fireplace and carport, Levitt is throwing in a twelve-and-a-half-inch television."

Betty, talking with her mouth full of Jane's homemade crumb cake, pointed out, "Well, those ranch owners are getting the same size loo as we have in our homes, so Alice isn't any better than us."

"She never thought she was better. And we call it a bathroom, not a loo. You are showing your English side again, Bets," drawled Norma, and then, turning to Ella, she sarcastically clarified, "Betty Carter, born and raised in merry old England as Elizabeth James, met her very sweet American husband, Bob, when he was stationed during the war at an English air base near her family home. They met at some dreary local dance and dated throughout the war. At least that's how her back story was described in our infamous local newspaper article. Isn't that correct, Bets?"

"Gee whiz, Nor," interjected Jane, clearly annoyed. "Let's not bring up that newspaper incident again!"

Ella noted the color rising in Betty's fair face. She was perplexed over the 'newspaper incident' but she could see there was some friction between Betty and Norma.

Before Betty could counterpoint, Anna calmly changed the subject. "I will miss Alice. I hope she comes back to this side of town to visit us. But now we have a new friend in Ella. Why don't you tell us a little about yourself?"

All eyes at the cramped kitchen table turned to look expectantly into Ella's anxious blue ones. She silently gulped and clasped her shaking hands together in her lap. However, before she could speak, one of the two babies, each situated in their own mosquito-netted carriage under a tiny newly planted tree in the side yard outside Jane's kitchen door, began to fuss. Betty's four-month-old, Robert Junior, and Anna's newborn daughter, Susan, had both been sleeping since the start of the group's meeting. The only other homemaker who had a child was Jane. Her two-year-old, Pamela, was quietly playing with her dolls on the floor of the living room next to the kitchen.

Anna leaped out of her seat to check on the babies, but Betty declared, "I'll go. That's Robby fussing. I recognized his cry. He probably lost his binky. I'll be back in a flash."

"So, Ella, I understand from Jane you're from Germany," prompted Norma, re-crossing her legs, and turning towards Ella. "That's fascinating. Tell us more, sweetie."

"Ja... I mean yes. I am from Berlin originally, but, when I was eleven years, my mother and I were evacuated out of the city because of the bombing. We stayed with my mother's cousin and her husband at their farm in the country until the war ended," explained Ella nervously in her lightly German-accented English. She suddenly wondered if any of them would resent her foreign nationality, and at that thought, her anxiety increased.

"Did you have any brothers or sisters? What about your father?" asked Jane. "I come from a big extended family from the Bronx, the O'Briens. I can't imagine a family consisting of just a mother and daughter."

"I had two older brothers killed in the war, as was my father. My mother died of complications from measles a few months before the war ended," said Ella without elaborating. The details of her life during and immediately after the war were too painful for her to share yet with these strangers.

"You poor thing. You have no immediate family remaining," said Anna, her deep brown eyes displaying great empathy.

"That is sad," Norma agreed wholeheartedly. "But, since all our spouses had to serve in the war to be eligible for these homes, I assume your husband was a GI that you met in Europe?"

"Yes, John was an English-German translator for the United States Army," Ella proudly supplied.

"That means you and Betty have a lot in common, seeing how you're both war brides and all," said Anna as Betty resumed her seat at the table after coming in from outside.

"I guess," replied Betty. "But at least I come from a country that fought on the same side as the USA."

"She's got a point," added Jane. "It might not be a good idea, Ella, to advertise you're from an enemy country that was led by that monster Hitler."

Mortified, a silent Ella immediately cast her eyes downward and wrung her hands which still lay helplessly on her lap.

Norma stared icily at Jane and Betty, then quietly said, "Hitler's dead and not every German was our enemy. Ella isn't responsible for her country's politics. My maiden name was Wolf, and my father's family came from Germany many years before the first world war because they didn't agree with the Kaiser. When the time came for the U. S. to join that war, Dad fought in the American army, even though my grandparents at home in New York were being given a hard time because of their foreign accents."

"Thank you, Norma," whispered Ella as she lifted her gaze and looked gratefully at the woman sitting next to her. "My family did not agree with the Third Reich, but we had no way out of our country."

"Well, you are very welcome here. We are definitely a nation of immigrants," pointed out Anna. "No one comes from bigger Italian American families than my Sal and me."

"I'm sorry for my stupid comment. I'm always putting my foot in my mouth," said a contrite Jane, her gray-blue eyes sincere. "And you're right, Anna. All our families at some point came from other countries. That's what makes up the good old U. S. of A! My ancestors and Danny's were all from Ireland, and boy-o-boy, were they ever treated poorly when they came over! 'No Irish Need Apply' and all that baloney."

"I'm sorry for my remark, too," apologized Betty, reaching over to pat Ella's arm.

Ella just nodded and gave them all a small smile. Although Norma and Anna had defended her nationality, Ella wondered if these four women could ever truly accept a German native as a member of their group, especially since their countries had been at war only five years earlier.

Betty turned towards Norma and said, "I didn't know you have German heritage, Nor. I've lived next door to you for two years, and I figured your ancestors came on the Mayflower."

"Why would you think that?" Norma asked coolly.

"I guess because you never tell us anything personal about yourself, so I had to assume," replied Betty equally coolly while raising her eyebrows.

Norma cast a haughty look at Betty and replied, "Well, Bets, you know what they say when you 'assume.' You make an ass out of you and..."

Anna cleared her throat and tactfully changed the subject to current events by swiftly asking, "What do you all think about this growing conflict in Korea?"

"I don't even know where that country is," exclaimed Betty, turning her attention back to the group. "Why get involved with some problem in the Orient?"

"Because Truman needs to look tough on communism. And weren't you glad in England when America got involved with your problem with Hitler?" challenged Norma.

Ella grew uneasy again. She did not want the conversation to stay on this track involving any talk of war, either from the past or possibly the future.

Anna interjected, "I think our president may be trying to send a message that the U.S. will do what it takes to prevent communism from spreading."

"And come to the aid of our allies in South Korea," added Norma.

"But at what cost, Nor?" said Anna wearily. "None of us want this to escalate into another war. We lost too many young men in the last one. The wounds are still too fresh."

"Anna, this could be the first step in a communist campaign to take over the world. As much as I don't want to see a war either, we might have to fight," said Norma.

"I just pray it can all be settled diplomatically without bloodshed," replied a hopeful Anna.

Ella was impressed with Anna's and Norma's knowledge of world events. She and John discussed the news all the time, but she did not feel confident enough yet to express her opinions to outsiders. She did, however, notice Jane and Betty did not seem as informed as the other two and avoided contributing anything further to the discussion.

Suddenly, there was a rumble of thunder in the far distance. The women noted the formerly sunny afternoon had started to darken and a spring storm seemed to be approaching. They decided to call it a day and began to collect themselves and their babies for their respective walks home.

As the group filed out to the side yard, Jane explained to Ella, "We try to do these afternoon gatherings at least once a week in good weather, during the babies' nap times. It keeps us from going batty until our hubbies get home. We just chat and indulge in coffee and treats. We should really give our little meetings a name...something more than just 'gatherings.' I don't know...what do you all think?"

"In England, you would call it teatime, I suppose," suggested Betty.

"But we aren't drinking tea. Just good old American coffee. Coffee Time sounds silly," said Norma.

Ella quietly offered, "In Germany, we had a word *Kaffeeklatsch*, roughly meaning 'coffee chat.' Literally, *klatsch* means gossip. When people anglicize it, they say coffee klatch, spelled k-l-a-t-c-h."

"As my Irish grandmother would say, that's a grand idea!" proclaimed Jane, eager to make amends to Ella for her earlier disparagement. "The Strong Lane Coffee Klatch it is!"

CHAPTER 2

Norma - 1950

Norma Lewis sat at her kitchen table stirring her Monday morning coffee and contemplating the most recent gathering of the women of Strong Lane. She should really think of it as last Friday's 'coffee klatch,' the name their new neighbor Ella had proposed. Norma liked the suggestion; it was a catchy phrase.

Dressed for the office, Gordon entered the kitchen. Just over six feet tall with an athletic build, he leaned down to give his wife a peck on her cheek, took a sip from her coffee cup, and said, "You look deep in thought, Nor. What's that beautiful brain thinking about?"

"I was thinking about our new neighbor, Ella Schmidt. I liked what I saw of her. The woman may be a little timid, but who wouldn't be when meeting the four of us?" Norma continued sarcastically, "After all, we've been together in the wilderness for almost two years now and pretty much know each other's good and bad points. Betty's gossipy but bakes a mean cake. Jane is always trying to boss us around but she's the fighter you want in your corner. And Anna is just a saint, maybe too good to be true."

"And you, my lovely wife? How do they summarize your pluses and minuses? Of course, I'm truly biased and see only your good side," said Gordon as he took the lunchbox Norma handed him.

Norma shrugged and replied, "I suppose those three consider me a bit opinionated, but they chiefly get my dry sense of humor. For the most part, we have fun and quite a few laughs."

"Seriously, Nor, it might help if you stop calling Levittown 'the wilderness.' I know it's not as posh of a Long Island town as where you grew up, but most of us on this street hail from the New York City boroughs. I think we're all proud of our status as new homeowners. Having a house on a bit of land is something I never thought I'd have after growing up in a Brooklyn apartment."

Norma noted the sense of achievement in his voice, although she also detected the hurt in his eyes. She grew serious and rose from her chair to give Gordon a hug and a kiss before murmuring in his arms, "Don't pay any attention to me and my silly mocking. I *am* proud of this home you bought for us. I know the town will eventually grow. And I'm enormously proud that you're the only husband on this block who's taking advantage of the G.I. Bill and going to college at night after a long day at work. There is something so sexy about being married to an engineer."

"I have another year and a half of schooling before I'll be able to call myself an aeronautical engineer. Is being married to a mailroom supervisor good enough for now?" he asked with amusement while nuzzling her ear.

"As I promised on our wedding day two years ago, Mr. Lewis, I'd follow you to the ends of the earth."

"As long as you were wearing a designer dress, a fur coat and some expensive jewelry on that journey," laughed Gordon, extracting himself from Norma's embrace. "Listen, sweetheart, I've got to run, or I'll be late for the office. Since I don't have school tonight, are we still on for our date night?"

"Yes. I'll find out what time that movie starts. I wish this little town would get its own movie theater, so we didn't have to drive so far west to find one..."

"All in good time, my impatient wife." He threw her a kiss and rushed out the door to their only car, a 1947 green Ford Coupe.

Norma watched her attractive husband leave. His dark hair and eyes gave him a movie-star quality. *I've dated many handsome men in my past, but my darling Gor has qualities way beyond his appearance,* she thought.

She resumed her seat at the table and sipped at her now luke-warm coffee. She mulled over what Gordon had said, but she still thought of this area of former farmland as a wilderness. She had been raised in a town with roots going back to the nineteenth century, located about ten miles west of Levittown. Her parents still lived in Garden City where Norma had been born in the magical summer of 1927. Her June birth was exactly a month after Charles Lindbergh departed on his famous solo transatlantic flight from her hometown's Roosevelt Field. As another nod to greatness, Norma was named after her mother's favorite American movie actress, Norma Shearer.

Norma had been raised in a comfortable mid-sized house. It was not among the larger manor homes in the incorporated village, but it certainly was not considered one of the smallest either. Her father was an accountant who currently directed his department at the Sperry Corporation, the same company where Gordon worked as the mail-room supervisor.

She frankly observed the compact kitchen surrounding her. It had a narrow stove featuring three electric-coiled burners over a small oven; white steel cabinets above the sink and stove; a short refrigerator with a freezer box inside; and a Bendix washing machine. The room was roughly half the size of the kitchen in her parents' home. Norma remembered being shocked at its small dimensions when she and Gordon had first toured the model Levitt home. However, if it was any consolation, her neighbors had the same exact kitchens in their identically sized houses. Norma amusedly pondered that due to Levitt's assembly-line styled houses, no homemaker on this street could think of herself as any better than the others, since the playing field among them was so even.

Norma's thoughts continued to whirl. *If I didn't worship that good-looking husband of mine so much, I'd have never agreed to live in such a small place.* Gordon had accepted and loved her despite what she considered her greatest shortcoming, and, because of that one unselfish act of his, she would do anything to make him happy... including agreeing to rent and then buy this affordable, yet lackluster, dwelling.

As Norma rose from her chair to wash her empty coffee cup, she observed through the window Anna Marino crossing the street and making her way towards Norma's kitchen door. With her sleeping daughter, Susan, cradled in the crook of her left arm, Anna opened the door. During the weekdays, all the Strong Lane women were usually informal with each other, walking through each other's unlocked doors throughout the day.

"Good morning, Norma! Mind if I come in?" Anna's greeting was cheerful but whispered so as not to wake her baby.

"Sure, Anna. Let's go in the living room so you can sit in a comfortable chair with that adorable angel of yours," suggested Norma after taking a quick peek at Anna's bundle. "What is she – almost two months now?"

Anna carefully sat down in the club chair Norma indicated and answered, "Yes, next week, and she's sleeping a good six-hour stretch now at night. Sal and I are so thrilled to get some consecutive hours of rest."

Norma liked babies and thought Susan was precious, but she didn't like to dwell on the subject for too long. Instead, she asked, "What brings you to my house this morning? May I help you with something?"

"No, I just came to have a discussion with you, and I'll cut to the chase because I don't know how long this little one will sleep."

"You've got me intrigued, Anna. What's up?"

"Nor, why aren't you and Betty getting along?" Anna asked quietly with a concerned look on her face. "I think it might have been obvious to our new neighbor this past Friday. It still can't be that silly newspaper article. That was a year ago."

"I don't know what to tell you, Anna," Norma started defensively. "I think Betty is still annoyed that the local paper used my photo in the article instead of one with her. But I can't help what was printed."

"Betty was the one who had contacted the newspaper when she read they were looking to interview a homemaker in our town. She wanted to be the sole subject for the article about coping with this new suburban life," Anna said.

"Yes, I know. I had no idea that a reporter was interviewing her about being an English war bride when I popped over to her house.

He decided to ask me questions too and use both our stories of how we ended up in Levittown. If you remember correctly, the final article's text was mainly about Betty since she has a more interesting backstory. But, the photographer with the reporter kept giving me lecherous stares and insisted on taking pictures of the both of us. There were shots taken of us separately and together, but only the one of me alone in front of my house ended up in the newspaper. It's not my fault the newspaper chose not to use one that included Betty."

Anna carefully added, "I'm sure you didn't mean it, but the way Betty tells the story, you flirted with the photographer, Nor. She also thinks you dressed extra nice that day because you knew the newspaper men were there and planned on stealing her thunder."

"Anna, you know that's not true! Betty never shared with any of us on this street that she had contacted the newspaper. When I went over to her house that day, it was to borrow something, not to be interviewed. And I would *never* have flirted with that sleazy shutterbug!"

"I guess it's all a matter of how each of you remembers that day..."

"It's beyond that one incident. I can sense when someone doesn't like me, and for some reason, Betty doesn't. I remember two years ago when Gor and I had moved into this house the day after Betty and Bob had moved into theirs. We walked over to meet our new next-door neighbors. Bob was as pleasant as could be, but Betty looked Gor and me up and down, like she was sizing us up. She had an annoyed look on her face and hardly spoke."

"Well..." paused Anna before finding the correct words, "You and Gordon are a handsome couple, and I think Betty can be easily intimidated by appearances."

"I know some women can be put off by the way I look. Some think I'll steal their husbands, even though that's ridiculous. I get it. I went to a high school with a lot of cliques, and since I was a cheerleader and, I admit, popular, I made some girls outside my circle feel insecure. But I had two best friends, Dorothy and Lillian, who were not in that cheerleading crowd. We three always had each other's backs despite being part of different groups. I can be loyal to anyone who accepts me and gives me a chance. Like you and Jane did when we first met, and hopefully Ella too as she gets to know me. But Betty doesn't even try to like me."

"But you do seem to pick on her sometimes," Anna countered thoughtfully.

"Because her dislike of me gets my back up. She and I will never see eye to eye."

"So, agree to disagree, but can't you try harder to get along? You two have been neighbors for almost two years now. It's difficult enough out here in a developing suburb. We wives need to stick together," soothed Anna.

"I did try, and I'll continue trying. She's not warm and welcoming like you are, Anna. Betty can be a fairly rigid person."

Anna nodded and acknowledged, "I agree. Betty is not fond of hugs or expressing her feelings. Maybe it's her British 'stiff upper lip' and how she was raised. Cut her some slack, though. You, Jane, and I didn't live through the war here in America in the same way Betty had to in England."

Norma considered this statement for a moment. She'd never thought about what it would have been like for Betty, spending her formative years with the war practically in her backyard.

Anna continued, "And Betty has many good qualities. She's a very good neighbor. When my Susan and I first came home from the hospital, Betty had called me each morning to see if I needed anything from the stores. She offered to put Robby in his baby carriage and walk up to the Village Green for me. Her baby isn't much older than mine, and, believe me, it's no easy task shopping with a little one! Betty can also be a good listener. I've had some new-mother frustrations with this first baby, and Betty is always there to offer advice since she has two months more experience at motherhood."

"Oh, Anna, you're too good! Of course Betty is a good listener," said Norma. "She's a gossip and wants the dirt on all of us. She's always digging so she can get an upper hand."

"I'll concede Betty is a bit insecure and tries to compensate for it by being inquisitive. I think she wants to know the details of other people's lives to make herself feel better about her own."

"Wow, Anna, you're like our group's own little Dr. Freud," Norma said and then wondered, *what does Anna hypothesize about me?*

Anna didn't seem flustered by this comparison. She just shrugged and offered, "Let Betty be nosey. What harm can it really do to answer her questions?"

It can do plenty of harm, agonized Norma internally, *to those of us who have secrets we don't want revealed.* Despite Anna's appeal for kindness and understanding, Norma needed to protect herself and not allow Betty to put her life under the microscope. Although Norma hid behind her sarcasm, her anxiety was at a constant high. She worried what the others would think if Betty uncovered her skeleton in the closet. *The best way to get Betty to stop asking questions,* theorized Norma, *is to put her on the defense, and the only way I know how to put Betty on the defense is to go on the offense.*

CHAPTER 3

Betty – 1950

Betty Carter finished diapering her five-month-old son, Robby, and proceeded to dress him appropriately for this warm and sunny June day. Since her husband, Bob, would be minding their son while she attended this afternoon's coffee klatch, Betty didn't dress the baby in one of his better outfits. Whenever she brought Robby with her to a neighborhood gathering, she wanted him to look his best.

Betty carried Robby from the small second bedroom at the rear of the house into the front living room and placed him on his stomach in his playpen. He had recently started to roll from his front to his back, and his parents were delighted with this new development.

Bob was lounging on the sofa with the heels of his feet resting on the coffee table in front of him. He had been reading yesterday's newspaper but looked up with a grin as Robby earnestly floundered to turn himself over.

"Bob, I wish you wouldn't prop up your feet on the furniture. It looks so working class," Betty lightly scolded as she picked up the feather duster she had abandoned before attending to Robby.

The affable Bob laughed and said, "We are working class so what's the difference? I don't own the Long Island Rail Road; I'm just a conductor on it."

Betty noticed Bob had pulled the table closer to the sofa to accommodate his legs, and she made a mental note to position the piece back in place later. Although sparsely furnished, her living room had to be just so. Betty picked up her husband's legs, dusted the table under them and then grabbed a stray magazine to place under his shoes. She dropped his legs back onto the table.

Although Bob was six inches taller than her, he was the shortest man on Strong Lane. Norma, Jane, and Ella's husbands were all six feet or more. And Anna's husband, Sal, despite being under six feet, still stood a few inches over Bob. Betty knew Bob was sensitive about his height, and she never brought up the matter. When they met in her hometown in England during the war, he told her he hadn't dated as a teen growing up in his New York borough. She assumed it was because of his height, but since she was only five feet without heels, his stature never bothered her.

"What time will you be home from Ella's house this afternoon, Betty?" asked Bob as he went back to his paper. "I'll have to leave at five to start my night shift."

"Oh, I'll be back before then. And don't forget to reheat those leftovers for yourself to eat before you leave," reminded Betty. "Honestly, Bob, aren't you a bit cheesed off with these night shifts? You've been doing them for the last five years."

"Cheesed off?"

"Don't be daft, Bob. You know what I mean. Aren't you annoyed still having to do these all-nighters? Did you ever look into applying for a supervisor position?"

"The occasional night shift doesn't bother me. There are less passengers, so the work is easier. And, as I told you before, I don't think I'd like being a supervisor. I'm happy doing what I'm doing," admitted Bob without animosity.

Betty gritted her teeth. Bob was a pleasant and soft-spoken man, the antithesis of the men in her English family. It was these character traits that had attracted her to the kind American serviceman. However, his lack of ambition greatly bothered her.

Frustrated, Betty attempted to keep her voice even when she responded, "A supervisor position would pay more money. We could use it now that we have a family, and our budget is tighter. Don't you want to buy nicer things for Robby and me?"

"Betty, I make enough money for us to live comfortably, even with an extra mouth to feed," Bob stated firmly. He disliked it when Betty started on these tirades about money. He was a simple man with basic needs. He sometimes felt his wife would never be satisfied with her lot in life, and the thought filled him with sorrow.

"Of all the chaps on this block, you must earn the least," continued Betty, warming to her argument, although still forcing her tone to remain calm. She knew Bob would not respond if she started to raise her voice. "I had to be frugal during the war living in England with all the shortages and rations. Is it so wrong to want more now, especially since we live in the 'land of plenty,' as everyone calls America?"

"Betty, honey, I do the best I can."

"My mum used to say to my brothers and me that sometimes you have to try harder than just your best."

Bob sighed and said, "I take extra shifts when we need a little bit more cash, like last month when we had that unexpected plumbing problem. But life is too short to put so much emphasis on money. We have our own home and a car. We have clothing, food, and modest savings. We're clunking along nicely."

"I don't want to 'clunk along' as you put it," wailed Betty finally losing her composure. "If I wanted to do that, I'd have stayed in England. I thought when I agreed to marry an American and move across the pond, I'd be whisked away to a more interesting life. I thought life would be easier, but it really isn't."

"I'm sorry if I disappoint you, Betty," Bob said sadly. "When we first met at that local dance near your family's home, you told me you wanted nothing more than to leave England. I was able to grant you that wish."

His disheartened look was not lost on Betty, so she relented with true affection and said, "Oh, Bob, you know you were my hero getting me away from my barmy home life. If it hadn't been for you, I probably would have turned into an old maid, unhappily minding my aging parents."

Betty's father and her two older brothers had been a pugnacious threesome. Argue first and ask questions later had seemed to be their truculent motto. Although they had always been respectful to women, the three men had inherited short fuses and had constantly picked fights with their male contemporaries. Betty's mother had been as quiet as a wren during her husband's and sons' tirades, letting them blow off steam at any perceived injustices. However, as a teenager, Betty, the only daughter, had found her voice and nastily ranted back at her brothers if they had dared to shout at her.

Looking back, she knew deep down she had loved her two brothers, but she wouldn't have been surprised if she ever learned their hot-headed tempers had led to their young deaths. Both were British soldiers who had died during the war. Betty had been dating Bob when her parents had received each of the telegrams from the war department. Stationed at an air base northeast of London, Bob had been wonderful, supporting both Betty and her parents during that traumatic period. Ironically, Betty's father's anger had seemed to disappear after the unjust deaths of both his sons. Her now subdued Dad and heartbroken Mum still resided in Betty's childhood home on the other side of the Atlantic Ocean.

Betty ventured one last attempt to spark a bit of gumption in her husband. "Bob, maybe the railroad isn't the right job for you. Have you ever thought of doing some night classes on the GI Bill, like Gordon Lewis? I asked him about it, and he graciously told me he'd give you all the brochures and research he has on how to get started in the veterans' college program. Maybe you can investigate a new career path? Norma says Gordon will get a big increase in salary when he finishes his degree and becomes an engineer."

"Gordon's a decent fellow. He's a good neighbor and always the first guy to lend a hand. I truly like him. And I give him all the credit in the world working a nine to five job and then going to college at night," said Bob. "It's not for me, though. I was never a great student and just about graduated high school before the war came along. And I was grateful my Uncle Charlie could get me into the LIRR when I returned from the war. A rail job with a pension like mine is hard to come by.

A lot of guys I served with would have done anything for such a good position right out of the service. I'm a lucky fellow!"

"Yes, dear," a deflated Betty conceded. *The lucky one in all this,* she thought to herself, *is Norma, since Gordon has an upwardly mobile career-path that Bob lacks. Norma will have the easier life that I desire, in addition to her good looks. It's not fair that some women have everything.*

A few hours later, Betty walked down the street to Ella's corner house. Ella was hosting her first coffee klatch, and Betty wanted to be the first to arrive. She hoped to speak privately with her new neighbor before the other three women walked in. She had something weighing heavily on her mind since she'd first met Ella at Jane's house the month before.

"Greetings, Ella," said Betty after she gave a quick knock on the door and proceeded to walk into Ella's kitchen.

"Good afternoon, Betty. You are very punctual," exclaimed a surprised Ella standing at the sink filling her coffee pot.

"I came to see if you needed any help setting up. You've attended quite a few of our gatherings, but I thought you might be a little nervous hosting your first one. Bob is watching my Robby until he leaves for work, so I'm a free mother hen today," quipped Betty.

"That is very kind of you. Would you like to fill the percolator with the right amount of ground coffee? I am not sure how strong the other ladies like it."

"Oh, sure. Leave it to me. I'll have it done in a jiff," agreed Betty, and she proceeded to scoop from the can Ella provided.

"Since my table in this kitchen is very small, I set up a fold-able table in my living room for our coffee klatch," explained Ella, returning to the kitchen after bringing the last of her baked goods into the next room.

"That sounds topping, Ella. And that chocolate cake you just brought in looks divine. You'll have to give me the recipe," Betty warmly noted.

"I will be happy to," beamed Ella. She looked around her kitchen and added, "I think I have brought everything we need into the living room. We will just wait on the coffee."

Betty set the coffee pot on the stove's burner and switched it on. Then she turned and said, "Ella, I also came early because I wanted to apologize for that remark I made at Jane's last month."

Ella had a puzzled expression, so Betty continued with, "When I first met you, I had compared how I came from a country that fought with America whereas you are from a country that fought on the other side. I feel terrible about saying it, especially now that I've discovered more about you."

"That is all right, Betty," Ella stated stiffly. "You apologized on that day."

"No, it was still wrong. And it was daft of me to harp on a difference when I now realize we two women have the most in common," pointed out Betty. "We were both war brides, born across the pond in Europe and not here in the USA. We both experienced the war as teenagers in a more direct way than any of the other gals on Strong Lane. We each lost two brothers in the war, our only siblings. Both of us were the youngest and only daughters in our families."

"I suppose I never thought of it that way," acknowledged an astonished Ella. "We *do* have many similarities in our lives."

"I'm glad you agree," said Betty with a smile. "It will be nice to have someone else to confide in. I'm close to Anna even though she was raised here in the New York area. She's such a dear. And Jane and Norma are good neighbors, but Jane is too wacky, in my mind, to be a true confidante, and Norma is just too different from me, from all of us really."

"How so?" questioned Ella.

"Norma grew up in a well-to-do family. Her father went to college and had a professional job. She lived in an upscale Main Street USA kind of neighborhood and had the better things in life as a kid. You and I are from simple people, and we struggled through the war during our adolescence. Jane and Anna were both born in America, but each grew up in blue-collar families in New York City boroughs. I guess what I'm trying to say is that Norma is in a different class than the rest of us. Frankly, I find her a little stuck up."

"I do not know this term 'stuck up,' and I do not know the four of you too well yet," Ella cautiously replied. She then thoughtfully added, "Nevertheless, to me, everyone seems to be helpful and friendly, always laughing and joking. That is important for good neighbors. Norma seems like a good person, and that is more valuable than how one was raised. Do you not think so too, Betty?"

Another fan for Norma, thought Betty with discouragement. Before she could answer, Jane, with her two-year-old, Pamela, in tow, burst through the kitchen door. Mother and daughter were wearing identical cobalt blue wide swing skirts. There appeared to be a large dog design applied to the fabric of each skirt.

"What on earth are you wearing, Jane?" asked Betty. "Is that a coiffed poodle on your skirt?"

"It's the new fad. It's called a poodle skirt. Aren't they darling? I saw the idea in a magazine and knew I just had to have it," Jane crowed. "And then at a store near my parents in the Bronx, I found mother-daughter matching ones! I had to get one for my Pammy too. I could not believe they made one in such a tiny size for her."

Just then Norma came in, and Jane turned her attention to the new arrival, repeating the fashion story. Betty, with mirth in her voice, whispered to Ella, "See what I mean? Jane is a little wacky. Sometimes I can't take her seriously."

That evening was warm and pleasant with the summer sky still bright at six o'clock. Bob had departed for his night shift an hour earlier, and Betty was out for a stroll pushing Robby in his baby carriage. As she made her way around the block of homes behind Strong Lane, she happily recalled today's meeting at Ella's. Everyone had had an enjoyable time, and she was glad no friction occurred. Betty thought Norma had been very pleasant and kept her usually snide observations in check. As a result, Betty had relaxed and tried to listen more to the other women instead of asking as many questions as she usually did. Overall, she was pleased the day was a success for Ella, who had initially seemed tense hosting the group for the first time.

As Betty now turned the corner and was back on Strong Lane, she approached the front of the fence-enclosed sump next to Norma's house. Inexplicitly, a sudden shiver ran down her spine, despite the mild weather. *That's odd,* thought Betty, *like a goose walking over my grave.*

She shook off the peculiar feeling and continued pushing the carriage on the sidewalk. She smiled when she noticed Robby had fallen asleep. "I adore you, my little angel," she murmured joyfully.

Looking ahead to the Lewises' plot, Betty spotted Gordon's car now parked at the curb. It had not been there when she had started her walk a half hour ago. As she approached her neighbors' home, she could hear soft music playing and laughter drifting through the open front living room window. When Betty came abreast of the window, she could see through its screen that Norma was in Gordon's tight embrace. The couple was dancing to their own slow rhythm with Norma's head bent back laughing and gazing up at her tall husband.

Betty watched, unobserved, for a moment. The smile slid from her face before she headed to her own house next door.

CHAPTER 4

Jane – 1950

It was the middle of July, and Jane Flynn was preparing to take advantage of the pleasant morning to walk to the local stores. Jane thought the seven Village Greens Levitt had built and scattered throughout his town were the most beneficial perks of the new housing development. The one located nearest to Strong Lane consisted of a row of small stores and businesses, a children's playground, a huge swimming pool and a smaller splash pool for little ones. Housed in the Green's long, single-storied, partitioned business building were a butcher shop, bakery, delicatessen, liquor store, drug store, dry cleaners, barber shop and beauty salon. During the week, Jane could accomplish most of her errands at the convenient Green. She only needed their one vehicle,

Danny's pick-up truck, once a week to drive to the brand-new super-market about two miles from Strong Lane.

Danny, dressed in blue jeans, a sleeveless chambray work shirt and steel toe work boots, entered the kitchen where Jane was writing a brief list of the items she needed to purchase. Two-year-old Pamela was finishing her breakfast in her highchair when Danny swooped in and gave his daughter a kiss on her cheek. The little girl giggled in delight.

The sight of her muscular six-foot tall, red-haired, blue-eyed husband never failed to give Jane's heart a little jolt. She was still as attracted to him as she had been when they first started going steady during their freshman year of high school. Apart from the interlude of three years during and immediately after the war, they had not been separated since the ninth grade. She had missed him terribly when, at the age of eighteen, he voluntarily enlisted in the United States Navy's Seabees.

Since he was old enough to hold a hammer and fit into a small hardhat, Daniel Flynn had apprenticed at his father's home construction company, Flynn and Sons. It had been a foregone conclusion that Danny and his two older brothers would enlist in the Seabees during World War II. The Flynn brothers had been three of the 325,000 men who served in this naval division of skilled construction workers whose task had been to assist in building naval bases in the theatres of war. Danny had served in the South Pacific from 1943 through 1946, completing an extra year in his tour of duty after VJ Day had been celebrated in August 1945. When he had been discharged in December 1946, Jane had been patiently waiting for him in the Bronx neighborhood of their childhood. They were married the following spring. One year later, they had moved with their newborn daughter to their house on Strong Lane.

"What-cha doing, Janie?" asked Danny as he picked up the steel lunchbox Jane had left on the counter.

"I'm making a list of a few things I need up at the Green. Pammy and I are going to stroller up there."

"I can drive you before I head off to the job site," offered Danny. "We can put Pammy's stroller in the back of the pick-up and then you only have to walk home after you're done."

"No thanks. We're not quite ready to go, and I don't want you to be late. You don't need your father's fury first thing on a Monday morning. It's not too warm outside yet. Pammy and I will have our little outing this morning before going to Norma's for coffee klatch this afternoon."

"Dad runs a tight ship, but he's okay if me or my brothers are a little late due to a family matter."

"We'll be fine," Jane said and rose from her chair to give her husband an affectionate hug and kiss.

Danny looked down at his much shorter wife and returned her kiss before he said, "And don't forget, babe, I'm going to that four o'clock Yankee game today with the guys after work. I should be home some-time after seven. I'm sorry I'll be missing dinner with you and Pammy."

Jane laughed and pointed out, "You're not sorry. When it comes to the Yankees, I know I come in second place."

Danny grew serious and said, "Never. You and Pammy mean the world to me. I can live without baseball, but I can't live without you two."

"Enough mushy stuff, you big red-headed lug. Off to work you go!"

An hour later, Jane helped her daughter into the powder blue and white Taylor Tot stroller with its little wood seat and metal tray. The two passed the Marinos' house next door where Anna was busy watering her prized front garden.

"Your flowers are looking great, Anna. Wish I had your green thumb!"

"Good morning, Jane," greeted Anna as she continued with her hose. "I'd be glad to show you what to do to get a flower patch started."

"Gosh, no. I'm too impatient to cultivate such pretty plants," Jane cheerfully replied. "We're headed to the Green. Do you need anything from there?"

"No thanks, Jane. We're good, but why don't you leave Pammy with me? She can help me water the flowers until Susan wakes from her morning nap."

Jane leaned down and asked her daughter if she would like to help Mrs. Marino, and Pamela started to climb out of her stroller with enthusiasm. Jane helped her down and the toddler ran to Anna's open arms.

"Thank you, Anna. I'll be back in a jiffy. I'll still take the stroller with me to carry my packages," said Jane with a wave before continuing on her way.

After buying a few items at the delicatessen, Jane headed to the butcher shop. She left the stroller with her package in front of the store, knowing both items would be there when she returned. As she walked into the shop, Jane noticed a woman at the counter and two other customers waiting in line to be served. Fred, a middle-aged balding man with an obvious paunch under his white butcher's apron, was speaking loudly, clearly agitated. It took Jane a moment to realize the woman standing in front of him was Ella Schmidt. Ella seemed upset, and the two women waiting for their turns were staring at Ella's back with clear looks of annoyance on their faces.

"Lady, speak up," Fred barked, his round face flushed. "I still don't understand what you want."

Ella, nervous and embarrassed, cleared her throat and meekly explained, "I am very sorry. I cannot think of the correct English term for the meat I need. It is what I use to make schnitzel."

"Schnitzel? Is that some kind of German food?" asked a sarcastic Fred. "You came to the wrong place, lady. I run a good American butcher shop. I don't supply no German specialties, especially since my son was killed by your people during the war!"

There was an audible intake of breath on Ella's part as Fred now stared at her with blatant anger. Just as Ella turned, as if to leave the shop, Jane pushed past the other two customers and stood next to Ella. She put her arm around her neighbor's shoulders and, in the process, turned them both to face the proprietor.

"What seems to be the problem here, Fred?" implored Jane, trying to keep her voice controlled. Inside, she was steaming over the way Ella was being treated.

"You tell me, Mrs. Flynn. Do you know this Kraut?"

Jane, seeing Ella wince at the derogatory term, gave Fred a piercing stare and said emphatically, "This *woman* is Mrs. John Schmidt, my neighbor, *and* she's an American citizen. Her husband served bravely in the US Army during the war. I'm sure I speak for everyone here in saying we are sorry for the loss of your son, but this good woman didn't kill him. How dare you treat a customer this way and call her names?"

"Now, hold on, Mrs. Flynn," Fred began, adding a conciliatory tone to his voice and appearing to back down a smidge. The Flynns were good customers, especially two weeks ago when they'd purchased a large amount of meat for a big Independence Day family barbecue.

"As I was going to say, there's a German butcher in the next town over that can help *her*," Fred finished, indicating Ella by pointing his chin towards her.

"No, *Mrs. Schmidt* lives a few blocks from here and should be allowed to shop at your store, Fred," Jane replied chillingly. Then she turned to Ella and calmly asked, "Ella, dear, what kind of meat do you need to make your dish?"

Red-faced, Ella only looked at Jane and explained, "Meat from a pig..."

"You mean pork. Is that correct?" prodded Jane quietly.

"Yes, that is the term I could not think of," agreed a relieved Ella. "And it must be cut thin... and hammered? But that is not right..." She trailed off and looked distressed again.

Jane turned to Fred, "So, Mrs. Schmidt needs boneless pork pounded thin with a meat tenderizer."

"How many pounds does she need?" a defeated Fred asked, looking only at Jane.

"You can ask *Mrs. Schmidt* how much she requires, Fred. And do so with a smile."

Fred sighed, directed his gaze at Ella, fixed an insincere smile on his face, and then inquired, "Mrs. Schmidt, how much of the pounded boneless pork fillets do you need?"

"Two pounds, please," responded Ella in a clear triumphant voice. Fred proceeded to retrieve the meat and locate his aluminum tenderizer.

Jane smiled at Ella and took her arm off the shorter woman's shoulders. Her smile vanished as she turned to the two female customers and said with abhorrence, "Shame on the two of you for standing there all this time, refusing to help a fellow homemaker being bullied!"

"Well, we had no idea what she wanted..." one started saying.

"Oh, *please*," mocked Jane. "You make me sick." And she turned her back on them again.

Fred returned to the counter with the package. Ella paid him, and then he asked with a smile, "And what can I do for you today, Mrs. Flynn?"

The two other women were about to protest that they were waiting before Jane had arrived. However, since neither wanted to face more of Jane's wrath, they remained silent.

Jane grinned sweetly at Fred and said, "You know what you can do for me, Fred? You can treat all your customers with the respect they deserve. Until I see that happen, I'll be serving a few meatless dinners." She looked him squarely in the eye, then looped her arm through Ella's and walked out of the store with her neighbor.

Once outside, Ella gushed, "Oh, Jane. You were wonderful! Thank you so much for supporting me. I do not know what I would have done without you."

"Listen, Ella," Jane advised as she collected her stroller and the two started to walk back to Strong Lane. "In this world, you have to always stand up for yourself. Especially against pea-brained men who try to make us women feel inferior. If there's one thing my sisters and I learned from being raised in the Bronx, it's that!"

Later, at the afternoon coffee klatch at Norma's house, Jane and Ella were jointly retelling the morning's encounter to the other three women. Ella made Jane sound like a warrior from a fairy tale, as if Jane was a slayer of dragons. Although Jane was trying to project a bit of humility, she couldn't resist feeling proud of herself, and she supplied verbatim her closing remarks to Fred.

"That's our Jane," enthused Norma. "Always taking command of a situation. Good job! I wish I could have been there."

"Me, too!" added Anna. "I've witnessed Fred being a little short with some of his female customers, but I never had the nerve to say something."

"This goes beyond being short," observed a defiant Betty. "That's just pure intimidation of women. How dare he! I have half a mind to bring my business to another butcher."

"Good idea, Bets! Let's boycott Fred's shop," agreed Norma wholeheartedly.

"I do not want you ladies to be inconvenienced because of me," declared Ella. "Fred's shop is so close to our homes. He is just a bully we must contend with."

"Ella, I know bullies. My two brothers and father were bullies," admitted Betty. "But they never gave women a hard time, only other blokes."

"Girls, Ella's right," Jane proclaimed. "Why make our lives more difficult seeking out another butcher? Let's make a pact that if one of us ever sees Fred being condescending and arrogant with any shopper, male or female, we call him out on it right in front of his customers."

"Agreed!" shouted Norma with glee.

"Absolutely," added a determined Anna.

"It would be my pleasure to give him a piece of my mind," said Betty.

"So, are you with us, Ella? Can you stand up to Fred, or any other store owner, who pulls this nonsense on you again?" asked Jane.

"I can be strong and advocate for myself. I can do it because of all of you," promised Ella.

"Cheers to not being pushed around!" proclaimed Jane, raising her coffee cup and clinking it with the other four.

Norma, Anna, Betty, and Ella started to amiably discuss other subjects. Jane, staying unusually quiet, took it all in, glancing at the four women with affection. Outside of her three sisters, she'd never felt so connected to a group of females.

CHAPTER 5

Ella - 1950

In the evening, after her expertly prepared dinner of authentic German schnitzel, Ella and her husband lingered over dessert at the tiny table for two squeezed next to the corner knick-knack cabinet in their small kitchen. Ella was carefully relaying to John the eventful details of her day. She did not want to worry him by repeating the butcher's more negative remarks about her heritage. Although Ella's German accent was now slight, she knew her sensitive husband had worried that living in this new remote suburban area might be a problem for his shy foreign-born wife. Instead, she put a positive spin on her anecdote, emphasizing Jane's defense and her own promise at coffee klatch to stand up for herself in the future. She divulged she felt accepted by the others and, for the first time, truly part of the group.

John smiled as he watched his wife's face light up. "That's my girl! You show them the very smart, beautiful fraulein I fell in love with on the day I first saw you."

Ella gave a little chuckle. "How could you tell I was intelligent? I was a frantic person when we first met."

"Well, you were definitely beautiful that day, prettier than any American girl I ever knew."

"And you were my knight in shining armor, John. Like a prince from the fairy tales I read as a child," Ella replied seriously, leaning over to give him a kiss on the cheek. "And the best teacher, patiently instructing me in your English language."

"You can't give me all the credit for being a good teacher," reflected John. "If Oma and Opa hadn't spoken German exclusively in our house when I was growing up, I never would have got to meet you."

Raised on a dairy farm in rural upper New York State, John had learned from his paternal grandparents to speak, read, and write their native German. Although his parents and three brothers spoke a little of the language, John was the only one in his immediate family who was fluent.

"But it was you, my darling Ella, who worked so diligently at learning English. You've made great progress in the last four years. I'm very proud of you."

"Of course, I worked very hard. I am a United States citizen now. I want my wonderful husband to be proud of me."

"Oh, I am, Frau Schmidt, I am," said John, and he leaned over to give her a tender kiss on the lips.

Ella smiled and countered, "That is *Mrs.* Schmidt to you! We only speak English in this house."

"Touché, Mrs. Schmidt!"

"What does this 'touché' mean, John?" asked a perplexed Ella.

"It means you made a clever point at my expense, my darling."

"I like this word. I will remember it," teased Ella with a grin.

She grew thoughtful for a moment and then disclosed, "Oh, John. It was a wonderful coffee klatch at Norma's house today. For once, everyone got along so well. It brought us together, this common struggle against the butcher who is a bully."

"Darling, on a regular basis, doesn't everyone get along well? No one has been nasty to you since we've moved here, have they?"

Ella hesitated. She had never revealed to John the remarks made by Betty and Jane at that very first gathering. Both had apologized, and Ella had never again heard a disparaging remark from any of the women. She had decided to move past that first meeting. She was beginning really to like each of her neighbors and did not want to hold a grudge.

"Everyone has been very pleasant to me since our coffee klatches began," said Ella slowly, and she felt truthful saying it. After all, it wasn't until the group's *second* meeting that it was officially called a 'coffee klatch.'

She continued with her explanation. "It is just there is some friction between Norma and Betty. I do not fully understand why. Betty had told me she thought Norma had an easy life and was 'stuck up,' whatever that term means."

"Betty is saying she thinks Norma acts superior," explained John. "Do you think this is so, Ella?"

"No, Norma has been nothing but kind to me. I like her. And I will not become involved in a squabble she has with Betty."

"Good! You make up your own mind about each of your new friends."

"I agree. Nevertheless, today was a good meeting with no dis-agreements between Betty and Norma," finished Ella with a smile. "Now, John, you go into the salon.... I mean the living room. I will clean the dishes and you read the newspaper you brought home."

"I'll help you, Ella. You had a big day today with the ladies, and I'm sure you're tired too," John offered. He brought their dessert plates over to the narrow counter next to the stainless-steel sink.

"No, no, no... I will do it. Please go and relax," said Ella as she started to fill the sink with warm water and soap. She began humming a tune to herself.

John gave his wife a peck on her cheek. He walked out of the kitchen, past the front door on his left and into the living room. As in all the houses on Strong Lane, the kitchen and living room were at the front of the house with the front door and the opposite staircase located between the two rooms. At the top of the narrow staircase was a push-up trap door concealing the unfinished attic space, a place to eventually construct additional bedrooms. On the ground floor, the two bedrooms, connected by a tiny hallway, were at the rear of the cape cod. The bathroom was at the end of the hall located between the front kitchen and the smaller rear bedroom.

In the kitchen, Ella efficiently organized the dishes in the order she would wash them, starting with the less dirty glassware and ending with the far grimier pots on the stove top. She remembered her mother showing her this technique when Ella was a girl living in the spacious apartment over her father's Berlin bakery.

Even now, all these years later, she could recall with vivid clar-ity the delightful aroma of the freshly baked breads and still feel the comforting warmth from the ovens as it rose into her family's upstairs quarters. She imagined she could hear her two older brothers arguing over a game of chess and teasing her about being an elfin-sized girl who couldn't keep up with them. She could almost taste her father's incredibly delicious apple strudel and see her mother compassionately assisting every one of the bakery's customers at the front counter. Life had been good then, although it had started to become extremely complicated.

"But, Mutter, they say at school you are not to associate with the people who wear the yellow stars," Ella recalled her ten-year-old self having asked her mother one day in 1938. A woman wearing such a badge had just exited the bakery after a purchase.

Checking the store was clear of customers, her mother, Greta, an intelligent former schoolteacher, had quietly answered, "And Ella, your papa and I have taught you and your brothers to think for yourselves. Although we warn you not to say anything to outsiders, you know we do not agree with Herr Hitler. I will serve any customer who comes in our bakery."

Hitler! Ella felt like spitting in her kitchen sink's sudsy water. When at that first gathering Jane had alluded to Ella 'coming from a country led by that monster,' Ella had felt she might have been physically sick at the association. For Ella, that hated name was synonymous with the end of her happy childhood, one that had been filled with love and security.

Because of Hitler, her only siblings had been unhappily drafted into the German army during the war, where the two young men were eventually killed. Because of Hitler, she had to evacuate Berlin in 1940 as part of the Kinderlandverschickung, instated to save children in Nazi Germany from the risks of the aerial bombings in the cities. Ella, accompanied by her mother, had to leave her father in Berlin where his bakery had to continue producing goods to feed the Third Reich's headquarters. Mother and daughter had relocated to a remote farm belonging to one of Greta's cousins. And because of Hitler, Ella had watched her usually positive mother grow depressed over their fractured family.

"Why is Hitler's appetite so insatiable? Why does he risk our country's young men to gobble up more European lands?" Greta had lamented after learning of the death of her older son in 1942. And after her second son was killed less than three years later, a dispirited Greta had lost her fortitude. She couldn't fight a case of measles that had spread through the farming community where there had been no doctor due to the war.

Ella had been devastated after her mother's death. Staying with Greta's kind cousins in the country until the war's end, Ella, at seventeen, had been determined to travel to Berlin and find out what had become of her father. Since the German postal service had been destroyed and correspondence had ceased, she had no idea if her father was alive.

Ella angrily scrubbed at the dirty pot in her sink as she thought back to all she had been robbed of because of Hitler's regime. She rinsed the pot clean, set it to the side and then released the dirty water down the sink's drain. As she watched the brownish water circle and then disappear, she took a deep breath and tried to release her fury. She remembered her well-read mother quoting Buddha when one of her children displayed anger. "Holding on to anger is like grasping a hot coal with the intent of throwing it at someone else; you are the one who gets burned."

When Ella grabbed a towel and started to dry her clean dishes, she allowed herself to daydream of the day she met John: the turning point of her life.

It had been the summer of 1946, and Ella had travelled from the countryside to the chaos that had once been Berlin. The war-torn metropolis had been divided into zones, and it had been at the border of the American zone where she had met a young, bespectacled U.S. Army serviceman. Ella, overwrought from waiting in several long lines that led to no answers, had worried she wouldn't be able to find help in locating her father in the bedlam that surrounded her. Then, this soldier had removed his eyeglasses, and she had looked into his steady hazel eyes.

"Sprechen Sie Deutsch?" the translator had asked. Ella recalled now how she had observed on his forehead a stray wavy lock of light brown hair that had escaped the rest of his Brylcreemed capless head, and how she had been tempted to reach out and smooth the lock back into place.

"Ja," Ella had replied wearily.

"Oh, good," he had continued in German. "The last woman I tried to help only spoke a Hungarian dialect, and I couldn't do anything for her. My name is John Schmidt, and I'd like to help you."

How kind and compassionate this man is, Ella had thought at the time. He had seemed genuinely disconcerted that he couldn't assist the person before her. Reinvigorated, she had smiled at him, gave him her name, and then told her story. As she spoke, he had diligently scribbled down the important facts.

"Well, Ella, I wish every German-speaking individual I've tried to aid was as concise and pertinently detailed in telling their story as you are. And to be honest, I wish everyone I've come across was as nice as you. Most of your fellow countrymen display some strong contempt for us Allied Forces. I'm usually an optimistic guy, but I admit I've been a bit discouraged with my duties here. I'll be pleased to try to find out what became of your father and his bakery."

As John had started to give her instructions to a nearby American Red Cross camp where she could stay while his investigation was completed, Ella had felt a calmness come over her that she hadn't experienced in seven years.

Drying the last of the dinner dishes, Ella further recalled the few weeks after their initial meeting. By then, she had made herself useful at the Red Cross camp, assisting the staff with the other refugees. John had visited her frequently with the pretext of asking more questions, but Ella had sensed he was carefully courting her. They both shared a love of books and had happily discussed the classics. She grew to trust him and had shared details of her happy childhood before the war. She had told John, for the first time without fear, about her family vehemently disagreeing with the Third Reich. He had started to teach her English and had been impressed with her intelligence.

However, a month later, he had come to her solemnly with his cap in his hands and empathy in his voice as he told her of her father's death from a direct bomb strike to the bakery in early 1945.

"I knew, deep down, that Papa was no longer alive. I am now an orphan and truly alone," Ella had said before quietly starting to weep. And although she had known this American soldier only for a brief time, he had taken her gently in his arms and comforted her with the words, "You will never be alone, Ella. Not while I'm on this earth."

Ella hung up the dish towel to dry. She looked around her orderly kitchen and knew she had stability in her life again. Yet, her security had little to do with her home or her American citizenship or even the mastering of her new language. It had everything to do with the loving and sensitive man in the next room, and she rushed in to join him.

CHAPTER 6

Anna – 1950

"Sal," began Anna as her husband poured a generous portion of cream into his coffee on an evening in late August. "I'm a little worried about Betty and Bob. Betty told me they had another disagreement about money."

After taking a huge gulp from his cup, Sal raised his thick dark eyebrows and replied, "Again?"

Before she could continue, Anna moved her daughter from the crook of her arm, where the baby had been guzzling the last of her evening bottle, to over her shoulder, where little Susan immediately produced a loud burp.

"That's my girl!" Sal, the invariably proud father, exclaimed. His dark eyes shone in his swarthy face as he beamed. "Here, pass her to me, Anna, so you can drink your coffee."

Anna gratefully passed Susan to Sal. While he patted the baby's back and joyfully murmured silly babble to his daughter, Anna stirred her own coffee and observed her husband. He was what some women would call a 'hands-on father.' He took no issue with diapering, feeding, or burping their first-born. Although one might assume Sal Marino, the youngest of seven children, would be inexperienced with the care of babies, he had a large extended Italian family where there had always been an opportunity to hold a little one.

Anna reflected, *Sal is a fine, competent husband and father.* Then she inwardly cringed and thought, *is that the way I should be thinking of the man with whom I recently celebrated a fourth wedding anniversary? Fine? Competent?* She wished she were more enamored with this good man who had been similarly raised in her old Italian-Catholic neighborhood in Williamsburg, Brooklyn. Her parents and Sal's had acted as matchmakers when Anna had turned eighteen. In the absence of any other prospects, she had dutifully married the pleasant Sal two years later without ever feeling the infatuation she expected a bride should feel. She supposed she loved him, but she had never felt besotted, then or now. She knew she didn't love him in the same way Norma and Jane seemed to love their husbands. Those two would blush and get sly grins on their faces when they spoke of Gordon or Danny in a personal way.

"Anna, where did you drift off to? I asked when you spoke with Betty?"

Anna brought her focus back to Sal. "Yesterday, she came over to borrow an egg. Remember, I told you she had mentioned to me a few months ago a discussion she had with Bob about going to college on the GI Bill? But he wasn't interested. Now she tells me she borrowed the government brochures Gordon Lewis offered and presented them to Bob this past weekend. With the fall college semester starting soon, she's still imploring Bob to sign up for courses. She said he had a bit of a fit, marched the pamphlets across the lawn to the Lewises' house, and returned them to Gordon."

Sal considered this information and speculated, "I doubt that Bob had that much of a row with Betty. We've known him for two years, and he must be one of the most mild-mannered guys I know. I've been in the bowling league with him for months now, and I've never seen him blow off steam, even when he misses a spare in a tournament! Still, I guess Betty can raise his temperature when she doesn't give up on an idea."

"I suppose," Anna said. "Still, Betty was quite upset, and I did feel a little sorry for her. She's sort of fixated on Bob earning more money by getting a better job ever since Robby was born this past January. She's always going on about the cost of raising a child."

"Well, we aren't millionaires either, but I guess I'm lucky Pop gave me a raise when little Susie here came along," Sal said, moving Susan from his shoulder onto her back across his knees.

Each morning, Sal drove to work at the Marino family-owned gourmet Italian foods and seafood shop in Williamsburg. The store, opened decades ago by Sal's father and currently run by the old man and his sons, was located on the same street in Brooklyn where his parents still lived, not far from Anna's parents' home.

Anna continued, "I think Betty also started to obsess about money when Norma mentioned to the group that Gordon will get a nice increase in salary once he finishes his course of study."

"That must have stuck in Betty's craw," interjected Sal, reaching for his coffee while rocking his knees side to side to soothe little Susan. "You and I know there's no deep affection between her and Norma.

Betty has told you many times she thinks Norma is 'too big for her britches,' as my Nonna used to say. Personally, I've never had a problem with either of the Lewises, and Bob has told me he likes them well enough, too."

"Yes, Betty and Norma get on each other's nerves. I spoke to Norma about it not too long ago and appealed to her to try to get along better with Betty. I plan on reaching out to Betty too, but I haven't found the right time yet."

"Well, sugar-pie, you'll find a way. That's why I call you my Little Switzerland because of your neutrality and calmness, especially in our families' frequent quarrels," joked Sal as he rose from his chair. "I'm going to put Susie down in her crib. She's falling asleep on my lap."

When he left the kitchen, Anna continued to reflect on Sal dubbing her a good negotiator. As the oldest of ten children, she had to be. Coming from a big family and then marrying into another large Italian American family, Anna had evolved into a good mediator. She could detect and defuse a potential argument before the heated words started flying. Her diplomacy also had been a great asset when she had been employed as a department store salesperson in New York City for the two years before her marriage. Crowded one-day sales at the huge, famous store had brought out the beast in most of the women shoppers, and there had been many times Anna had to moderate disputes between two warring females.

Anna decided she would make it a point to speak with Betty the next day. Although there had recently been some coffee klatches where Betty and Norma had not snapped at each other, those gatherings were still outnumbered by ones where there was obvious discord. It was important to Anna for all five women to be compatible. During the weekdays, they depended on each other; not just for practical matters but, most importantly, for camaraderie. It wouldn't do having any animosity between two of them.

The next morning, Anna and Betty were taking a neighborhood walk, pushing their babies in their respective carriages. It was a sunny day with a warm breeze, a slight relief from the previous humid stretch of summer days.

"How's it going, Betty? Are you and Bob getting along again?" asked Anna.

"Yes, he's forgiven me for pushing the college brochures on him. And I promised not to bring the subject up again. I guess I just have to accept my hubby doesn't want to move up in the world," replied Betty with a heavy sigh.

"College isn't for everyone. Actually, Gordon Lewis is the only husband on this block pursuing an education. My Sal works for his family's food business, as does Danny Flynn working for his father's construction company. Neither of them has college; they learned their skills on the job. And although Ella's John seems like an intellectual with all those books he and Ella have in their home, he doesn't have a college degree either."

"Really?" questioned Betty with her eyes widening in surprise. "John looks so smart and wears those eyeglasses. He works at the United Nations headquarters as a translator. With such an important job in such an impressive agency, I figured he was college educated."

Anna noted Betty almost looked pleased that John Schmidt didn't hold an advanced degree. For not the first time, Anna thought, *Betty is always comparing her own situation to others' and weighing who has an advantage.*

Even so, Anna kept her impressions to herself and replied, "Nope. I discussed it once with Ella. John comes from a family of dairy farmers, but he knew his translating skills, honed during the war, could lead to a better job. So, right after his service, he applied to the UN as a German-English translator. And like your Bob working for the Long Island Rail Road, John will get a nice pension someday. You're very lucky, Betty. Sal and Danny won't get a pension working for family businesses."

"I never before thought of Bob's benefits as such an advantage," marveled Betty with a smile. Then a cloud came over her face, and she added, "But Gordon, as an engineer someday, will make the most money, even without a pension."

"Yes, he may, but why let that bother you? When I experience jealousy, I always remind myself of the Proverbs quote from the Bible. 'A heart at peace gives life to the body, but envy rots the bones.'"

"I'm not envious of Gordon," Betty said sincerely. "I like him, and he always treats me kindly. I know he's working hard going to school after a full day in the office. I admire that."

Betty stopped walking for a moment to give Robby back the pacifier he had just flung to the far corner of his carriage. She resumed strolling and said with more fire, "It's just that Norma will continue to have her easy life married to him. Do you know, Anna, I actually saw the two of them dancing one night in their living room? They had the hi-fi playing a romantic song, and they were cheek-to-cheek. Who has time for something like that when already married?"

Despite having just quoted Proverbs to Betty, Anna's jealousy raised its ugly head. *I wish Sal would do something spontaneously romantic like that. Maybe then I would feel more passion for him.* However, she had never mentioned to Betty, or anyone else for that matter, how she felt about

Sal. She swatted away her envy of Norma and instead remarked, "I think that's very sweet, trying to keep the romance alive."

"I guess," conceded Betty. "But Norma will have her trouble-free life while the rest of us struggle."

"Betty, you don't know if Norma's whole life has been uncomplicated."

"How *would* we know? Norma is very tight-lipped whenever we try to ask her about her background. Even when that newspaper reporter questioned her and me about our lives before moving to this development, Norma glossed over her happy childhood, her time living in New York City with friends while attending secretarial school and her years working as a secretary at a Long Island company where she met Gordon. That was it, no details. Anytime the rest of us girls tell stories about our formative years before marriage, she adds nothing personal to the conversation. You have to admit it, Norma is very secretive."

"Well, I guess you have a point, Betty. You, Jane, and I have known her for two years now, and she hasn't revealed much. But that's her prerogative."

"Maybe she confides in Jane," wondered Betty. "After all, I feel like I'm closer to you, Anna, and am more confident telling you some private things, like my rows with Bob. I trust you don't tell the other gals everything I tell you."

"Believe me, I don't," assured Anna. "But I also don't think Norma necessarily tells Jane anything more than she tells us. Jane has told me she's also perplexed by Norma's secretiveness."

"Then you're with me in not liking Norma," Betty challenged.

"I didn't say that!" Anna responded, exasperated. "I like her well enough. She's witty and fun when we women get together. She's intelligent and always up on the latest news. I like it when she and I have a friendly debate over some current issue. And sometimes, Betty, I feel sorry for her. On the nights Gordon drives directly to school after work, she must feel very lonely eating dinner by herself."

Zeroing in on only one word of what Anna had just said, Betty pouted, "Sometimes her 'witty' remarks are at my expense."

"I talked to her about that, not too long ago," shared Anna. "Norma thinks you dislike her, and you don't give her a chance. She also gets upset with your inquisitiveness. It gets her dander up and makes her defensive."

"Are you taking her side, Anna?"

"I'm not taking anyone's side! I just want us all to get along."

"For the most part, we do," acknowledged Betty, backing down. "It's not like there's a brawl every time Nor and I are in the same room."

"I know, but sometimes there is obvious tension. Can you at least attempt to get along better with Norma? Maybe stop peppering her with so many questions."

"I'll certainly try, Anna. Like you, I want our little group to succeed and be congenial. But mark my words, there is more to Norma Lewis than we know..."

CHAPTER 7

Norma - 1950

Before slipping into her beige wool swing coat, Norma donned a chiffon headscarf over her meticulously styled chestnut hair. As she knew it would, the new scarf's muted autumn colors in shades of brown and green complimented her complexion and hair color. She had not planned to wear anything on her head, but then she heard the early morning wind rattling the windows of her house and decided her hairstyle needed protection. The hairspray alone was not enough on this last Monday morning in October. She hoped the wind would cease and the temperature would grow warmer by the next day. She didn't want to see the neighborhood children wearing jackets over their Halloween costumes.

As she left her house at noon and unlocked the car's door, she was glad today was a carpooling day for Gordon. Having his Ford Coupe at her disposal a day or two a week was a true blessing. The company where Gordon worked was situated in the town of Lake Success. It was the same location that temporarily housed the United Nations where John Schmidt was employed as a translator. The two men had discovered this coincidence a few weeks after the Schmidts had moved on to Strong Lane this past spring. Since then, Gordon and John would save gas and carpool on the days Gordon didn't attend college classes at night.

Norma was happy Gordon got on well with John. To an outsider, the two men seemed like total opposites. Gordon was the tall, athletic, out-going type with a quick sense of humor whereas John, although equally as tall, was slighter in build, cerebral and serious. Norma knew, though, that her husband could have a good relationship with anyone because he was an inquisitive man who made others feel important. Gordon exhibited equally keen interest whether talking about sports with Danny, cars with Sal, home repairs with Bob, or world events with John.

As she slowly maneuvered the car down Strong Lane, she passed the Schmidts' house on her left. Ella was stooping at the side of her house, removing the recently delivered glass milk bottles from the shiny aluminum milk box sitting on the ground next to her kitchen door. Ella stood, arched her back, and rolled her shoulders. In this position, Norma could observe the growing bump in Ella's slim mid-section. During their last coffee klatch, Ella had shyly announced her pregnancy. Her due date was in mid-March, and she was only now beginning to show.

From her seat in the car, Norma tapped the Coupe's horn in greeting and waved gaily to the mother-to-be. Ella smiled and waved back.

Norma genuinely liked sweet Ella and was happy for her. However, if Norma was being truly honest with herself, she was also a little resentful. Ella would be joining the other three women on Strong Lane in the experiences of motherhood. Until Ella's timid announcement, Norma had felt a special affiliation with the young German woman since they had shared the common bond of being the only childless women on the street. Now Ella would be involved in the endless discussions Jane, Betty and Anna had about child rearing. Dr. Benjamin Spock's bestseller, *The Common-Sense Book of Baby and Child* Care, was constantly quoted by the three mothers, and Norma knew Ella would also become one of its disciples. Norma imagined herself being ostracized.

Norma took a deep breath to shake off her blue mood. She willed herself not to think of motherhood and babies right now. She was on her way to pick up her mother for a day of clothes shopping and lunch, two activities that always cheered Norma. She started humming Nat King Cole's new song "Mona Lisa" as she sped west on Hempstead Turnpike towards her parents' home.

Thirty minutes later, Norma drove down her familiar childhood tree-lined street and noted the leaves had almost completely disappeared from the autumnal branches. As her car approached the curb in front of the white-shingled colonial, Mary Wolf came through the front door and walked swiftly down the brick path to the passenger side. Although now in her late forties, Mary had the same youthful chestnut hair color as her daughter. Norma's hair was her natural color whereas Mary's came compliments of her weekly visits to her beauty parlor, Salon Dionne. Mary, dressed in her best navy daytime suit, was clutching her gloves and leather purse in one hand while holding onto the tiny fashionable hat perched on her head with the other.

"This wind is horrific," exclaimed Mary after she settled herself into the passenger seat and air-kissed near the cheek her daughter offered.

"Maybe you should have skipped the hat today, Mother, and went with a headscarf like I did. It's more practical on a day like this."

"Norma June Wolf, as I've told you since you were a little girl, appearances are what set us apart from the riff-raff of the world. A hat and gloves are always necessary items for a woman when she is lunching and shopping, no matter what the weather," declared Mary. "And what are you wearing under that coat? Please tell me it's your good autumn suit."

"My last name is not Wolf any longer, and I'm wearing the perfectly nice forest green shirtwaist dress that you helped me select the last time we shopped," countered Norma as she started to drive. *Honestly,* she thought, *I can't believe my mother still thinks she can dictate my wardrobe!*

Norma quickly changed the subject and asked, "How is Daddy? And what do you hear from Stewie?"

"Your father is fine, as I'm sure Gordon can tell you since he sees him at the office. And your brother Stewart never calls. He claims his junior year at that New England college is so much more difficult than his first two years, so he doesn't have time to ring us. Afterall, we *are* the ones paying for his education, but heaven forbid that he thinks of us once a week to let us know how he's doing!"

Technically, contemplated Norma, *Daddy is paying for Stewie's school since Mother has never worked a day outside her home since she married twenty-five years ago.*

However, she was not about to correct her mother. Instead, she said, "Gordon hardly ever sees Daddy at work. It's not as if the head of Accounting has weekly meetings with the Mailroom."

"When is Gordon going to finish that degree and move up to the engineering division?" asked Mary as she slid her dove-gray gloves over her slender fingers.

"He thinks he should be done by next year and graduate in December. Hopefully, he'll begin 1952 with a new title. I can't wait. It would be nice to have a husband come home every night for dinner. The days he goes to night school directly from the office are the longest and loneliest for me. On those nights, Gor doesn't get home until at least eleven, and, as much as I try, I'm not always awake when he gets in. It would be different if I had a baby to occupy me. But with just me, the television and the four walls, there are nights I could go crazy."

When she mentioned the word 'baby,' Norma felt her mother physically stiffen and an uncomfortable silence hung in the air. *Darn it,* thought Norma, *I can't believe I brought the subject up. It had to be seeing Ella earlier that brought it into my thoughts and inadvertently out of my mouth!*

"Well... well..." Mary finally stammered before regaining her composure. "I'm glad that television at least gives you something to do. Frankly, I thought it was a silly Christmas gift for us to give you last year, but your father insisted. I rarely ever watch ours, but your father finds it amusing. And Stewart, when he's home, thinks it's the greatest invention. How that boy can stand watching Milton Berle dress up like a woman..."

Norma wasn't listening any longer. She was too caught up in her thoughts and her mother's unspoken sentiments. She knew Mary believed her and Gordon's lack of children was completely Norma's fault.

And I guess it is, surmised Norma. *If only I had done things differently...*

CHAPTER 8

Anna - 1951

Making her way from the frigid backyard into her warm kitchen, Anna carried a wicker laundry basket overflowing with soggy clothes. Only two hours ago, just before Sal had left for work, she had neatly clothes-pinned the wet garments onto her metal umbrella clothesline anchored in the muted winter grass of their small rear yard. The early morning had been gray and cold, but the radio's weather report she had heard during breakfast had not predicted precipitation on this first day of March. However, at a few minutes before ten o'clock, as Anna had placed Susan, freshly bathed and diapered, into the play-pen in the middle of the living room, she noticed that snow had started to fall. Hence, the laundry needed to be brought back inside. Anna set about hanging the clothes on heavy twine that she had capably strung in a zigzag pattern across her toasty kitchen. Although Anna's home included a small front-loading washing machine, an automatic clothes dryer was still an unknown luxury for her and her Levittown neighbors.

As Anna finished hanging the last piece of laundry on her make-shift clothesline, she looked out her front kitchen window at the already snow-covered Strong Lane. Her house was located at the end of the block, directly across from Betty's, and she observed the Carters' front door was barely visible through the dense sheet of falling flakes. Due to the sudden blizzard-like deluge, she wondered if Betty would still host this week's coffee klatch, scheduled for two in the afternoon. She supposed the ladies would all bundle up in their snow boots and warm coats and trudge the short distance to Betty's. The five neighbors all looked forward to the few hours of 'girl talk and goodies,' as Betty would say.

Anna's thoughts turned to their expectant neighbor. Ella, situated two houses down the street from Anna, would have to walk the farthest to Betty's, but Anna estimated that would only be about one hundred feet. Yet, with Ella's due date only two weeks away, Anna thought it would not be prudent for her to chance a slip on the snowy pavement. *Maybe I should telephone Norma and suggest she escort Ella down the street later,* thought Anna.

Still glancing out the window, Anna anxiously wondered, *will Sal even be able to drive that old car back home tonight with this continually mounting snow?*

As he did each weekday, her husband had coaxed their 1938 Dodge sedan to start this morning and then drove approximately thirty-five miles to the family store. Sal had been talking about replacing the thirteen-year-old car since the beginning of the winter, but Anna knew he wanted to wait until he saved a little more money so he wouldn't have to buy a used automobile again. Sal, who loved to tinker with cars in his spare time, was looking forward to buying a brand-new model, something he had never done in his twenty-six years. Ironically, despite Sal's extensive knowledge of cars, it was his experience in his family's food business that had secured his occupation for the duration of the war. During his stint in the U.S. Navy, he had constantly been assigned to food preparation duties on various submarines roaming the Pacific.

Anna looked in on Susan, who had fallen asleep in the playpen, splayed out between her stuffed animals and the colorful jack-in-the-box. Anna had been so pre-occupied with hanging the clothes and observing the weather that she had forgotten to place the baby into the crib for her morning nap. Anna could not help grinning as she watched her curly-haired daughter sleep, one untamed lock of springy black hair falling across her tiny forehead. Her firstborn would be turning one at the end of the month and had recently begun tentatively cruising around the playpen, using its wooden bars as support in her walking attempts. Susan would be joining Betty's Robby, who had started walking the day of his first birthday this past January.

Startling Anna from her thoughts, the telephone started to ring. Before the sound could wake Susan, Anna dashed to the black instrument perched on the mahogany gossip bench's small writing table. She plopped down on the bench's attached padded seat, picked up the heavy receiver and whispered, "Hello?"

"Hey, sugar-pie. How are my two best girls doing?" shouted Sal over the din at his family's store.

"Susan is sleeping. That's why I'm whispering. Is it snowing in Brooklyn?"

"It's coming down like a son-of-a-gun. And the shop is nuts! Everyone is coming in to get last-minute food in case they're snowed in for a few days. All anyone is talking about is how steadily this stuff is coming down. The weatherman on the radio now claims the storm blew in directly off the Atlantic Ocean. So, they couldn't predict it on the earlier reports since it didn't come in over land from the west like most of our storms do. I'm telling you Anna—I don't think I'm getting home tonight in my old car. It's only getting worse."

"Sal, just plan on staying at your parents' house tonight. Susan and I will be fine if the electricity stays on. And we have plenty of candles just in case we should lose power. You brought home so many groceries last night, I could feed the neighborhood if necessary."

"Yeah, I guess I will stay here. Are any of the neighbors' cars home? Did Gordon go in with John?"

"I'm looking out the front window, Sal, diagonally over to the Lewis house and I don't see their car. It's Thursday, and I think Gordon only carpools with John on Mondays and Wednesdays. And there's no car across the street at the Carters. Bob must be on a LIRR shift today because Betty is hosting our coffee klatch, and I know she never offers to have it if Bob is home."

"And I saw Danny Flynn drive off in his truck when I was eating breakfast this morning. I was talking to him last night when we were both putting out the trash. He's on some big job in the Bronx this week," countered Sal. "So that means you gals are sort of stranded on Strong Lane today. Will you be going over to that hen party at Betty's later?"

"If she still wants us, which I'm sure she will. What else can we do today? I'll bundle up Susan and go on over. Maybe we can have Ella watch the kiddies, and then Betty, Norma, Jane, and I can work together to shovel paths to our houses."

Sal laughed and said, "Good luck getting Mrs. Carter to push a shovel! Every time we had snow this winter, I only saw Bob out there shoveling it. All you gals chip in and help but never Betty. For crying out loud, even Ella with her huge belly was out there sweeping the snow off the sidewalk during the last snow!"

That is true, thought Anna. *Betty shuns heavy physical labor at all costs. She expertly does her family's cooking and housecleaning, but when it comes to any outside work, Betty draws the line. The rest of us wives will garden and wash windows, but Betty has Bob do all the outside chores.*

"Listen, Anna," Sal said seriously. "Don't worry too much about shoveling. I don't want you girls to hurt yourselves. This is some nasty, heavy stuff coming down. I'm already seeing some cars get stuck outside the shop. Just stay warm and have some fun at Betty's. If it all ends by later tonight, hopefully I'll start home early tomorrow morning. The rest of my brothers can help Pop run the shop tomorrow."

"Okay. Say hello to your parents for me. And don't worry about us. We'll be fine. Good luck with the car tomorrow. And remember, Susan and I love you," Anna dutifully replied.

"Back at you, sugar-pie. Call me at the shop 'til six and then at Mama's after that if you need anything. Not that I can do anything for you from here but call me tonight after Susie goes to bed and let me know how your day went."

"Will do, Sal. Good-bye." Anna sighed and hung up the telephone just as Susan started to stir from her nap.

However, before Anna rose from her seat, the telephone started to ring again. This time it was Betty.

"Good morning, Anna. How do you like this crazy weather? I called the other gals, and they all agreed to come over at noon instead of two. I have some fresh cold cuts if anyone wants a lunchtime sandwich in addition to the goodies. I figured we can meet earlier so you all can get back home sooner if this whiteout gets worse."

"Thank you, Betty, but are you sure you still want us to come over today?" asked Anna as Susan started to get very verbal in her pen.

"Blimey! Of course, I want you all to come. I'll lose the plot if I stay inside with Robby and the telly all day."

Anna was not sure what losing the plot meant, but she guessed Betty was talking about going stir crazy in the house with just her son and the television as company. *Betty sure has some odd phrases from her English upbringing.*

"I'll be there, Betty. Susan just got up from her nap, so I'll just give her an early lunch, bundle us up and head on over. I'm a little worried about Ella making her way over with this…"

"Nor said she'd walk over with her," interrupted Betty. "See you at noon. Toodles!"

"Goodbye, Betty."

Within the hour, Anna, awkwardly carrying a snow-suited Susan, trudged across the street towards Betty's house. The flakes were still falling heavily, and the wind had started to increase. She estimated there must have been at least four inches of snow on the road. Along the way, she met Jane making a similar clumsy trek holding the hand of a struggling Pamela. The two mothers greeted each other warmly as they arrived at Betty's side kitchen door. Their hostess quickly ushered them indoors and started to help the women unbundle the two little girls. Robby toddled into the kitchen from the living room. The adorable boy's coloring was exactly like his mother's: creamy skin, soft brown hair, and light gray eyes.

"Nor and Ella aren't here yet?" inquired Jane.

"Nope. Does anyone fancy a sandwich?" asked Betty.

Both Jane and Anna said they would wait for the other two ladies, and they proceeded to set up Pamela and Susan with some of Robby's toys in the living room. The three neighbors were making small talk as they supervised their children when they heard the kitchen door reopen and Norma's voice call out.

As the three women made their way back to the kitchen, Betty said to Norma, "Take off your boots, Nor. You're dripping all over the place. And where's Ella?"

"I left her at her house. You are never going to believe this, but I'm fairly certain her labor started," announced Norma after removing her boots. She followed the others back into the living room.

"Are you kidding?" said Jane. "She's not due for another two weeks. And it's her first baby. You're always late with the first one, aren't you?"

"Not necessarily," Anna replied. "I had Susan a few days before my due date. Did you call her doctor or the hospital, Nor?"

"Apparently, you girls haven't checked your telephones lately," said Norma. "I think the lines are down. I tried the phones at both Ella's and my house, and they were dead."

Betty picked up her receiver and confirmed they were all without outside contact.

"Does anyone have a car at home today?" asked Jane.

Each confirmed that her husband had the sole family vehicle. Anna mentioned that Sal would not be making it home today, and she doubted the other husbands would be home anytime soon with the heavy snow continuing. And with that new fact, the color disappeared from Betty's face, and she started to panic.

"What are we going to do? She can't have that baby today. She just can't!"

"Well, she might just do that, Bets, and there's not much you can do about it. So, get a grip!" demanded Norma. "We will all just have to combine our experiences to figure out a way to help her."

"Don't pretend to be all calm and collected, Norma Lewis. You're worried too," insisted Betty. "And what could you possibly know about delivering a baby? You don't even have one."

Norma's face darkened. Betty had obviously hit a nerve.

"Ladies," interjected Anna. "Arguing isn't going to solve anything. Let's think this through rationally."

"Well, I'm heading back over to Ella's house. I told her I wouldn't leave her for too long, and I've already stopped at my house to check the phone. *Someone* has to help the woman," said Norma looking pointedly at Betty.

"All right, girls, let's stay calm," began Anna. "Betty, do you think you can handle the three children for a little while so Nor, Jane and I can go over to Ella's? On the way over, Jane and I can check our telephones just to make sure the whole block is out. Thank goodness the electricity seems to be holding."

"Yes, I'll watch the children, and I'll keep checking the telephone," answered a relieved Betty. "I would much rather stay with the little ones than deal with a potential birth."

"I have some experience with births," explained Anna calmly. "All my siblings and I were born at home in Brooklyn with our female relatives acting as mid-wives. The youngest of my siblings was born just five years ago. I assisted my aunts a bit during my baby sister's entrance into the world. And then I helped with the birth of a cousin last year."

"Well, that's impressive! Sometimes you just utterly amaze me, Anna," said Norma.

"Okay, let's get this show on the road and check out the situation," demanded Jane. "Maybe it's just false labor."

After donning their outerwear, Norma, Jane, and Anna made their way out into the storm. Norma headed straight to Ella's house at the end of the street, while Jane and Anna stopped at their own homes to check their telephones. As Norma had surmised, the block was without outside communication. Since there would be no one else to turn to, Anna grabbed some items from her own home that she thought might be useful. She then met Jane outside, and they trudged to Ella's. As the two women pulled off their snow-encrusted boots in the kitchen, they could hear a low groan from the back of the house followed by words of comfort from Norma.

"Jeepers!" exclaimed Jane. "That doesn't sound good. What are we going to do, Anna? It's not like we really know anyone very well outside of our street. It's just the five of us!"

"We are going to help our friend have her baby. If there are no complications, Ella will be fine. What do you remember about having Pammy?"

"Not much after the initial pains at home. At the hospital, I was a twilight sleep delivery and happy to claim it!"

"Well, I didn't want to be put out for Susan's birth, so I had her mostly naturally," said Anna.

"More power to you, sister. I just don't know how you made it through," wondered Jane as the two of them made their way to the back of the house and Ella's bedroom.

Lying on her side, curled in a fetal position on an outside edge of her queen-sized bed, petite Ella looked like a small child enveloped in the mattress and linens. Her damp fair hair was strewn across her forehead and cheeks. Her eyes were opened wide, and she was staring at Norma who was crouched on the floor directly in front of Ella's face. Norma's calm green eyes held Ella's scared blue ones as the brunette murmured encouraging words.

"Well, how are we doing in here? Are we going to be welcoming the newest member of the Schmidt family today?" asked Anna in her jolliest tone. She was doing her best to sound confident and professional although she was shaking inside. She wished at least one of her aunts were with her. "Let's take a look at our little mother-to-be. When did the pains start, Ella?"

Norma helped Ella turn onto her back as Ella told her neighbors that she thought she felt something odd early this morning as John was getting ready for work. She didn't know if it was actually labor starting, and not wanting to worry her husband, didn't say anything to him.

After examining Ella as well as she knew how from her past brief midwifery experiences, Anna took note of how often Ella thought her contractions were occurring. Norma dampened a washcloth from the bathroom and proceeded gently to wipe Ella's flushed forehead and cheeks. She gave the patient little sips of water and gently rubbed her back. As instructed by Anna, Jane searched for as many towels as she could find and positioned them under the mid-section of the mother-to-be. Anna continued to monitor the new contractions and encouraged Ella to breathe deeply and steadily.

Gaining some confidence with the preparations, Anna said, "At this point, there isn't much more we can do but wait."

"I was never a person who could sit still for long," proclaimed Jane. "I'm a woman of action! I'm going to bundle myself back up, check on Betty and the children and then hike off this street to see if anyone on the next block has telephone service or a car to help us."

"Do you think that's a good idea?" asked Norma. "We don't want to have to rescue you from a snow drift."

"I'll be fine. I was a Girl Scout when I was a kid. Besides, you two seem to have everything under control. I'd just be in the way."

After Jane left, Ella progressed steadily. The contractions were coming more frequently, and Anna and Norma did what they could to help her breathe through each episode. Between contractions, the two coaches kept up a constant chatter to distract Ella from thinking of her pain.

At one point, Norma mentioned the current event that was monopolizing the newspapers. "The Rosenberg trial is starting in a few days. Federal espionage charges! Such a serious crime. I wonder if those two will get the death penalty if convicted."

"God help their poor little boys if they are sentenced," said Anna, glad to talk about something other than the birth for a few minutes.

"That's why they should never have gotten involved in spying," countered Norma. "If I had two lovely children, I would never have jeopardized my family. Ethel, at least, should have steered clear of her husband's dealings with the Soviet Union. If Julius got sentenced to death, at least Ethel could have raised her boys."

"Maybe the Rosenbergs are just victims of Cold War paranoia," pondered Anna.

"The evidence is stacked heavily against them, Anna. Don't you agree Ella?"

But Ella had stopped following the conversation due to another labor pain.

Later, when she had exhausted the latest news to discuss, Norma suddenly admitted, "I'm so enthralled being a part of your childbirth, Ella. And I'll confess, very jealous too."

"How so?" questioned Ella quietly.

Norma hesitated briefly before continuing. She busied herself with smoothing the bedcovers and, not looking directly at Ella or Anna, calmly said, "Just between us three girls, as much as I'd like to have children, I'll never be able to experience this personally."

Anna was shocked. The private Norma had never mentioned anything before about her desire to become a mother. Once, Betty had speculated to Anna that Norma did not have children because she did not want to compromise her lovely figure. Anna had told Betty she could not believe that; doesn't every woman want to be a mother, she'd asked.

Ella, forgetting about her own pain for a moment, whispered, "Norma, can you not have a baby?"

"No, I had a medical issue before I was married, and I found out I can't have children. Gordon knew this when he proposed, but he married me anyway," Norma replied with a hitch in her voice.

That is true love, thought Anna. She went over to Norma, enfolded her in a hug and said, "Oh, Nor, I'm so sorry."

With this display of genuine affection, Norma's reserve broke, and she started to tear up. "It's okay. I'm used to the idea now and try not to let it consume me. Still, I feel so guilty that Gor won't have a child of his own someday. I've always felt like I'm letting him down. He's such a great guy with wonderful qualities that he won't see replicated in a child." She grabbed a lacey handkerchief from the pocket of her wool trousers and dabbed at her eyes.

"Norma, I am so sad for you two," Ella quietly empathized. "Maybe you can adopt a baby."

"Yes, that's what Gor says," Norma responded, and she started to smile through her tears. "He said he saw so much unhappiness in war-torn Europe when he served in the army. So many orphans. He thinks all children deserve a loving home. Once he's done with night school, we'll look into adoption."

"And that will be soon, right? Isn't he finishing his degree before long?" asked Anna gently.

"Hopefully by the end of this year," Norma answered, a smile returning to her face. Then she grew concerned and said, "Please don't mention this to anyone else. I don't want too many people to know."

"Of course, Norma. Your secret is safe with us," Anna promised.

"Yes, me also," agreed Ella just before she began to writhe silently in pain.

Norma, apparently bringing her thoughts back to the matter at hand, took one look at Ella and coached, "For God's sake, darling, scream if you want to. We're not in a hospital where you must be polite and worry about what others think. It's just us, so let it all out if it makes you feel better!"

And Ella did just that, causing the hairs on the back of Anna's neck to rise.

Around three o'clock, with the snow and wind still raging, Jane returned to Ella's house. As she removed her boots in the warm kitchen, she told Anna and Norma she had initially checked on Betty and the children and then made the slow trek to the next block of homes, the ones located perpendicular to Betty's house at the end of Strong Lane. She'd knocked on several doors and at first found only young mothers, also without telephone service.

"So, no one had a car at home either?" asked Norma.

"There was one family with a car. The husband sleeps in the day and works a night shift someplace. His wife woke him to tell him our story, but he said he would never be able to drive very far with the streets not plowed. And he didn't have chains on his tires. He's not even venturing out to work tonight. However, he did have something better than a car! He had one of those CB radios," exclaimed Jane triumphantly.

"What good does a radio do us?" Anna asked.

"He called it a Citizens Band radio. I don't really understand it, but he said he could talk with other users through a radio band or something. Anyway, it took a long time but with a lot of back and forth, he was able to contact Meadowbrook Hospital in East Meadow. The hospital said they would send an ambulance with a doctor, although they don't know how long it will take," explained Jane.

"Ella's obstetrician is located at Nassau Hospital in Mineola, but I guess that doesn't really matter anymore. Mineola is too far away and East Meadow is just the next town over from us," observed Norma before she excused herself and went back to Ella.

"How's the little mother doing in there?" Jane asked Anna.

"It's going to be a fast birth. She's in active labor. Last time I checked, her cervix was well dilated, too. I think she's almost in transition. I don't think that doctor will be here in time to deliver the baby, but I hope he can at least get through soon after the birth so the ambulance can take the two of them to the hospital for recovery."

"Golly, I never heard of a first-time mother delivering so fast. I guess it's her strong German background or something," wondered Jane. "Listen, Anna. It looks like you and Nor have things under control here. If it's okay with you, I think I'll go back and help Betty. Last I checked, she wasn't having the easiest time keeping three kiddies under control. At Betty's, I'll keep an eye out for the ambulance and direct them here when they arrive."

Anna could tell Jane was growing anxious and was not comfortable with all the medical terms Anna had just used. She knew Jane would not really be any help with the birth, and Norma was undeniably the more competent assistant.

"I agree, Jane. You should go help Betty. Thank you for your trek out in this nasty storm to find help. You're a real trooper."

"Glad to help!"

Before leaving, Jane went in to see Ella, gave her a kiss on the cheek and, in her best optimistic cheerleader voice, said some words of encouragement. Then she got redressed as quickly as she could in her snow-encrusted outerwear. Anna amusedly observed that Jane seemed more than grateful to retreat to the Carters' house.

Within an hour of Jane's departure, Ella's labor became intense and more painful. Her contractions were coming very close together and lasted longer than a minute each time.

"My back hurts! There is so much pressure," gasped Ella with tears in her eyes. "I cannot do this."

"Yes, you can, sweetie," encouraged Norma squeezing her hand. "You're almost there. You've been so brave, and soon you'll meet your baby."

"You're doing wonderful, Ella," added Anna who was positioned at the end of the bed monitoring the progress. She was more than relieved that all seemed to be going well. "This looks like a textbook delivery. I don't see any problems at all. I think you can start pushing with the next contraction."

Outside, the gray light was starting to fade, and the bedroom was growing darker. Norma brought the two lamps from the living room and plugged them into sockets near the end of the bed so Anna could have a brighter surveillance of the birth.

"It stopped snowing," observed Norma as she glanced out one of the bedroom windows on her way back to her position next to Ella.

"Ella, you've got to gather all your strength now so you can gently push this little one into the world. When you start to feel an overwhelming urge, just go with it and push," instructed Anna.

With her sweaty hands, Ella clutched Norma's left hand tightly. Through clenched teeth, Norma calmly pleaded, "Ella darling, ease up a bit on the grip. You're leaving me with very little sensation in my fingers."

"Sorry," panted Ella.

"That's okay, sweetie. Here, seize a hold of this dry washcloth instead."

"I think I have to push!" gasped Ella, ignoring the washcloth and still clasping Norma's hand.

The progression of the infant's birth became controlled and steady. Anna felt like she was on autopilot as she remembered terms her aunts had used during the births she witnessed. She told Ella to slow down her pushing when she started to see the baby's head crown. Soon the baby's head completely emerged.

"The head is out. Nor, hand me one of those clean hand towels. I have to wipe the baby's mouth and nose," said Anna.

With her free right hand, Norma passed Anna a towel and excitedly asked, "Well, is it a boy or a girl? Don't keep us in suspense, Anna!"

"It's just a head right now, Nor. But a beautiful, perfect head, Ella," Anna answered patiently. "I've got to turn it a little to the side so the shoulders can rotate and come out. Ella, on the next contraction, you can push out the rest of your baby."

And then, everything happened at once. First there was a commotion from the kitchen as the women heard the door slam open and Jane's voice shout, "They're here! The ambulance just pulled up!"

Then, Ella cried out, "I have to push," as she bore down and let out her last big groan of the day still tightly grasping Norma's bruised left hand.

Next, Anna exclaimed, "It's a girl!" as she wrapped the newborn in the last of the clean towels. With the umbilical cord still attached, she passed the baby over Ella's raised knees to Norma who gently placed the infant into her mother's arms.

They heard Jane say, "This way, gentlemen," before she burst into the bedroom with the ambulance attendant and doctor following close behind her.

Jane took one look at the scene in front of her, froze in her tracks at the doorway, and could only gasp, "Holy cow!" before the men gently moved her aside so they could reach Ella.

Seeing there would be limited space in the bedroom, Anna vacated the end of the bed and went to stand next to Norma near Ella's head. She was thankful for the arrival of professional help but a bit disappointed she couldn't complete the task. The doctor took over, clamping the umbilical cord in two places and then cutting between the clamps. He examined the newborn and gave her back to her mother. He returned to his position at the end of the bed and told the attendant they would wait for the placenta to be delivered before transporting mother and baby to the ambulance. The attendant went outside to prepare the vehicle. Jane remained still, transfixed against the wall next to the bedroom door.

The doctor looked up at the two women standing by the infant on Ella's chest and said with heartfelt admiration, "You ladies did a wonderful job. I don't think a doctor could have done any better with the circumstances you were in."

"It was all my friends' doing. They were perfect nurses to me. I do not know what I would have done without the two of them. I am so grateful," answered a euphoric Ella while her eyes never left her daughter's small face.

Jane finally broke from her mesmerized state and made her way past the doctor to admire the baby. "Oh, Ella, she's beautiful. Did you and John have a girl's name picked out?"

"We did, but I have changed my mind. I was hoping it would be a girl because her name is to be Noranna Greta Schmidt. She will carry a combination of the names of the three bravest women I know - the wonderful friends who brought her into this world and my mother."

Eventually, mother and daughter were transported to the hospital. After the ambulance had left, Norma claimed she alone would clean up the bedroom. She was in the process of insisting Anna and Jane go back to Betty's to retrieve their daughters when John Schmidt walked through the front door. He was surprised to find the three women there after his harrowing drive home. Anna quickly explained what had happened that day, told him he was a father and sent him back out to the snow-covered streets to make his way to the nearby hospital to join his wife and daughter.

Later that evening, just before midnight, Anna was still awake as she lay in bed attempting to rest, finally, after an exceedingly long day. She had put an exhausted Susan in her crib hours ago but sleep eluded

Anna as she reviewed the events of the fateful afternoon. She was proud of herself for handling the birth with an external composure and confidence that internally she never fully felt. It was only now, in the stillness of her own bedroom, that she allowed herself to think of what could have gone wrong today. She knew she was not a certified midwife; only a woman who had assisted and observed the birthing process several times in the past. A devout Catholic, Anna silently thanked God. He had stood by her and Norma all day in their efforts to deliver a healthy daughter to Ella.

The next morning, with the sun shining on the pure white landscape of Strong Lane, Sal's old car, complete with tire chains, pulled up in front of the Marino house as close to the curb as was possible. Earlier, at daybreak, a sanitation truck with a plow in front had swept down the narrow street pushing mounds of snow to either side. Sal made his way from the car and up the unshoveled path to the kitchen door. Inside the warm kitchen, he found Susan in her highchair and Anna sipping coffee as she tried to spoon cereal into the baby's mouth. He gave them each a kiss and poured himself a cup of coffee. He proceeded to tell his wife about his vexing journey home that had started at sunrise and had, along the way, included many stops to dig his stuck car out of snow piles on corners.

"It was unbelievable, Anna," concluded Sal. "Hey, you never called me at Mama's last night. I guess your last twenty-four hours stuck here on Strong Lane were pretty boring in comparison to my day."

"Well, Sal, you could say we had a little bit of excitement here, too," remarked Anna with a sly grin on her face, and she launched into her own tale of the March blizzard.

CHAPTER 9

Jane - 1951

The temperature outside had already reached ninety degrees at eleven o'clock on this hot and humid first Tuesday morning in August. Jane Flynn was standing at her kitchen counter busily preparing an assembly line of ham and Swiss cheese sandwiches as she occasionally wiped her damp face with the back of her hand. She had a dozen slices of Wonder Bread lying in two rows of six on her counter, and she was slapping deli-sliced ham and cheese on each piece of white bread as fast as she could. Two of the sandwiches would be for her and Pamela to take with them as their picnic lunch. The other ten would be placed on a plate in her refrigerator for the work crew to eat on their noon break.

Jane could hear the buzz of handsaws and the pounding of hammers above her head. She could not wait to leave the noise behind and take her daughter to meet the block's coffee klatch members at the local public pool. Danny and his construction crew of three men were framing out an upstairs rear dormer that would eventually provide a second floor with two bedrooms and an extra bathroom.

Jane was thrilled to be the first family on Strong Lane to expand her small Levitt house. Nevertheless, she wished the construction could magically be done in a day. Today was only the second day of a project that could take several weeks to complete. Danny had explained to her that once the outside structure was completed, the inside work would not be as noisy. However, Jane knew once the men moved inside, they would have to traipse all day through her front door and march up the stairs opposite it to reach the work site. She did not relish the thought of cleaning up the constant dirt and debris the crew would be carrying through her usually spotless house. Currently, with the men working exclusively from the outside, the closed trap door at the top of the narrow staircase blocked the outside mess from the rest of the house.

Jane felt sorry for the men working outside on such a sizzling summer day. The sun was particularly brutal this morning. Despite wearing a thin sleeveless shift over her cotton bathing suit, Jane felt as warm as she imagined the men did on her sweltering roof. It did not help that her body was acting as a little incubator for the future member of the Flynn family. She was glad she was past the three-month mark and not experiencing any more nausea as she had during the first trimester. Extreme heat and queasiness did not make a good combination.

Just as she completed her task and was covering the plate of sandwiches with a clean dishtowel, Danny came bustling through the kitchen door.

"Hey, babe. How's it going? Do you have enough grub for the guys and me?" asked Danny as he stooped down to give his wife a peck on her flushed cheek.

"Yup, the sandwiches are on this plate, and I'm putting them in the fridge with a pitcher of lemonade. There's cold water in a jug, too. You all should take frequent breaks to cool down. I'm leaving in a few minutes with Pammy for the pool. How's the work going up there?"

"It's coming along. I wish my brothers could have come to help today, but Dad couldn't spare them with that big site they're all working on in Queens. The crew I have with me are good guys, though; no problems so far."

"I have to tell you, Janie," continued Danny, "the Levitts built a darn good house. Considering it was a reverse assembly line kind of construction, everything I'm seeing with part of the roof off is good quality. Remember how annoyed Dad was when we came out here and originally rented this house and didn't wait for him to build us one?"

Jane recalled all too well the argument Danny and his father had had just before Pamela was born in April 1948. Father Flynn, as Jane called her father-in-law, had not wanted the couple to move from their tiny two-room Bronx rental to another rental property, even though the Levitt house would give the expectant parents more room. Father Flynn had argued that if they could just tolerate their apartment for another year, he could build them a bigger house near both of their families. Although Jane would not have minded living closer to her folks, she had wanted to put some significant miles between her anticipated baby and Danny's overbearing parents. Her in-laws were good people but a little too controlling for Jane's comfort. Before Pamela was born, Jane had observed how Mrs. Flynn would constantly get involved in the rearing of her grandchildren from Danny's brothers. Jane thought her two spineless sisters-in-law might tolerate the elder Mrs. Flynn's interferences, but she was not going to endure it. It was Jane who had discovered the Levitt advertisement in the newspaper and pushed her husband to investigate the details. She had caught him at the time he had the highest sympathy for his very expectant and uncomfortable wife, and she knew he would do anything to make her happy.

After Pamela had been born in the Bronx, the new family of three had moved onto Strong Lane and eventually had bought their house after a year of renting. Sometimes Jane felt a little guilty because most days Danny had a long commute in his truck to whatever job site Flynn and Sons were working. However, Jane hoped other local homeowners would take note of this significant renovation to their house. She had insisted Danny should advertise with a company sign on their front lawn during the project. She secretly wished that someday Danny could break from his father's company, form his own home improvement business, and then exclusively work in suburbia.

When Danny headed back outside, Jane packed her canvas beach bag with the items she would need at the pool. She knew the nearby public pool at their local Village Green would be a godsend on a sweltering day like today.

She left the house, slinging the beach bag over her shoulder and taking Pamela by the hand. The two walked down the flagstone front path and as they turned left onto the sidewalk, Jane noticed Ella in front of her corner home placing mosquito netting over a beautiful navy blue and white Perego carriage. She called out to her neighbor and approached the carriage. She peeked inside to look at five-month-old Noranna, or as the baby was commonly called by the neighbors, Nan.

"Good morning, Ella. Nan is getting so big and looking more like you every day! She has the most beautiful blonde hair."

"Thank you, but I think she will be tall like John and not so small like me. I am afraid she will outgrow this carriage quickly."

"Oh, you'll have a good two years of use of the buggy before you need to switch her to a stroller. In February, when my new baby is due, I'll have to get my carriage back out of storage." They started to walk. "Boy, it sure is hot out today! Do you know if the others left for the pool yet?"

"Yes, I saw Norma, Anna, and Betty walk by my house a short time ago. How are you feeling, Jane, with this heat?"

"I'm okay. I'm not queasy any longer. It's funny, I never felt nauseous when I was expecting Pammy. Maybe this one is a boy. Wouldn't that make Danny happy to have a little addition to his construction crew!"

"Boy or girl, we just want them to be healthy," replied a serious Ella.

"Amen," countered Jane.

They reached the Village Green's fence-enclosed pool area and quickly found the other three ladies sitting at the edge of the children's splash pool with their legs in the cool water. Between Anna's feet sat a splashing sixteen-month-old Susan. At nineteen months, Robby Carter was a bit more independent, standing at one of the six sprinklers that was shooting water from the shallow pool's wall back into the center. Betty was within an arm's length of her sturdy son. Pamela immediately joined Robby at the sprinkler as Jane settled herself between Anna and Betty. Ella parked her carriage, with a sleeping Nan, steps away from the group on the shady part of the concrete patio surrounding the splash pool. Then she squeezed in at the end of the group, next to Anna. Behind the women, on the other side of a short dividing chained link fence, they could hear shouts and splashes coming from the larger main pool, complete with diving boards at its deepest end.

Despite the dozens of mothers and children occupying the splash pool area, Norma took up a small section at the corner next to Betty. Sitting at the pool's concrete edge, the striking brunette had her legs placed gracefully in the shallow water and was leaning back on her elbows cushioned by a beach towel she had placed behind her seat. Soaking in the sun's rays, Norma had a pair of fashionable sunglasses perched over her eyes on her upturned face. She was the only one in the group wearing a two-piece bathing suit, a summery lime green-and-white polka-dot number with a ruffled flounce around the bottom.

"Blimey, Norma! Do you have to look like a tart modeling for a swimsuit advertisement?" scolded Betty. "You've got the teenaged lifeguard staring at you."

Norma sat up, lowered her sunglasses a smidge down her tanned nose and looked over the rims at the young man seated on a chair at the center of the opposite side of the splash pool. She flashed him a brilliant, flirty smile, and he quickly looked away blushing. She said with a laugh, "Well, I guess I still have it, even at the old age of twenty-four!"

"I don't think it's funny to try to corrupt the young," reprimanded Betty. "What's the matter with you? You're not in high school anymore."

"Jealous, Bets?" questioned Norma as she resumed her reclined position.

"Of you, Norma Lewis? Never. I'm a secure adult who doesn't have to relive my younger glory days."

"Did you ever *really* have any glory days, Bets? I wonder..." drawled Norma with her face still pointing towards the hot sun.

Abruptly, Betty stood up from the pool lifting Robby with her and placing him firmly on her ample hip. She stepped onto the cement patio, tugged at the bottom of her one-piece black bathing suit with her free hand, and snapped, "I'm going to the loo," then made her way towards the far end of the adult-sized pool where the restrooms were located.

When she was out of earshot, Jane vehemently observed, "Jeez, Nor, you've gotta lay off of her. She's really beginning to hate you." Jane noticed Anna nodding her head in agreement.

"Oh please, Jane," said Norma as she sat up again and looked at Jane, now sitting next to her since Betty left. "Bets knows I'm only teasing. I'm just having some fun with her. Don't be so serious."

"I don't know, Nor. I'm starting to feel sorry for Betty. Being British, I'm not so sure she gets your sarcastic wit."

As a response, Norma just silently shrugged her shoulders with an annoyed look on her face.

Jane continued with a warning, "And Betty can be a little vindictive. I wouldn't want to be on her bad side."

"Let's change the subject," interjected Anna. "How's the construction going, Jane?"

I know Anna agrees with me, thought Jane, *so why isn't she also calling Norma out on her nastiness? But I'm not going to start an argument over this. It's too hot of a day for bickering.*

Instead, she sighed and said, "It's going. I'll be glad when it's done. Danny is already talking about the next project. He wants to build us a garage. Although I asked him, what would that be for...his old pick-up truck? Honestly, we've got to get a regular family car. The three of us fit on the front bench seat of that truck now, but what are we going to do once this new baby comes? We can't fit a family of four in a truck! I'd also like to have a car to use during the week for doctor visits, food shopping, and other errands. Ever since little Nan was born during that huge blizzard, I don't like the idea of being out here in the 'burbs without transportation."

"Yes, I agree," added Norma, apparently happy now that a new topic had been broached, and the spotlight was off her treatment of

Betty. "Since the United Nations completed their first structure in Manhattan, Ella's John can no longer carpool with Gor. That means, as of last week, both guys drive themselves each morning, and I've lost the use of our car. Even though I only had it a day or two each week, I really miss it."

"Well, since Sal bought our new car at the beginning of the summer, I have the old Dodge sitting in front of my house at our disposal... that is, in case Jane's February baby comes during another blizzard," said Anna with a grin.

"Bite your tongue! And, no offense, Anna, but I don't think I'd trust that old piece of junk to start during a snowstorm and get me to the hospital on time," countered Jane.

"No offense taken. I don't really trust it as a reliable second car either, despite all of Sal's tinkering with it. But when I can get it going, it is a wonderful thing to have the freedom to drive somewhere when I want to."

"Actually, we should all have second family cars for that freedom. We all know how to drive, right?" asked Jane.

"I do not," admitted Ella quietly. "I never did learn, although John has said he would show me."

"You should definitely let him teach you, Ella," encouraged Norma. "Do it on the weekends and leave little Nan with me when he takes you out. It's an important skill to have in this godforsaken area we live in."

"What's important to have?" asked Betty as she returned from the restrooms and pointedly sat at the end of the group next to Ella, as far away from Norma as she could be.

"A driver's license. I think we all need to petition the hubbies for a second family car," said Jane. "Actually, I've been tooling around with an idea to make some extra money. I could use the cash to buy a second-hand car, and then Danny can't refuse the idea."

"Do tell, Jane. How are you going to make money out here in the potato fields of Long Island?" inquired Norma.

"Tupperware!" announced Jane.

"Tupper what?" asked Betty.

"Tupperware. One of my timid sisters-in-law is making a killing selling the stuff in my old neighborhood in the Bronx. I'm sure I could outsell her any day of the week. And I just read that the company used to sell it in department stores, but now they've taken it off the shelves and are exclusively selling it through home demonstrations. With the thousands of new homes in Levittown, I could be a top seller."

"But, Jane, what is it?" an exasperated Betty asked again.

"It's those plastic bowls and containers that store food and keep airtight. Remember when I had coffee klatch last month, and I showed you girls the bowl with the burping lid? I bought it from my sister-in-law's home demonstration party. There was a company representative at the party trying to recruit future demonstrators. I took a promo package from her describing the whole process. I would manage a demonstration party at someone's house. I make a commission and the woman who is hosting the party gets a prize based on the number of sales at her party. The more sales, the bigger the prize. Then, I try to get other women at the party to agree to host their own party with a different group of women so they can get prizes, and so on and so forth."

Betty, with a gleam in her eyes, said, "Well, that doesn't sound too difficult, making money during a gathering of women. I'll host your first demonstration, Jane. I could use some storage bowls, and I'm *always* looking for a discount or bargain!"

"As is evident from her out-of-style clothes," murmured Norma for only Jane to hear.

"Did you say something, Nor?" asked Betty, ready to resume their earlier argument.

"I just said we'd all support Jane in her little business," Norma loudly replied for all to hear.

"It sounds like a very good idea, Jane," stated Ella.

"I'll host a future party, too," added Anna. "With my big family and Sal's, I'll have plenty of customers for you, Jane."

"That settles it. I'm going to call that rep tomorrow and get the ball rolling for my future business! Thanks for encouraging me, ladies."

Checking her wristwatch, Betty started to rise from her seated position and said, "You're welcome, Jane, but does anyone realize it's one o'clock already? Let's take the kids over to the playground and eat our lunches. I'm just about starved to death. If I don't get a sandwich in me soon, I'll pass out!"

Norma, obviously biting her tongue, dramatically rolled her eyes for only Jane to see.

Jane telephoned the Tupperware representative the next day. She was told she would need to visit the local distributor's office to complete a consultant training program and receive her display items. Jane made an appointment for the following Monday. With Danny working on their home's construction, Jane figured she would be able to use his truck to drive to her appointment. Now all she had to do was discuss the idea with her husband.

The following evening, Jane prepared Danny's favorite dinner of macaroni and cheese. She had fed dinner to their daughter earlier, and Pamela was now situated in front of the television watching a cartoon. After working a long day with his crew on the upstairs extension, Danny was happy, although suspicious, when his wife poured him a cold beer into a frosted glass. It was a Thursday night, and he normally saved any intake of alcohol for the weekends, when he could kick back and relax.

"Okay, Janie. What's up?"

"I'm serving my handsome, hard-working husband a much-deserved ice-cold beer," she responded after finishing the pour. She followed this with a quick kiss to his cheek and then turned to the casserole on the kitchen counter to start spooning it onto plates.

"Babe, you fed Pammy before us, and you made my favorite dinner *with* a beer. You must want something. I've known you for too long to think otherwise."

"Well…" began Jane as she placed the plates on the table and took her seat. "I do want to talk to you without Pammy interrupting."

"You can't be telling me you're expecting a baby because we both know you already are," joked Danny. He began to dig into his plate of food with enthusiasm.

"Ha-ha," mocked Jane, then quickly stated, "Danny, I want to get a little job."

"What?" spluttered Danny, gagging on his mouthful of food before he took a chug from his beer. He regained his composure and continued, "We have one kid and another on the way. We're expanding the house, so there will be more rooms to clean. A job too, Janie? That's taking on a lot."

"Hear me out, you big lug!" implored Jane and she launched into her explanation of the job of a Tupperware representative. She made a point of reminding him that she got the idea from the wife of one of his own brothers.

"And you know I can outsell her any day of the week. Think of it, Danny. Money will be tighter when this new baby comes, and we'll really need a bigger car. Four of us can't fit in your truck. And I'd like to have a car to myself for errands during the day while you have the truck at a jobsite. With my earnings, we can get a good used car, maybe one of those station wagons!"

"What about the kids? You said the parties would be in the evenings. You can't take them with you," Danny pointed out.

"That's when I'll be counting on my tall, handsome, wonderful, generous, and did I mention handsome, husband! I'll have the two kids all fed and ready for bed. You'll just have to read them a story and put them down for the night."

"How often will these parties be and how long will you be gone?"

"I wouldn't do more than one party a week, and I'll probably be gone about three hours all together. Please agree to do this for me, Danny. It would mean a lot to me. You know I have more energy than I know what to do with. This Tupperware business will not interfere with anything at home, I promise. Cross my heart and hope to die," a reverent Jane vowed and made an x on her chest with her right index finger.

"Great," guffawed Danny. "Now, you're going to leave me a widower with two kids!"

"You'll never get rid of me, Mr. Flynn. You're stuck with me for the long haul! So, seriously, what do you say?"

Danny thought for a moment, then sighed, and said, "I'm willing to support your little venture and do my part with the kids. I know once you, my determined and bossy wife, have set your mind on something, there's no way me or anyone else can talk you out of it. However, you've got to promise me that if we find your job is causing problems here at home, we'll have to rethink the matter."

Jane jumped out of her chair and gave him a big smack on the lips. "I promise, you big lug, cross my heart and hope..."

"Don't say it!" interrupted a superstitious Danny, and they both burst out laughing.

Norma volunteered to watch Pamela on the day Jane went to her Tupperware training session. Jane brought her daughter across the street to Norma's house at nine in the morning and returned home full of excitement at four in the afternoon. As Jane entered Norma's front door, Pamela came running towards her with a big smile on her face, waving her little hands.

"Look, Mommy. Nor-Nor painted my fingernails! Isn't they pretty?" demanded the thrilled three-year-old.

Jane laughed and said, "Yes, my darling, you look very glamorous, but you mustn't call Mrs. Lewis by her first name. It's not very nice for children to do that."

"Don't scold her, Jane. I told her to call me Norma, but she concocted Nor-Nor. I'm fine with it," said Norma, coming up behind the child.

"I'm so glad you had a fun time today, Pammy, but you must call her Mrs. Lewis from now on. Okay, sweetheart?" asked Jane.

"Okay, Mommy. Tank you, Missus Lewdwis," chirped Pamela. "I'm gonna get my toys to bring home."

"I hope you don't mind the manicure," Norma said as Pamela disappeared into the small back bedroom to gather her belongings. "I thought it would be a fun thing for us girls to do, and she got such a kick out of it. She was profoundly serious about not touching anything while her nails were drying. I read her three books as she sat as still as a statue with her hands splayed out on my kitchen table, even though I told her she didn't have to be that careful. But she said, 'No, this is how Mommy sits after she paints her fingers.' She is such a delight, Jane. You're so lucky!"

"Thanks. You should have one, too. You'd make a great mom! You know, once kids get past the infant stage, they actually become good company and a lot of fun."

Jane immediately noticed a shadow and a look of sadness cross Norma's face. *Stupid me*, thought Jane. *Why did I let that slip out?*

"I'm sorry, Nor. It's none of my business why you and Gor don't have children yet. I'm always sticking my foot in my mouth."

"It's okay, Jane. I'm sure you've wondered why I'm the only one on this block who isn't a mother by now."

"You don't need to tell me, if you don't want to."

"I had a medical issue before I was married. I can't have children. Gor and I are going to investigate adoption after he graduates from college this December. Hopefully, a year from now, I'll be a mother, too."

"Oh, I'm sorry, but that would be wonderful. Adopting, I mean. That Gordon is quite a guy," stammered Jane. She didn't know what to say in a situation like this. Then she added, "Your secret is safe with me, Nor. I won't tell anyone."

"Anna and Ella already know. I told them when we were delivering the baby during the blizzard. Of course, my family and Gor's know....and my two best friends from high school. I don't really like to advertise my personal problems, but I know you three neighbors will keep it quiet. However, please, don't tell Betty. She has a big mouth, and I don't want her to know my business."

"No, of course not, my lips are sealed. I won't even tell Danny," Jane promised.

Pamela emerged from the back of the house with her toys and books gathered in her small arms. Norma bent down to help the child organize her bundle. She gave Pamela a big hug and said, "Anytime you want to have a play date with me, Miss Pammy, you just ask Mommy. Okay, darling?"

"Yes, yes, yes," shrieked Pamela. "Pleeeaassee Mommy, can I come again?"

"We'll see, Pammy. Thanks again, Nor. I really appreciate it. And now since I'm a fully accredited Tupperware Consultant, I'm going to telephone Betty and take her up on that offer to host my first party. You'll come, won't you, Nor?"

"I wouldn't miss your debut for anything, Jane. I'm proud of you. You've even got me thinking of getting a little job for myself."

True to her word, Betty hosted an evening gathering two weeks later for Jane's first organized home party. All the coffee klatch ladies were in attendance. Betty had invited Bob's mother and his two sisters from Queens. Jane's mother and two of Jane's sisters drove out from the Bronx for the occasion. Jane's third sister, the eldest of the four O'Brien girls, abstained since she had asked Jane to run a similar party at her own home in Floral Park the following week. As the Carters' house was at the corner of Strong Lane, Betty had also invited a few of the homemakers who resided on the street perpendicular to her own.

It was a good-sized group for Jane's first demonstration, and although she was nervous, she did a splendid job describing the products. The sales were substantial, which made Betty happy with her prize of free Tupperware items. Afterwards, two of the women from the next street agreed to host future parties, and Anna planned one at her house in October.

By the time she supervised her fourth party at Anna's, Jane was exuberant. She was no longer nervous and, with each party, grew more proficient in organizing successful demonstrations. She was proud of herself for setting a goal, working hard, and achieving it. With Danny's assistance, she was on her way to a successful part-time career. Her constant mantra was *I can visualize that second family vehicle within my grasp!*

CHAPTER 10

Norma - 1952

It was the afternoon before Valentine's Day, and Norma was hosting a coffee klatch in her kitchen. The women were gathered tightly around the table discussing the special meals each of them planned to prepare for the following evening.

"...and so, I'm making macaroni and cheese. It's Danny's favorite," concluded Jane.

"That's not a very special Valentine's dinner, Jane, compared to the dishes Ella, Anna and I are cooking," observed Betty.

"I'm nine months pregnant and running Tupperware parties on an average of twice a week. I don't have the time or energy to make some elaborate dinner like you gals," was Jane's retort. "And besides,

Danny is no gourmet. He'll be happy with it, and mac-n-cheese is something Pammy will eat too. I'll throw a candle on the table and make it romantic."

"Leave the candle out of your scenario, Jane. You and fire don't mix well," interjected Norma.

"What is that supposed to mean, Nor?" demanded Jane.

"Oh, come on, Jane. Have you already forgotten the beginning of last summer? Remember when you almost burned down your house?" began Norma with an impish grin.

"I did not!"

"You did so," countered Norma warming to her tale. "It was when Gordon and John used to carpool together. The men were returning home from work in John's car and had just turned onto our street when they suddenly saw a huge fireball of flames coming from the side yard of your house, Jane. You thought you would get a start on dinner before Danny came home and went to light that portable outdoor barbecue grill of yours. But you used way too much lighter fluid. Gor dashed out of the car and grabbed your garden house, putting out the inferno. And then you got mad at him because you'd used the last of the charcoal briquettes, and he had flooded the whole grill base with water making the last of your charcoal unusable."

They all started chuckling except for a mildly offended Jane who replied, "Norma Lewis, you exaggerate! It was *not* an inferno or fireball. Just an unusually loud whoosh and high flame, nothing I couldn't handle. I didn't need to be saved by any man."

"Oh, please," Norma chortled. "Gor and John both said afterwards that before Gor dashed over, you were jumping up and down and trying to put out the flames by taking big breathes and blowing on it!"

"She is correct, Jane," confirmed Ella, giggling. "John told me the same account of your mishap."

They were all laughing harder now, and even Jane couldn't keep a smirk from her face before adding, "Well, I had the last laugh. I made Gordon clean out my grill and give me some of his fresh charcoal. Of course, he insisted on lighting the new set-up."

"I wonder why?" Anna asked with feigned sincerity as tears of mirth slid down her face. "I'm just glad you keep that grill on the side of your house adjacent to Ella's home and not mine."

"What makes you think I want my home burnt to the ground?" Ella gleefully added.

"Ha-ha, ladies," said an unamused Jane. "Like you all don't do some screwy things. I can find things to pick on, too."

"Oh, Jane, we love you," conceded Norma after wiping the tears of laughter from her face. "That's why we tease you in jest. Don't be mad."

"I'm not mad. I can roll with the punches," Jane rebounded and then, taking on a highbrow attitude, declared, "And thank you, Mrs. Carter, for being the only kind one here and not verbally mocking me like these other three. It's nice to know who my friends are…"

"It *is* a wickedly funny yarn," Betty acknowledged, still chuckling. "But seriously, it's true we've *all* done some daft things. You wouldn't know this, Ella, because it happened before you moved here, but one of the first times Norma hosted a gathering, she made the ghastliest cake."

Of course, Betty would have to bring up a faux pas of mine, thought Norma. However, beating Betty to the punch, Norma quickly disclosed with good humor, "I remember that. I confused the salt for the sugar while mixing the batter and almost poisoned you all! Most of you were trying to be polite and take a second bite before Betty finally announced,

'This is bloody awful! What did you do to the cake, Nor?' It was then I realized what I'd done. You girls know that baking isn't my forte. That's Betty's strong point."

So there, Betty! surmised Norma. *I not only confessed my own mistake without your negative depiction, but I also threw in a compliment to throw you off the hunt.*

Betty raised her eyebrows with an indifferent attitude and asked, "So what are you going to cook for Gordon for Valentine's dinner, Nor? We've each said what we plan on preparing."

"This is a special Valentine's Day for you, Norma," said Ella. "It is the first one you will be celebrating since Gordon received his college degree."

"Yes, I've spent a few Valentines' nights alone in the past when he was in school. I want this one to be extra special. He and I also have something important to discuss, and I'd like to do it over a candlelit dinner," Norma stated mysteriously.

"What would that be, Nor?" questioned Betty.

Wouldn't you like to know, Norma thought. She ignored nosey Betty and instead said, "Actually, girls, I have a little problem. What I want to do is make a meal with the new pressure cooker my in-laws gave me at Christmas. Gor keeps asking me when I'm going to use it, but truthfully, I haven't even removed it from the box."

"Why not?" asked Anna.

"Frankly, I'm afraid of the stupid thing. I read in the newspaper that some woman used it incorrectly, and she got burned when it exploded!"

"It's not that difficult, Nor. That woman probably didn't adequately vent the pot," said Betty. "Bob bought me one for Christmas, too. I love it; it drastically cuts down the cooking time when I make beef stew."

"Do any of you other girls have this new contraption?" inquired Norma.

Ella and Anna responded in the negative, and Jane said, "I don't even know what it is!"

Betty explained, "It's a big pot you seal with a lid. You start it on the stove with high heat to build up steam, and the pressure increases. At the right time, you must lower the heat and release some steam. In addition to shortening the cooking time, it keeps the food tastier because you don't lose so much flavor boiling in an open pot."

"Well, I'm still intimidated by the directions," confessed Norma. "And I already purchased the meat, potatoes and veggies to prepare a pot roast dinner in it for tomorrow."

"I'll come over tomorrow afternoon to show you, Nor," Betty offered unexpectedly. "Bob is off from work tomorrow. He can watch Robby for an hour. If you have the meat and veggies all prepped before I get there, I can get you started and explain what you need to do to finish the task."

"That's a perfect solution. Don't you think so, Nor?" Anna, looking incredibly pleased, asked enthusiastically. Norma knew amiable Anna would love nothing more than for Norma and Betty to bond over something, even if it was just instructions in using this idiotic kitchen gadget. *I just hope Betty doesn't sabotage the process on purpose, so I do end up with an exploding pot,* Norma worried.

Anna, Ella, and Jane looked at her hopefully while Betty's expression was, as perceived by Norma, an obviously forced neutral one. Norma knew she had no choice. She replied in an overly honeyed voice,

"That is exceedingly kind of you, Bets. What time would you be able to come over?"

At the agreed time, Betty walked through Norma's kitchen door. Norma had already cleaned and prepared the vegetables, and the roast, wrapped in brown butcher paper, sat on the counter. Norma had the brand-new pot out of the box and on her stove. She had a pad of paper and a pen to jot notes on the instructions Betty would share with her.

It had occurred to Norma this morning that over the past few years, she and Betty rarely conversed alone. Ever since Betty had gotten perturbed over the ridiculous newspaper interviews, Norma had socialized with her only among the other neighbors. *It's sort of a shame,* Norma pondered, *since we live right next door to each other, and our husbands get along well enough.* She decided she would truly try her best today to receive the gift of Betty's assistance with grace and gratitude.

"Thanks for coming, Bets. I really appreciate it," Norma now greeted her with sincerity.

"That's okay, Nor. Glad to help a homemaker who lacks some skills that I possess."

I will not make a snide remark, I will not make a snide... Norma kept repeating to herself, doing her best to remain controlled.

"So... we will start with the roast and brown it on all sides in the cooker," instructed Betty.

"That's the same thing I do when I cook a pot roast in a regular pot," said Norma and took to the task.

After the browning, Betty showed her how to add liquid, seal the lid and bring the cooker up to full pressure. Once that was done,

Betty reduced the stovetop heat to low while maintaining full pressure. Norma furiously scribbled detailed notes for herself. She was grateful Betty was providing her with the means to use the pot confidently on her own in the future.

"Okay, now the meat will cook for thirty minutes, and then I'll show you how to use the quick-release method to lower the pressure so you can open the lid and add your spuds and veggies."

"Great, Bets. Do you want to run home and get some of your dinner prep done in the thirty minutes?"

"I don't need to, Nor. I made my dinner this morning and have it in the fridge, ready to just bake later. That's what's so brilliant about making stuffed peppers; it can all be done ahead of time."

What a haughty smart aleck, fumed Norma. *She acts like I have no idea how to cook just because I needed some help. She's enjoying that I'm at her culinary mercy.* Norma sighed and repeated to herself, *I will not make a snide...*

"Do you have any tea or coffee for us?" asked Betty. "Then we can have a good chinwag while we're waiting for me to show you the next step."

Norma loathed that British term of Betty's. When Betty said 'chinwag' instead of 'chat,' Norma always pictured a big wild turkey with its bright red wattle flapping on its neck. And the last thing she wanted to do was to have a one-on-one chat with her inquisitive neighbor. *Time to put my guard up,* she warned herself.

"Sure, Bets. I'll put the kettle on. I don't have any leftover morning coffee, and there won't be time to brew another pot."

"I'm fine with a cuppa," replied Betty pleasantly.

After the water boiled and the tea was brewed, they sat at the table while the kitchen's minute-timer quietly ticked off the designated thirty minutes. Norma was willing it to go faster when Betty coyly inquired, "So, Nor, did you do much cooking before you were married?"

"Yes, some," responded a wary Norma. *This is where the interrogation starts, and where I need to sidestep the deeply personal grilling.*

"Did your mother teach you?"

"My mother wasn't much of a cook. We had a housekeeper who came in on weekdays and prepared most of our meals."

"Why am I not surprised?" replied Betty with raised eyebrows.

I will not make a snide remark...

Norma continued with forced cordiality, "My grandmother taught me how to cook."

"Was that your German grandmother?"

Oh, Bets, you don't forget a thing, do you? I mentioned only once my father's parents were from Germany...

"No, it was my mother's mother. I guess the desire to cook skipped a generation," Norma lightheartedly answered.

"Did you cook many meals when you lived in that apartment in New York City with your girlfriends? I would imagine secretarial school was expensive, so you needed to economize and cook at home. Or were attractive men taking you out to dinner every night?" Betty questioned with a feigned playfulness.

And there it is, predicted an unsurprised Norma. *Betty's constant attempt to find out more about my life right before I married Gordon.*

Norma was saved by the bell when the timer started to ring. She jumped up and retrieved her pad and pen to write down the next instructions. "Show me what to do next, Bets."

Betty reluctantly dropped her line of questioning and demonstrated how to release the pot's pressure and safely open the lid. Norma added the other ingredients, and Betty again sealed the lid.

"You'll need to bring the cooker up to full pressure again and cook it all for an additional fifteen minutes," Betty directed. "Then you use the quick-release method again and... voila! You can transfer the roast and veggies to a serving platter."

"Thank you, Bets. I genuinely appreciate your help. I have it all written down." Norma remained standing by the stove. She did not want to resume their seats at the table for additional conversation.

"You're welcome," said Betty as she grabbed her cup of tea from the table to finish it. She looked at Norma over the rim of her teacup and asked, "So, Nor, what's this important issue you and Gor need to discuss tonight over this lovely dinner I've helped you prepare?"

If you think that just because you instructed me today, I will now share with you the anticipated discussion concerning adoption I'm planning to have with my husband, you are sadly mistaken, Bets!

In an easygoing voice, Norma laughed off the inquiry, "Questions, questions, Betty Carter! You have so many today! But seriously, it is getting late, and you should go home and start baking *your* lovely dinner. I can take it from here."

"Are you sure you don't want me to do the last pressure release with you?"

The only pressure I want to release is this false cheerful demeanor I'm projecting, Norma thought handing Betty's jacket to her.

"No thanks, Bets. I have all the steps written down. I'm confident I can do it," Norma gaily replied while opening the door. "Happy Valentine's Day to you, Bob and little Robby."

CHAPTER 11

Betty - 1952

B etty Carter jumped when she heard the boom of a firecracker in the near distance. Although it was only nine o'clock in the morning, her living room's two windows were wide open to cool down the house from the early morning heat. The firecracker's reverberation resonated clearly through the mesh window screens. She quickly surmised the sound had come from the front yard of the house located directly behind her own. Her 'back-door neighbors,' as she called the Keller family, had two teenaged sons. Betty was sure it was the two boys testing some of the fireworks they would be using in full force on Independence Day this Friday.

The Fourth of July was Betty's least favorite American holiday and not only because of the noise that would be a constant in her neighborhood during the upcoming three-day weekend. Betty would never admit this to her patriotic husband, but she secretly disliked the Fourth because she felt like a hypocrite celebrating it in her adopted country. After all, it commemorated the United States' independence from her native Great Britain. Most of the time, Betty thought the thirteen colonies should have stayed under British rule. Maybe then Americans, like the Kellers, would have better manners.

"What dat, Mommy?" asked Robby as he ran to her from his small bedroom at the back of the house.

"It was a firecracker, my little love," replied Betty, giving her two-and-a-half-year-old son a hug. "There will be more over the next few days for America's birthday. Remember Daddy was telling you about it last night?"

"Yup, I remember. Did the boom make baby scared?" asked Robby, pointing to his mother's tummy.

Betty and Bob had just last night shared the news with Robby that he was going to be a big brother. Betty was only ten weeks along and had not wanted to tell her son this early. She had told her husband that Robby had no concept of time and would never understand that his sibling would not arrive until January. Nevertheless, Bob had been bursting with excitement and had insisted on explaining the happy news to his son. He had painstakingly explained that when Robby turned three, a baby brother or sister would arrive as an extra birthday gift. This had led to a discussion on Robby's part of how many birthday parties he might attend before his own. Bob had told his son the next birthday they would celebrate would be the one for the United States on Friday. Betty had rolled her eyes and had told Bob he was creating a nightmare for her; she predicted her son would be pestering her every day asking when January would arrive.

"The baby is just fine, Robby. Did you gather your shovel and bucket to bring to the beach today? We're leaving soon. We'll be going in Mrs. Flynn's car with Pammy."

"Baby Mark come too?"

"No, Robby. Pammy's baby brother will stay home with his grandma. Now find your bucket and shovel, and please clean up the toys on the floor in your room before we leave."

"Okay Mommy. But I sad baby Mark not wit us. He's gonna miss all the fun," Robby said quietly.

"That's very nice you are worried about him, but Mark will be happy at home since he can't walk yet," replied Betty as Robby scampered into his room.

Betty had to smile. Her son's ability to converse at two and a half years was really progressing. In her opinion, he was very advanced for his age. And he was learning to be as compassionate and soft-spoken as her husband. Although it still annoyed Betty that Bob didn't have a desire for career advancement, he was, more importantly, the type of man who could not bear to see anyone hurt or unhappy. And that was what Betty loved about him.

Betty focused on the day ahead. The Strong Lane women and their children, except for Jane's five-month-old son Mark Daniel Flynn, were headed to Jones Beach, the big, beautiful New York State Park on the south shore of Long Island. Since Bob was working a day shift on the Long Island Rail Road and using the Carters' car, Betty and Robby would be travelling to the beach with Jane and Pamela in the Flynns' prized second vehicle.

Betty had to hand it to Jane. When that Flynn woman set her mind on something, she didn't stop until she got it. Since starting her Tupperware business last fall, a pregnant Jane had worked a whirlwind of home parties and had barely stopped to deliver her son on the last day of February. The Irish Tornado, as Betty secretly thought of Jane, had actually managed a demonstration party at a Levittown home two nights after she came home from her week's stay in the maternity ward. By May, Jane had saved enough of her commissions to buy a used 1948 Pontiac wood-sided station wagon. The car was a little banged up, since it had belonged to one of Danny's friends who had used it for his plumbing business. When Danny had learned that the guy was trading the wagon in for a truck, he had negotiated a deal for his wife. Jane had cleaned up the wagon until it sparkled and drove her treasure constantly.

Betty admired Jane's tenacity and hard work in obtaining a second vehicle for her family. But in contrast, she resented the fact that her next-door neighbor had a second car handed to her without lifting a finger herself. This past winter, Norma had acquired a five-year-old car from her parents. Apparently, Mr. and Mrs. Wolf traded in their automobile every five years for a brand-new model. At the time, Betty had silently contemplated, *Norma probably whined to her parents that she needed a car. And, as if by magic, a 1947 sedan suddenly appears in front of Nor's home.* At the time, Norma had claimed she and Gor had worked out a deal for the car with her parents. This way, Norma had explained, she would have her own transportation for her new part-time job in the admissions office of the maternity wing at the nearby Meadowbrook Hospital.

Betty fumed that each of the women on Strong Lane had a second vehicle except for her, and the non-licensed Ella. And John Schmidt had just recently started giving Ella driving lessons whenever the two could spare an hour and get Norma to keep an eye on little Nan. Betty was certain John would eventually buy his wife a car too, and then even Ella would join the two-car club. Betty was even jealous of Anna and her old clunker of a second car that practically had to be resurrected each time she wanted to use it.

Betty repeatedly mentioned to Bob that she needed her own vehicle. She thought this request might also spur him to try for a railroad supervisor position and earn more money. She had promised Bob two years ago that she would never bring up the subject of college again, but she still heavily hinted to her husband about looking into a promotion. Unlike Jane, Betty had no desire to try to earn the money herself for a car purchase. She had enough to keep her busy at home, and she was raised to believe that the husband should be the sole breadwinner. But Bob saw no need for a second car for the Carter household, since Betty had their car at her disposal during the days when he worked a night shift.

Therefore, on this very hot first day of July, Norma and Jane would act as the drivers chauffeuring the women and children to the cooler haven of the Atlantic shoreline. When these plans were secured at yesterday's coffee klatch at Ella's house, Betty immediately claimed a place in Jane's wagon. There was no way she wanted to be driven by Norma!

At ten o'clock, the women met outside and loaded the two automobiles with all the items they would need for their day at the beach. Jane's parents, the O'Briens, would babysit their new grandson, Mark. The older couple were staying with the Flynns for the week to assist with the big Fourth of July gathering on Friday. Every Independence Day, since they had moved into their home, Jane and Danny hosted a huge backyard barbecue for both their extended families. They always invited their Strong Lane neighbors, too.

After a twelve-mile ride, the two drivers secured spots for their cars next to each other in the large parking lot adjacent to the Zach's Bay area of Jones Beach. Before they left Levittown, the ladies had agreed the calm water and lack of waves in the bay area were better suited to their young children as opposed to the rougher ocean side of the beach. The women would have rather planted themselves, as they did when they were younger, before starting families, on the pristine sand between the ocean and the front of the beautiful East Bathhouse. However, with their children's collective ages spanning from sixteen months to four years, they knew the safer choice was the bay.

As the mothers unloaded the cars and made their way, with belongings and children, to claim a spot on the bay's beach, Norma walked to the nearest nautical-themed hut to rent two of Jones Beach's signature striped umbrellas. She was able to coax one of the hut's male attendants into carrying and setting up the umbrellas at the mothers' chosen sandy location near the water. With several old quilts spread under the shade of the large canvas umbrellas, the women and children had an oasis of comfort from the hot sun.

For the next hour, the older two children travelled back and forth from the shade to the bay's gentle lapping water where Jane and Betty stood chatting and supervising. Pamela and Robby collected water in their beach buckets to dump into a hole Norma had dug near the quilts. The girl and boy were amazed that no matter how many times they poured water into the hole, the salty liquid would disappear as it soaked into the sand at the bottom. They finally gave up and plopped down to dig in the damp mixture they had made. Norma showed them how to make sandcastles with their buckets.

Two-year-old Susan held Anna's hand as they slowly walked along the shore collecting little stones that had washed up on the sand. And Nan, at sixteen months, held both of Ella's hands from above and toddled in front of her mother from the island of blankets to the edge of the bay, shrieking with joy each time her tiny toes touched the water.

By noon, all the little ones were looking to devour the food and cool drinks their mothers had packed. After their lunch, the children lay down for a rest under the protection of the umbrellas. One by one, they started to doze as the adults sat near them on the quilts quietly chatting.

Gazing out to the bay in front of her and then to her left at the northwest corner of Zach's Bay, Norma commented, "I wonder when the new marine stadium will be completed. They tore down that old wooden structure rather quickly. When I was seven or eight, I remember my parents taking me to see a water circus in the old open-air theater. They actually had elephants on that flimsy wooden stage. I remember wondering if it would hold their weight. Did any of you girls ever go there as a child?"

"I remember when I was a kid my parents piled us O'Brien girls into an old, borrowed auto—my parents didn't own a car back then— and drove out for an entire day at Jones Beach. During the day at the old stadium, we watched a water show, complete with an Olympic swimmer, and then at night there was a fireworks show. It was a really good day; one of my best childhood memories," reminisced Jane.

"Was the Olympic swimmer Johnny Weissmuller?" asked Anna. "I used to love him in those Tarzan movies when I was a girl."

"No, I don't think so. He was too famous as a movie star when we were kids. I don't think he would've been doing some rinky-dink water show out here in the mid-1930's," replied Jane.

"I read in the newspaper, the new stadium will have a revolving center stage and an underwater tunnel connecting the shore to the stage," said Ella. "It said there would be a lagoon separating the outdoor stage from the seats opposite it."

"Wow, imagine that! I think I heard it would be ready for shows next summer," added Jane.

"Speaking of shows, what do we have to do to get a handsome young man in a bathing suit to walk by us on this beach?" commented

Norma. "I love you gals and your children, but spending time on the family beach is a bore. This beach is ninety percent mothers, and the few men are harried-looking fathers. Even the lifeguards they place here are the older, uninteresting ones since no one drowns in this dreary bay. Now, if we were sitting over on the Boardwalk in front of one of the bathhouses, we would hopefully have a parade of movie-star quality men!"

"Oh, for goodness sakes, Norma! You're married," scolded Betty. "And Gordon is one of the best-looking husbands. As a married woman, how can you have such cheek?"

"I may be married, Bets, but I'm not dead! I love Gor, and he is a dreamboat. But I'm just talking about looking, not acting on it. God knows, married men ogle bathing beauties all the time. Why can't we enjoy ourselves too?"

"Here, here," cheered Jane.

Anna laughed and asked, "If you had your choice of any film actor to walk by us in a bathing suit right now, who would you choose, Norma?"

"Oh, hands down, it would be Marlon Brando. Did you see him in that torn undershirt in *A Streetcar Named Desire?* I'd like to see that brooding guy in swim trunks," answered Norma.

"You would go for the bad boy, Nor," chuckled Jane. "I'd be happy if William Holden suddenly walked by. I thought he was adorable in that movie *Born Yesterday* a few years ago."

"I like Gregory Peck. The first film I saw in America had him in it fighting social injustice. I find his serious, straight-minded approach very reassuring," said Ella.

"You would," countered Betty, rolling her eyes.

"For me, it would have to be Dean Martin," stated Anna. "What can I say? I'm a sucker for Italian men, especially one with wavy dark hair and a smoldering singing voice."

"And, what about you, Bets? Is Dino's goofy comedy partner Jerry Lewis your ideal movie star?" asked Norma with a saccharine grin.

"Ha-ha, Norma. No, I always liked John Wayne. I remember seeing one of his earliest movies, *Stagecoach*, when I was a teenager in England. He was my ultimate model of a living American cowboy."

"Who knew that little Elizabeth James dreamed of being swept off her feet by a cowboy on a horse?" countered Norma. "But I'm not really sure if John Wayne is a good choice for a man in swim trunks. He's got that strange, swaggering walk. Sexy enough when wearing the cowboy outfit, but in a bathing suit?"

Anna diplomatically changed subjects and asked, "How is the part-time job at the hospital, Nor?"

"I still only work two days a week, but it's been a great four months so far," gushed Norma. "Right before I was married, I had volunteered for a few hours each weekend at a similar position in a maternity hospital located near my parents."

Strange, Betty thought, *that is one of the few times Norma has ever shared an incident from her recent past. She'll reminisce about her childhood but gives little insight into her years between high school and marriage.*

Norma was still talking, "This job, though, is much better since now I get paid! Gor is making a nice salary since he became an engineer after graduation last December, but it is nice to have some mad money of my own. Most of all, I adore helping the expectant parents come in and get settled before the birth. The mothers-to-be are all calm, but the husbands can't even remember their own names to write on the paperwork I give to them. Some days, it's a real hoot!"

Betty's obstetrician was located at the same hospital where Norma worked. Betty just hoped when she delivered her baby next January, it would not be on a day Norma was at the admissions desk. However, this conversation about the maternity ward was a perfect springboard for Betty to make her big announcement, since she had not mentioned her pregnancy to any of her neighbors yet. However, just before she could open her mouth, Jane spoke.

"By the way, who's coming to my big July Fourth shindig on Friday? I hope the weather is good. I don't want a rainout."

"Thank you for inviting me, Jane, but John, Nan, and I are leaving on Thursday to go upstate for the long weekend. We will be staying with John's parents at the dairy farm and visiting the entire Schmidt family. They have not seen little Nan since we drove there for Christmas," explained Ella.

"Was Nan walking when they saw her last?" asked Betty.

"No, she was just holding on to furniture then, so they will be very pleased with her progress."

"I'm afraid we can't attend either, Jane," said Anna. "Sal, Susan, and I will be driving bright and early Friday morning into Brooklyn. Sal's parents will host a big outdoor party for all his relatives. They also invited my parents and my younger siblings that still live at home. My in-laws are closing their store for the whole three days of the weekend and will use most of the food inventory for the party. My father-in-law thinks it's a clever way to restock the store the following week with fresh goods for the start of the summer. There will be fireworks to watch on the East River in the evening, so we'll probably stay overnight at my parents' house afterwards."

"Well, I'll miss having you, but with all the O'Briens and Flynns, I'm not so sure I'll notice your absence," laughed Jane, then, looking at Norma and Betty, said, "What about you two?"

"Gor and I will come. I love your family. They're so much fun," raved Norma.

"I'll come with Robby. Bob is going to work the entire day for double-time pay. The railroad still runs on a holiday," began Betty, before pausing dramatically and adding, "…And besides, we'll need the extra money. Our little family of three will be expanding in January. I'm expecting a new baby, ladies!"

Jane let out a celebratory whoop, waking most of the children. The others started excitedly questioning the expectant mother. Betty, who loved to be the center of positive attention, was in her glory. The rest of the afternoon passed in a happy, golden haze for her.

Jane's wish for the weather was granted, and Friday dawned hot and sunny with a perfect holiday forecast. Betty rose from bed early so she could have breakfast with Bob before he left the house at eight for his ten-hour holiday shift. Immediately after her husband departed, Betty washed the breakfast dishes. Before Robby awakened, she wanted to start the baking preparations on a special holiday-themed cake to bring to the Flynns' party. Betty would always bake a celebratory cake to bring when invited to someone's home. She and Robby would be heading to Jane's backyard around noon.

As Betty reached for her shiny chrome flour canister sitting on a shelf above her stove, she felt a sharp pain in her abdomen. Alarmed, she stopped and sat down on one of her kitchen chairs. After a few deep breaths, she felt better. She was about to resume tentatively her task when Robby walked into the kitchen, rubbing his eyes and asking for his breakfast. Simultaneously, Betty busily attended to him and began her baking project.

An hour later, the cake was in the oven and Robby had been washed and dressed. He was playing quietly in his bedroom when Betty felt a second pain. This time it was like the type of strong cramp she usually experienced during her monthlies.

Oh, God, no, thought Betty, and she went into the bathroom to make sure she wasn't spotting. When she discovered that she was, panic set in. She grabbed a towel, went to her bedroom, and lay down on her bed. She willed herself to calm down and think. She remembered Anna saying once that she had spotted a little during her early pregnancy with Susan and that such occurrences could be perfectly normal. Betty respected Anna's intelligence about birth, and she wished the Marinos were home so she could telephone Anna to ask her opinion. However, this morning while waving goodbye to Bob, Betty had seen Anna, Sal and Susan in their car driving down Strong Lane on their way to Brooklyn.

Just then, Robby walked into her room and said, "Why you sleeping, Mommy?"

"I'm just resting, my little love. I think I did too much work this morning, so I'm just having a quick lay down. I'll be better in a jiffy. You get back to your toys, and I'll let you know when it's time to go to Pammy's house."

"Okay, Mommy," said Robby and he scooted back to his room.

I must call Bob, thought Betty. She realized, though, that she had no way of directly contacting her husband. At best, she could leave a message at the Jamaica Queens main-branch train station and hope he checked in on his mid-day break. Then Betty realized, with a skeleton crew for the holiday, there probably wouldn't be anyone staffing the telephones in Jamaica. Betty contemplated calling Bob's parents or his sisters, but they were all in Queens. It would take them too long to get here.

When Betty felt another strong cramp, her mind turned to closer assistance. Anna and Ella were out of town, and Jane had enough on her plate with the big barbecue. That left only Norma and Gordon next door. Asking Norma Lewis for help was the last thing Betty wanted to do. Betty thought about calling an ambulance for herself, but she didn't want to upset Robby. What would he think about a siren and men in white jackets taking his mother out on a stretcher? And he couldn't very well come with her to the hospital. She had no choice; she had to call Norma.

Betty gingerly slid off the bed and started to make her way to the living room. She grabbed the telephone and took it with her to the corner of the room where Robby could not observe her. She dropped slowly to the floor and tried to get comfortable as she started to dial Norma's number. Her neighbor answered on the second ring.

"Nor, you've got to help me," whispered Betty without a preamble.

"Who is this?" asked Norma.

"It's Betty. Something is wrong with the baby. You must come over right away and bring Gordon. Come quietly through my kitchen door so as not to upset Robby."

"We're on our way," said Norma and the telephone clicked off. Two minutes later, Norma and Gordon were standing in Betty's living room listening to her story.

"I'm going to call the hospital for an ambulance," said Gordon quietly as he started to reach for the telephone by Betty's side.

"No, please don't. It will upset Robby terribly. If one of you could watch Robby and the other drive me to the hospital, I think that would be best," whispered Betty.

Norma calmly took charge. Looking directly into Betty's troubled eyes, she said, "Meadowbrook Hospital is less than ten minutes away with a shortcut I use when I go to work there. I'll drive you, and, overall, it will be a lot faster than waiting for an ambulance to drive here and then make the return trip back to the hospital. Don't you worry, Bets." She turned her attention to her husband and said, "Gordon, you can bring Robby over to our house for a little while and then go over to the Flynns. The women there will help you look after him. And Gor, go shut the oven off and put that cake I smell on the counter while I help Betty get up."

"Okay, but before I take Robby, I'll go get your car, Nor, and pull it up onto Betty's side lawn so she doesn't have too far to walk from the kitchen door," said Gordon before he dashed into the kitchen for the oven and then ran out the side door to get the car.

With the two women left alone in the living room, Norma asked, "Do you want me to explain to Robby what is going on?"

"No, I'll explain it to him. Just help me to stand and get to a chair in the kitchen before you bring him to me," said Betty.

"You're a very good mother. You always put that boy before anything else, and I admire that," remarked Norma earnestly as she assisted Betty off the floor.

Betty could not savor the compliment because she immediately let out a soft moan. "I don't know if I can walk, Nor."

"Of course, you can. Come on, Bets. What was that advice you told us your mother always gave you during the war? Something about when things get tough…"

Betty grimaced and finished with, "Pull yourself up by your bootstraps and keep going."

Norma put her arm around Betty's waist, and they started to make their way to the kitchen. "That's right, Bets. You keep going!"

Norma delivered Betty to a kitchen chair and then fetched Robby. Betty explained to her solemn-faced son that Mrs. Lewis would be driving her to the doctor because she didn't feel well. But she would be "perfectly fine" once the doctor gave her some medicine. Mr. Lewis would bring Robby to the party at the Flynns'. He was to be a good boy and heed the adults until she or his daddy could get home to him.

"But I want go wit you, Mommy," said Robby as Gordon returned through the side door handing Norma's pocketbook to her.

"No, my little love. I don't want you to miss all the fun at the big party today. You go with Mr. Lewis, and I'll see you later when I'm all better."

"Come on, Buckaroo," coaxed Gordon. "I have a neat army helmet at my house that you can try on. If you like it, you can wear it to the party. What do you say?"

"Okay," said Robby, "but can I bwing big Teddy Bear, too?"

"Absolutely," replied Gordon. "Kiss your mom goodbye, and then let's go get him. Maybe we can find a hat for Teddy too."

Robby gave Betty a peck on the cheek and then grabbed Gordon's hand, leading him to his bedroom. Despite her pain and despair, Betty observed that Gordon would make a capable caring father, one who would be emotionally involved in his child's life. As she had in the past, she again wondered why Norma had not yet given this good man a child.

Breaking into her reverie, Norma exclaimed, "Okay, Bets, that's our cue to go. I have your purse and mine. And I grabbed your personal telephone book so we can call who we need to at the hospital. Let me help you out the door."

As they stepped outside, Norma observed, "Looks like Gor backed my car up your side lawn so the passenger door is right here for you. I don't know what Bob will think about the tire tracks on his lawn, but..."

Betty interrupted her to ask, "Nor, do you really think I'm miscarrying this baby?"

Without contemplation, Norma hastily replied, "I don't know what to think, Bets. I lost a baby once, and there was a lot of blood, so I guess it's possible. Let's just get you to the hospital and see what they say."

Despite Norma's speedy drive to the hospital, Betty did experience a miscarriage later that afternoon. Betty found out afterwards that while the doctors had attended to her, Norma had used the Carters' telephone book to call both the Long Island Rail Road office, where there was no response, and Bob's parents in Queens. One of Bob's two brothers-in-law had been able to physically hunt down Bob on the train branch he was working that day. The brother-in-law had then driven the distraught Bob and his parents to the hospital. Once they had arrived, Betty's in-laws had requested Norma drive them to Strong Lane so they could take over minding their grandson. The brother-in-law had waited to drive Bob home when he was ready to leave. Betty would need to remain in the hospital for a few days to recover.

The day after the miscarriage, Betty lay in her hospital bed devastated. She experienced a roller coaster of emotions: numbness, disbelief, sadness. Atypically, she lost her appetite, even when Bob tried to entice her with a favorite bakery item, a chocolate-iced donut.

"This can't be happening," Betty lamented as Bob sat in the visitor's chair gripping the unopened white bakery bag. "Did I do something wrong? What if I could have done something differently to prevent this loss?"

"Betty, honey, the doctor said it was just one of those things. You did nothing wrong."

"But, Bob, I had been feeling the same way as I did when I was expecting Robby. And he was a model pregnancy. Nothing seemed different. I didn't fall or get hurt to make this miscarriage happen."

Bob sighed. With great empathy, he said, "I know, honey. I'm so sorry this has happened to you...and to our little family. I was looking forward to another little one just as much as you. Even so, it's just something we will have to accept. At least you weren't too far along in the pregnancy."

Betty reached out her hand to hold Bob's. She had tears in the corners of her light gray eyes. "I'm sorry I failed you, Bob," she sobbed. "And how will we explain this to Robby? We already told him about the baby."

"You didn't fail me, honey. Don't ever say that again. And we'll figure out how to tell Robby. You just rest and get better so you can come home to the two who love you the most."

On the day Betty was discharged, she was still despondent. However, her mood instantly changed as soon as she slowly walked into her home. Robby, with his grandparents' assistance, had made a large "Welcome

Home" sign. Her son ran to her and gave a fierce hug to her legs. She prudently bent down to receive his kiss and heartfelt, "I missed you, Mommy!" Her spirits rose. She told herself she would put on a happy face for her son.

As the days went by, Betty grew stronger. Bob's parents finally returned to their own home, and Betty's neighbors began taking turns bringing meals for the Carters. When stopping by with a covered dish, each of the four ladies asked if they could do any housework or heavy lifting for her. Betty accepted the meals with sincere gratitude, but graciously refused the offers of help. It had always been a matter of extreme pride that her home be just so, and she did not want her friends to see it in any form of disarray. She also kept her conversations with the women short. Since she assumed none had experienced a miscarriage, she believed they could not relate emotionally to her. She asked herself, *why me and not any of them?* She refused to share her feelings, even with Anna, the neighbor Betty perceived as her closest friend. Deep down, Betty still felt as if she was a failure.

It was not until many weeks later, when Betty was feeling like her old self again, that she remembered what the usually private Norma had revealed to her on that Independence Day. Betty now wondered when her neighbor had lost a baby. The Lewises had lived next door to the Carters since the beginning of Gordon and Norma's marriage. Perplexed, Betty pondered, *how could I, who always kept a close watch on all my Strong Lane neighbors - especially Norma, have missed this piece of information?*

CHAPTER 12

Norma - 1952

It was a sunny, mild day in September, and Norma had a joyful spring to her step as she made her way from her home to Anna's. Afternoon Coffee Klatch was beginning in a few minutes, and Norma did not want to be late. She had exciting news to share with her neighbors and had waited impatiently all morning for the gathering to commence.

As Norma walked up the Marinos' new concrete driveway to the side kitchen door, she admired the home's recently completed remodeling project. Anna and Sal had contracted Danny's newly formed company, Daniel Flynn Construction, to expand their kitchen eight feet forward to create a spacious dining alcove complete with a large picture window. Anna's once ten-foot by ten-foot standard Levitt kitchen was now a roomy ten-by-eighteen space.

Norma knew that to Anna this project was a necessity to host occasionally the big Italian Sunday dinners with either side of the two families. On the contrary, Norma also knew Anna did not think the Marinos' equally new single-car garage and driveway were essential additions. However, Anna had understood the importance of them to her car-tinkering husband. Once Sal had inspected the garage the Flynns had added to their home, he'd been adamant about combining his garage and driveway with the kitchen remodeling project.

Anna greeted Norma, the first neighbor to arrive at the kitchen's door. The new garage was situated next to the house, starting a few feet behind the kitchen's original front corner. The construction company had extended the garage's roofline forward a bit to incorporate a shallow portico across the front of the garage connecting the coverage to the side kitchen door.

"This is so handy," remarked Norma pointing up at the portico roof over the door she was entering. "You can make your way from the kitchen door to the car in the garage without ever having to get wet during a rainfall."

"I must admit, I do love the convenience, even though I was against increasing our home improvement loan to add the garage set-up. But with Sal and his oldest brother hoping to open a second location of Marino Specialty Foods out here in Nassau County, my husband seems to think we'll be rolling in money soon."

"I think it's great he's planning on branching out on his own, just like Danny did with his construction company. You'll be so much happier, like Jane, to have your husband's commute each day shortened."

The two entered Anna's expanded dining area with its brand-new dinette set that included comfortable seating for eight adults. Norma enthusiastically complimented her hostess. "Oh, Anna. It's just beautiful! So spacious! You must really be pleased with the results."

"I am. Danny did a wonderful job," said Anna just as they heard another voice coming through the kitchen's exterior door say, "Did I just hear a recommendation for my husband's business?"

Jane, with her right hand balancing her chubby seven-month-old son, Mark, on her hip and her left one holding the hand of four-year-old Pamela, burst into the room. In addition to her children, she had a large green canvas diaper bag slung over the right shoulder of her slender frame. Although the day was not especially warm, Jane had small beads of perspiration scattered across her fair forehead. She looked like she had walked a mile instead of just across the lawn separating her house from Anna's.

"Holy smoke! This room looks great, Anna. Last time I saw the place, it was just a shell. I love the buttery yellow paint you chose for the walls. Sal did a wonderful job. Maybe he can start a second business as a housepainter," joked Jane.

"No, Sal has enough on his plate planning a second store," countered Anna. "Jane, would you like to put Mark in Susan's old playpen? I'll get it from the garage and set it up in here for him."

"That would be fantastic, Anna. This son of mine better start walking soon. I can't lug him around much longer. I'm only five feet, four. He's exhausting me. Pammy was never this heavy. Of course, Danny thinks Mark's size is wonderful. He wants him to be the next linebacker for the New York Giants."

Anna made her way out to the garage to fetch the folded playpen just as Betty, Ella and their children arrived. After the new arrivals admired the renovation and congratulated Anna on her home's new addition, the five women settled around the table. Anna had set an old clean tablecloth upon the floor next to the table for Susan, Robby, and Pamela to have some cookies and play with her daughter's toy tea set. Eighteen-month-old Nan had insisted on sharing the playpen with baby Mark.

"This pineapple upside-down cake is scrummy, Anna," observed Betty.

"Scrummy?" questioned Norma with a grin. "That's one of your British slang words I've never heard you use before, Bets."

"It means scrumptious," replied Betty coolly. "Anyway, Anna, you'll have to give me the recipe."

"Of course," said Anna and then added, "By the way, ladies, I think this afternoon is our turn to have the library's bookmobile stop on our corner. Is that correct, Ella? I know you usually keep track of its schedule."

"Yes. I noted on my calendar that we should have a visit sometime around three o'clock today. We will have to listen for its arrival bell. It is such a wonderful program having books come to you. I appreciate it so much since the library is not walking distance from here, and I love to read. They also have so many nice children's books for me to borrow for Nan."

"I agree. Even though I sometimes drive the kids across town to that tiny storefront library, Pammy thinks it's so much more fun to climb aboard the bookmobile and choose her books from there," commented Jane. Then she added, "Not to change the subject, but did any of you watch *I Love Lucy* on TV Monday night? That program just cracks me up!"

"Bob and I never miss it. That Lucille Ball is a comic genius," replied Betty.

"Yes, Gor and I watched it, too" added Norma. "It's so nice to share the evening television shows with my husband again."

"Yet the education was so worth it, was it not Nor? Now he is an engineer and happy in his work, yes?" said Ella.

"Yes, he definitely is. After four years of marriage, it's good that he finally feels settled in his desired occupation. In fact, because we are so settled as a couple, we have decided to pursue, at long last..." and here Norma dramatically paused to get everyone's attention and then continued, "becoming a family! Six months ago, we contacted an adoption agency. Can you believe it, darlings? I'm on my way to becoming a mother!"

"Oh, Nor! That's such wonderful news! Tell us all about it," Anna encouraged as Jane simultaneously shouted, "Fantastic, but six months ago? How did you keep this to yourself this long? If I were you, I'd have burst from excitement!"

"I am so happy for you," added Ella.

"Adoption?" questioned a puzzled Betty. "Why adoption?"

Norma hastily gave Betty her practiced response about her past medical history, the same explanation she had given Ella, Anna, and Jane over a year ago. "We've always talked about adoption, but Gor asked me to wait until he was established in his career. He wants to be a hands-on kind of father. He has always admired the fact that Sal helps Anna with all the tasks, even the messy ones, involving Susan. Gor doesn't want to miss anything, as he might have when he was working *and* attending college at night."

"You and Anna are lucky ladies to have hubbies who want to be involved in childrearing," said Jane. "I mean, Danny does his part watching the kids when I do my Tupperware gigs, but he's not really onboard when it comes to diaper-changing, unless it's absolutely necessary."

"All the men on this street are good fathers, and Gordon will hopefully learn from all of them," acknowledged Norma before continuing, "So, we put our names into an official agency back in March. You would not believe the scrutiny we've gone through as prospective parents. The endless paperwork and so many rules, regulations, and questions! A caseworker even had to come to our house and judge my housekeeping!"

"Well, no problem there. Your house is always spotless, but that's because you don't have any kids yet," teased Jane whose own house, since baby Mark had come along, was never quite as neat as it had been when the Flynns were just a family of three.

"Yes, you've probably got a point," laughed Norma. "I haven't mentioned this all before because I didn't want to tell anyone until we were approved. But we received the authorization letter on Monday. We are officially on the wait list!"

"So, when a baby becomes available, they'll let you know?" asked Anna, clearly happy for her neighbor.

"Something like that. I also keep my ears and eyes wide open at my hospital job. I'm hoping working in the admissions office of a maternity ward might help me be aware of an unmarried mother-to-be contemplating adoption. In fact, I discovered the name of the agency we are using through the hospital. The caseworker told me if I hear of anything before she does, to let her know so she can look into the situation for me."

"I assume you will leave your position when you receive your baby, Norma?" asked Ella.

"Oh, yes. That's one of the conditions of the adoption, that I will be a full-time mother. And that's fine by me. I enjoy the job, but one of the main reasons I pursued it was to have a possible advantage on an adoption. I know that may sound selfish, but I've waited so long for this and wanted to increase my chances."

"Well, I think any baby entering your family will be one fortunate little person," said Anna. "And now that I have this big kitchen space, you must let me throw your baby shower here when the time is right."

"Oh, please let me host the shower, Anna," requested Ella. "After all, you and Norma helped bring my little Nan into the world. I would be so honored to do something for her new baby as a symbol of my appreciation."

"Hey, I want in on this, too," demanded Jane. "Why don't we all throw the shower? But I think Anna's offer of having it in her bigger kitchen makes the most sense."

"You gals are wonderful," said Norma with tears in her eyes. "I couldn't ask for better friends and neighbors. I don't have any sisters, just a younger brother. You're like the sisters I never had."

Just then, they heard the distinctive sound of the Levittown Library's Bookmobile's bell announcing its arrival on Strong Lane. As Jane, Anna, and Ella gathered their children and made their way outside to the street's corner where the huge vehicle was parked, they happily chatted about ideas for the forthcoming baby shower. Norma, the last to leave Anna's house, noticed Betty taking Robby by the hand and following a few steps behind the group. With all the excitement, only Norma seemed to notice that Betty had been uncharacteristically silent since her announcement. Norma wondered if Betty was feeling a bit melancholy since her miscarriage had been less than three months ago. *Perhaps I should have waited to share my news,* Norma thought, *I may have appeared hard-hearted.* She rushed to catch up with Betty to try to make amends.

"Are you okay, Bets? I'm sorry if my adoption story may have brought up sad thoughts, you know, after what happened in July."

"I appreciate that, Nor. I really do. But having a baby and adopting are two different things, don't you think? I've put my loss in the back of my mind. I rarely think of it."

From the hurt tone in Betty's voice and the downcast look on her face, Norma considered this not to be a truthful statement but did not say anything.

"Besides," Betty continued, "I'm very happy that Gordon will finally have a child. I always thought he would make a spiffing father." They reached the bookmobile, and Betty climbed onboard with Robby, signaling the conversation was over.

Norma still felt a bit guilty that she'd reminded Betty of her recent unhappiness. Then she contemplated Betty's sentiment and realized her neighbor had only expressed happiness for Gordon, not for both of them. And instantly Norma's guilt was replaced by annoyance.

CHAPTER 13

Betty – 1952

The day after Norma's important announcement, Betty was a bit dispirited. Although she had claimed she rarely thought about her July miscarriage, truthfully, the event was never far from her mind. She still wondered what had gone wrong. Furthermore, even though Betty's doctor had given the green light months ago for her and Bob to try for another baby, she hadn't yet had any success.

Then when Betty reexamined the group's conversation at Anna's, she found herself in a state of bewilderment. She was trying to make sense of what she had learned of Norma's medical situation at yesterday's coffee klatch compared to the information Norma had given her on July Fourth. If Betty remembered correctly, as she was leaving her house on that awful day, she had asked Norma if she thought Betty was losing her baby. And Norma had said she'd "lost a baby once and there was a lot of blood." However, at coffee klatch, Norma explained she had experienced a past medical issue that prevented her from conceiving children. And Betty recalled Norma had said this "medical issue" was before she had met Gordon. Hence, Betty thought, *how could Norma have lost a baby if she is barren?*

Maybe, pondered Betty, *I heard her incorrectly yesterday. Perhaps Norma can conceive a baby, but physically cannot take the process to the whole term. Norma could have possibly miscarried once after conceiving. After all, I experienced the same heartbreak in July.*

Even so, Betty prided herself on being a good listener. She was also careful to pay close attention to any tidbits of information the usually secretive Norma let escape. Betty was almost certain Norma had said she had discovered she could not conceive *before* she met Gordon.

Perhaps Jane would know more about this, Betty contemplated. Luckily, this morning, she was on her way with Robby to Jane's house. Betty had promised to keep an eye on Mark, who was napping, while Jane took Pamela for a haircut at the beauty salon in their local Village Green.

At the agreed-upon time, Betty and Robby knocked on the Flynns' front door. Jane greeted them with her pocketbook in one hand and Pamela's hand in the other.

"Thanks a million, Betty. Mark just went down, and he'll sleep at least two hours. Considering that kid doesn't move around too much yet, he sleeps pretty soundly, as if he just ran a marathon. I'll be back in less than an hour. Do you need anything at the Green? I'm going to run into the little deli while I'm there to pick up a few things."

"I could use a loaf of Wonder, if you don't mind."

"Okey-dokey! See you in a bit," said Jane as she made her way, with Pamela in tow, out to her station wagon.

Over the next hour, Betty kept herself busy. She read Robby some of Pamela's storybooks. She then set her son up with a basket of blocks, and, while he was busy building, she snooped around Jane's house. She felt a pang of guilt doing this, but convinced herself it was just her way of achieving her goal of fully acclimating herself to the American homemaker's way of life. Although she had been living in the USA for the past six years, she still harbored some of her initial insecurities and considered herself an outsider when it came to some of the practices Jane, Anna, and Norma took for granted.

On the kitchen table, Betty discovered an invoice for some dresses from Best & Company in Garden City. *This statement is quite extravagant,* she thought, *considering all I ever see Jane wearing is pedal pushers or slacks. I guess she wears dresses when she runs her Tupperware parties. Nevertheless, Danny must be doing well financially as the owner of his own construction company. Either that or Jane is making more in commissions than I thought.*

Betty then looked in a few of the kitchen's cabinets and drawers, keenly observing the multitude of plastic containers the Flynns now owned from Jane's little business. She peeked in Jane's freezer and saw boxes of the newly advertised 'TV dinners.' Betty had to laugh. Jane was always the trend setter of the block, happily embracing all the latest fads. Betty herself could never adopt this current one of purchasing an individual frozen dinner in an aluminum compartmented tray. She only served Bob and Robby homemade meals.

Betty returned to the living room to play with her son and, shortly after, heard Jane's car door slam.

"We're back," whispered Jane as she made her way inside with two paper sacks in her hands. Pamela ran in sporting a new pixie haircut for her reddish-blonde hair, and the little girl joined Robby with the building blocks on the living room floor.

"Here's your bread, Betty. Is Mark still sleeping?"

"Never heard a peep out of him," replied Betty. "What do I owe you for the loaf?"

"Not a thing. Consider it a gift to my good neighbor for making my errand easier. I'm going to reheat some leftover morning coffee. Would you care to join me for a cup of joe before my bulldozer wakes up?"

"Sure, that would be nice, Jane. And thanks for the bread."

The two women settled with their coffee cups at Jane's chrome kitchen table. The hostess put the cookie jar between them, and then brought two oatmeal cookies into the living room for each of the children. When she returned to her chair, Betty was on her second cookie.

After she polished off the treat in her hand, Betty asked nonchalantly, "So what did you think of Norma's news?"

"Oh, I thought it was wonderful! Nor is great with kids, and she'll make a good mother. I'm so glad she and Gor found a way to have a family. I felt so sorry for her when she told me she couldn't have children."

"When *did* you find out she was barren?" prodded an annoyed Betty while attempting to keep her voice neutral.

Jane hesitated, a guilty look on her face. She seemed acutely aware that Betty now realized Norma's announcement was not the first time Jane had heard about their neighbor's fertility status. Avoiding the question, Jane said lightheartedly, "Barren? That's such an old-fashioned term, Betty. Is that what they say in England when a woman can't have kids?"

"I'm sure you've heard the term before, Jane," said Betty, backing down a bit on her line of questioning. It really didn't matter to her when Norma had shared her information with Jane. Betty decided to change tactics and use a more considerate tone when she noted, "I feel incredibly sad for Nor, too. I can't imagine never being able to conceive a baby, and worse yet, knowing that before getting married. Believe me, from my own experience, it's bad enough to get pregnant and then lose the baby. But to never be able to have life grow inside you, even for a brief time, is just tragic. Is Nor sure she's never been able to conceive?"

"From what I understand, Betty, she couldn't ever. I'm guessing maybe she's missing one of the important reproductive parts. And she knew all this before she met Gordon. I admire her for being honest with him before they married. A lot of women might not have admitted they can't have children. And I really have to hand it to Gor. He must have truly loved her to..."

Betty tuned out the rest of Jane's prattle. She'd gotten the confirmation she needed. Betty knew she could trust her own recall. *So,* she wondered, *when did Norma have a miscarriage?*

After her first pregnancy, Betty had rigidly planned the time frame of her future, deciding to have children three years apart. Now that the idea of presenting Robby with a sibling on his third birthday would not be a reality, she hoped, at the very least, to conceive as soon as possible. Yet, as each month passed fruitlessly, she grew frustrated. Subconsciously, she began to displace the anger she experienced from her own situation to Norma, the woman who, in Betty's opinion, breezed through life. Therefore, it was much to Betty's exasperation that she learned things were moving along swimmingly for Norma's adoption process.

By October, Norma discovered, through her hospital sources, an unwed sixteen-year-old girl named Amy, from a small town in Ohio, was expecting a baby in the middle of January. To avoid inevitable gossip, the girl's parents had sent her during the past summer to live with a maiden aunt on Long Island. The plan was for her to deliver her baby at Meadowbrook Hospital, recover, and then return to Ohio alone. Neither Amy nor her parents wanted to raise this child. The baby's father, an eighteen-year-old boy Amy had briefly dated, didn't want any part of parenting either.

Betty learned at coffee klatch that the caseworker from Norma's adoption agency and a lawyer had worked out all the details for the Lewises' adoption. Amy, her parents, and the teenaged father had agreed to sever all rights to the baby. As was the norm, it was agreed the adoption and original birth records would be sealed. Amy had confirmed she had no desire to see the baby after the birth. She just wanted the whole ordeal over as quickly and painlessly as possible so she could resume her life in Ohio.

Norma now had a due date for her baby's birth. She was cheerful at the weekly coffee klatches and, much to Betty's surprise and pleasure, less cynical and acerbic. The women listened to Norma's plans for a nursery in the small second bedroom in her house. She decided on a yellow and white color scheme, and Gordon was happily painting the walls to her specifications. Mary Wolf, excited at the prospect of becoming a grandmother, was constantly visiting with new purchases for the room. Norma humorously told the ladies she had to convince her mother to slow down on the shopping sprees or there would be no gifts remaining for her friends to give her at the baby shower.

Anna was planning to host the shower at her house on the Saturday afternoon before Thanksgiving. The event would start at noon, commencing with the opening of the gifts and then a sit-down luncheon at Anna's roomy new dinette table. As promised, Jane and Ella became involved with the planning and food preparations. Betty offered to make a special cake.

It was decided that the husbands would mind their children on the day of the shower. Sal and Susan would vacate their home and spend the day at the Carters' house with Bob and Robby. Jane asked if Pamela, now going on five years, could attend the shower. The little girl loved anything related to babies, and Mrs. Lewis was her favorite neighbor. Norma, who held a special place in her heart for the well-behaved child, readily agreed declaring, "My shower would not be complete without Pammy."

With little Pamela, there would be eleven females attending the shower. In addition to the five Strong Lane neighbors, there would be the two first-time grandmothers, Mary Wolf and Louise Lewis. Also attending would be Alice Martin, the former neighbor who had rented Ella's house before buying another home in Levittown, and Norma's girlhood friends, Dorothy and Lillian. Betty discovered these were the two women who had shared a New York City apartment with Norma when the three were attending secretarial school after graduating together from high school.

On the morning of the shower, Anna set her table beautifully with her best linens, sparkling dishes, and gleaming silverware. Jane drove to a local florist and purchased a festive autumn centerpiece. Ella had created inventive party favors to set on the plates.

Shortly before noon, Betty, wearing her best navy tailored suit, made her way over to Anna's house balancing between her hands her homemade sheet cake housed in a large box and, perched on top, a wrapped gift. She was certain the coconut cake, with white icing and the traditional pink and blue decorations, had to be her finest baking accomplishment. She was extremely proud of it.

However, despite the pride and her previously happy anticipation of the party, Betty was no longer in a festive mood as she crossed the street. When she had been dressing that morning, an upsetting notion had occurred to her and still lingered at the back of her mind. *Norma would have a new baby in January, the same month the baby I lost was due to arrive. It's so unfair! The Lewises will have a blessed event in the new year, and Bob and I will be reflecting on what could have been.*

As she walked up Anna's driveway, the hostess met her outside. Anna was wearing a new red tea-length dress with a full skirt and black patent-leather pumps with kitten heels.

"Let's put the cake on a card table in the garage, Betty," suggested Anna. "I have no room in the kitchen, and the cake will stay nice and cool out here until we're ready to serve it."

"Cracking good idea," responded Betty trying to appear cheerful and not ruin Anna's party. Although she wasn't one to necessarily appreciate or covet the latest fashions, she complimented, "My goodness, Anna, that's a smashing dress!"

Anna smiled and gave a quick twirl around. Betty was glad she'd made her cherished friend feel glamourous.

After depositing her cake in the garage, Betty entered the kitchen and caught Jane in mid-conversation with an older dark-haired woman. The perpetually trim Jane was wearing a dark green, three-quarter sleeved, sheath dress with a short string of creamy pearls around her neck. Betty assumed the dress was one of the purchases she'd seen on Jane's receipt from Best & Company.

"It is so good of you ladies to run Norma's baby shower, especially Anna hosting it in her home," the woman was saying.

"Oh, it's our pleasure," responded Jane. "We've all taken our turns with the baby showers since we moved on this street. When Betty and Anna were expecting their firstborns a few months apart at the beginning of 1950, I hosted a combined shower for them. And Norma hosted Ella's before her little Blizzard Baby was delivered right here on Strong Lane. I'm sure you've heard *that* story...."

"Oh, yes! That was really something! You girls were all so brave. But who hosted a baby shower for you, Jane?"

"My daughter was born before we moved here. I had a shower in the Bronx. But after I gave birth to my son at the beginning of this year, the girls bought me some lovely boy items since all I had were pink ones." Then Jane, turning to Betty, said, "Louise, have you met Betty Carter? She lives directly across the street and next to Norma. Betty, this is Gordon's mother, Louise Lewis."

After the introduction and a few pleasantries, Betty made her way into Anna's crowded living room. Norma sat like a queen in a decorated chair of honor between the front two living room windows, surrounded by gaily wrapped gifts. She was beaming in a deep pink angora twinset that had white pearl buttons on the cardigan, a navy pencil skirt, and stiletto heels. Betty guessed Norma had purposely worn pink and blue as a nod to the theme colors of the baby shower. Next to Norma sat Ella, dressed in a teal-colored circle dress that included a black cinched-waist belt and petticoats for fullness. On Ella's lap was a pad of paper and a pencil to keep track of the gifts and their givers.

On the other side of Norma's chair was the large gift from Betty, Jane, Ella, and Anna. It was not wrapped but sported a big yellow bow and streamers. The four of them had collectively purchased a Baby Bathinette, a combination baby bath and changing table. Danny had used his truck to pick up the large box from the store and deliver it to the Marinos' house. Sal had put the contraption together last night so the ladies could open the changing table lid and place small 'wishing well' gifts in the flexible tub portion. It was here that Betty deposited her small, wrapped gift of terrycloth baby bibs.

"All right, ladies," announced Anna. "If we all have with us a glass of punch from the bowl in the kitchen, we can settle in the living room so we can see Norma open her gifts. I know it's a tight squeeze, but I'm sure we can all fit in and have a good view."

Betty looked around the room. There were two folding chairs located at the back corner under the small archway that led to the rear bedroom hallway. One of the chairs was unoccupied, and Betty sat down next to a dark-haired woman around her age. Betty introduced herself.

"Glad to meet you, Betty," said the other woman. "I'm Dorothy, a friend of Nor's from high school and from her secretarial days in New York City. Lillian, the third girl who shared our Manhattan apartment, is the blonde sitting next to Mrs. Wolf on the sofa."

Oh yes, Betty recalled, *the two old friends of Norma's*. Despite Betty's persistent questioning, Norma had never elaborated about her life before her marriage beyond telling the group she had briefly worked in a city office after secretarial school. Without giving a reason, Norma had said she had eventually moved back to Long Island to work as a secretary at the Sperry Corporation, where she met Gordon. Betty had always thought it was odd that Norma would have surrendered a position in New York City, where the salaries were known to be higher than those in its suburbs.

"Do you and Lillian still share an apartment in New York?" asked Betty.

"Oh no, Lillian got married two years ago and now lives up in Westchester County. I still live in Manhattan, but on my own. I'm still single and have a position as the office manager in the same bank where I started as a secretary, back when Lil, Nor and I graduated from the Katharine Gibbs School." Dorothy then proudly added, "It was, and still is, one of the best schools for training executive secretaries. The three of us completed the one-year program and got great jobs."

"Yes, I've heard of the Gibbs School. I know Nor told me this story, but I can't remember all the details. Did the three of you all work for the bank after graduation?"

"No, we were employed at different companies. Lil worked for an art gallery, and Nor worked for an up-and-coming advertising agency. Since you neighbor gals are all so close, I'm sure Nor has told you about the very handsome, but very atrocious, partner she worked for at that agency?" inquired Dorothy cagily. The woman seemingly held her breath while waiting for Betty's confirmation.

"Yes, of course Nor has confided in us," lied Betty. She was amazed at this newly discovered piece of news.

An obviously relieved Dorothy continued, "I figured she disclosed her past to your little group. All of you have been friends for almost five years now and seem like a tight-knit bunch. Lil and I were her closest pals for the longest time, but we don't see as much of each other as we would like. We currently live in three different locations. I think you are closest to the people you see daily. Don't you agree, Betty?"

However, before Betty could respond, Jane loudly clapped her hands and asked for quiet. Norma was starting to open her gifts, and Jane wanted everyone to hear the guest of honor read the cards aloud.

For the next hour, Norma opened gift after gift, with all the guests, except Betty, appropriately oohing and aahing over the more adorable items. Betty, deep in thought, just plastered a fake smile on her face as impressions were spinning through her head. *Norma worked under an attractive man during a time before she met Gordon. If I know anything about Norma, it's that my neighbor cannot resist a good-looking man. Is it possible Norma had an affair with this boss? Had the man been single or married? Is that the reason she left a lucrative job?*

After the gifts were all unwrapped and Norma made a small speech of thanks, Anna encouraged everyone to make their way into her kitchen's dining area to start the luncheon. Dorothy had gone to use the bathroom in the hallway where Betty and she had been seated. As all the chatting women except Dorothy walked out of the living room, Betty held back and busied herself by picking up stray discarded wrapping paper. She wanted to have another private word with Norma's friend before they joined the rest of the party. She didn't know, though, what to ask to confirm her suspicions about Norma.

As Dorothy emerged from the back of the house, she approached Betty who stood alone in the living room attempting to clean up some of the debris. Dorothy started to help saying, "Thank you for waiting for me before going into lunch, Betty."

"No problem. I just wanted to straighten up a little for Anna," replied Betty and, deciding to take the approach of Norma's caring friend, said to her new acquaintance quietly, "Nor looked very happy today. I'm so glad our friend found a way to start a family after all the tragic sadness she experienced earlier in life. Not being able to have children is such a heartache."

"Yes," agreed Dorothy, and, obviously thinking Betty had a mutual knowledge of Norma's complete biography, she added in a heated whisper, "That abortion was just ghastly! Lillian and I tried to talk her out of it, but Nor's mind was made up. She was heartbroken, of course, after her boss wouldn't get a divorce and marry her, as he originally promised. And that weasel of a man even had the nerve to give her the name of the illegal abortion doctor! I'm sure Nor never would have gone through with the procedure if she knew its horrific complications would leave her unable to conceive. I'm just grateful she didn't die!"

Fortunately for Betty, she had been stooping down for the last piece of trash, so her shocked face was hidden from Dorothy's view. As she stood slowly, and before she could make an attempt at a reply, Anna called from the noisy kitchen, "Betty, Dorothy, please leave the mess as it is and join us. We're waiting for you gals to sit down before we start."

Dorothy and Betty joined the party. Betty took a seat between Ella and Jane, and Dorothy sat in the last available chair, between Lillian and Alice Martin. Luckily, it wasn't necessary for the shocked Betty to engage in any conversations with her seatmates; Ella's body was slightly turned and engaged in a discussion with Norma's mother at her left, and Jane was preoccupied with helping Pamela on her right. With all the new discoveries swirling in her head, Betty, for one of the few times in her life, didn't have much of an appetite.

Betty's Thanksgiving came and went in a blur. For a week, she mulled over the information she now possessed. She didn't share it with anyone, not even Bob. From her conversation with Jane in September, she figured the other neighbors had no idea that Norma had an abortion before she married. The others were all satisfied with the vague medical issue Norma had mentioned as the reason for her infertility. Betty guessed that only Lillian, Dorothy, and Norma's parents knew the truth. Betty could not fathom that Gordon had any idea his wife had partaken in an illegal procedure after participating in an extramarital affair. She knew no woman would ever confide in a husband about such a squalid past.

It was these thoughts of Gordon, blissfully unaware of his wife's past transgressions, that pushed Betty out of her state of rumination and finally into a planned course of action. Betty liked Gordon and thought he was a decent and honest man. She'd never forgotten that he'd offered information about the GI Bill for Bob or that he'd cared for Robby during her miscarriage. She felt strongly that Gordon had a right to know about his wife's past before he embarked on an adoption with her. What if it made him want a divorce? He should have a chance to do so before a child becomes involved. For his sake, Betty decided she had to tell him what she knew.

Betty's unexpected opportunity came on an unusually mild Saturday morning in December, exactly two weeks after the baby shower. Bob had just left to take Robby to the local barbershop to get both much-needed haircuts. Betty was outside by the narrow strip of a vegetable garden she kept along the side of her house next to her kitchen door. Although Betty loathed most yard work, she had found, to her surprise, that she'd enjoyed maintaining a little garden of tomatoes and herbs over the past summer. She had gathered the last of her crops in October but had never had the chance to clean out the dead plants and debris.

As she started her raking, she heard a male voice shout a friendly greeting from the vicinity of her front door.

"I'm out here at the side of the house," called Betty.

Gordon Lewis walked around the corner of her house and into her view. He had on blue jeans and a heavy flannel plaid work shirt. He greeted her warmly and asked if Bob was at home.

"No, he's at the barbershop with Robby. I'm just getting my garden cleaned out since it's such a lovely day. It looks like you're dressed for outdoor chores, too."

"Yeah, Nor is waiting for her mother to pick her up so they can do more baby shopping, and I'm going to try to pull out that dead shrub we have in the front yard. I was wondering if I could borrow Bob's pickaxe."

"I'm sure Bob wouldn't mind. I guess it's in the garden shed out back."

Gordon walked past Betty, heading for the backyard. She turned towards him with her back now to the front yard, as she nervously continued, "But, before you fetch it, Gordon, I'd like to speak with you. There's been something I've wanted to tell you, but I haven't had the opportunity to get you alone."

Gordon turned to face her with a big grin on his face and jokingly said, "You're not going to declare your secret love for me, are you Betty? Because I'm taken—unless you want to fight Nor for me."

Gordon stopped laughing when he saw the solemn look on Betty's face.

"It's funny you should mention Norma because that's who I wanted to talk to you about," began Betty. "How much do you know about your wife's past? I unfortunately heard something at Nor's baby shower that I think you have a right to know, especially before you start a family."

The smile completely disappeared from Gordon's once affable face, and he quietly said, "What exactly are you talking about, Betty?"

"I'm sorry to be the one to tell you this, Gor, because I think you're a great guy," Betty began. Then, in her anxiety, Betty's voice rose a little louder as she blurted out, "I found out your wife had an affair in Manhattan with her married boss, before she met you. She got pregnant, and he wouldn't divorce his wife and marry her, so she got an illegal botched abortion. That's the real reason she can't have children."

Gordon's dark eyes stared intently at Betty, so she looked down at his shoes. She felt a temporary sense of relief now that the information she had been concealing was finally released from her troubled mind. However, she oddly did not feel the satisfaction she'd thought she'd have in finally exposing Norma.

When Betty returned her gaze back to Gordon's face, she noticed he was not looking at her, but at a point beyond her left shoulder. She was about to turn when she heard a female voice growl, "Betty Carter! How *dare* you?"

Betty spun around to see Norma standing on the grass just past the front corner of the house. Betty would find out much later that Norma had forgotten to ask Gordon a question she needed answered before she went out for the day with her mother. Norma had followed her husband's path across the front lawn to the Carters' house, and, hearing the voices in the side yard, had just rounded the corner when Betty made her proclamation.

"Nor, I… I… I didn't know you… you were there," stammered Betty, staring at Norma's shocked face. "But I think Gor had…"

"Shut up, Betty," demanded Gordon as he walked past his neighbor towards his wife. When he reached Norma's side, he took her hand before facing Betty again.

"To answer your question, Mrs. Carter, because it *will* be the last time I speak to you," started Gordon tersely, "I know *everything* about my wife. Not that it is any of your business, but nothing you said today is news to me."

And with that, the Lewises turned and walked back to their own house. Betty, with her mouth still open, watched them go.

When Bob returned home, he told Betty that Anna had invited Robby to play with Susan in the Marinos' backyard. Betty was grateful her son was occupied outside their house because she wanted to tell her husband the whole story of her confrontation with the Lewises.

She was pale and trembling, pacing the kitchen and refusing to sit down while telling her tale. She was still convinced her intent had been just. Bob sat at the table, listening to her without saying a word, until she exhausted herself. Before he finally spoke, he took a deep breath.

"Betty, I love you," began Bob quietly. "But for some reason, you didn't get a clear sense of right and wrong during your childhood. Maybe it was because your father and brothers had such short tempers. Maybe it's because your mother was too passive and quiet to teach you more compassion. I don't know. I do know you've had your issues with Norma in the past, but you must realize you stepped way out of bounds today, right?"

"How can you not take my side in this, Bob?" whispered Betty. "Norma has always been so mean to me."

"I know when she teased you, it made you angry. And if you remember correctly, I suggested you talk to her about it and ask her to stop. However, telling her husband something about her past, that you assumed he didn't know, is ten times worse than teasing. You had no right to do that, Betty."

"But don't you think he should have known..." began Betty.

"That was not your decision to make," stated Bob firmly. "And why did you feel the need to hurt them, Betty? Both Norma and Gordon were so good to you the day we lost our baby. Norma was there for you when you needed her. That should have surpassed any gossip you may have heard and felt the need to repeat."

"But it wasn't gossip, Bob. It was the truth. Nor was lying about why she couldn't have children," insisted Betty mulishly.

"It was her truth to tell, not yours."

Betty changed tactics and continued heatedly, "Well, it appears Gordon already knew all his wife's dirty secrets, so what harm did I really do? They're just worried I'll tell the neighbors. The Lewises will try to get the others on their side without telling them what I know. Maybe I should clear the air and tell all of Strong Lane about Norma. Maybe I should..."

Bob interrupted her with a voice raised in anger. "I have never told you what to do, Betty, but I'm telling you right now! I FORBID you from ever saying another word about this to anyone, ever. And furthermore, you will go to Norma's house on Monday when things calm down and ask for forgiveness. She probably won't accept your apology, but I demand you at least try. Now, that's the end of it. I don't want to hear another word. I'm going to get my pickaxe and personally take out the Lewises' dead shrub. I hope Gordon at least lets me do that."

Bob put on his jacket and walked out the kitchen door. A shocked Betty finally sat down with a thud in the chair nearest to where she had stood. She started to sob. Her tears were not due to shame or remorse for what she had done. She cried because she had made her usually peaceful husband raise his voice to her for the first time since she had met him.

CHAPTER 14

Norma - 1952

Monday morning was cold, dark, and dreary, perfectly matching Norma's foul mood. She was still livid over the incident at Betty's on Saturday.

Immediately after it had happened, she had been so upset, she had refused to go shopping with her mother. Mary Wolf had already arrived at the Levittown house to pick Norma up and, with her son-in-law, had tried to convince her daughter to continue with her plans for the day. Norma had apologized to her mother that she'd made her car trip in vain, but she just could not go out and enjoy herself. Mary had then wondered aloud who had told Betty the story at the baby shower, because it certainly hadn't been her. Norma had guessed it had been Dorothy since she had noticed Betty sitting with her old friend during the opening of the gifts. Consequently, Mary had told her daughter she should also be equally furious with Dorothy.

Mulling it over while drinking her Monday morning coffee at the kitchen table, Norma realized she wasn't as angry at Dorothy as her mother thought she should be. Norma felt Dorothy would not have offered the information if she hadn't believed Betty had already known the story of Norma's past.

Norma, Dorothy, and Lillian weren't as close as they used to be. After she had married Gordon and moved to Levittown four years ago, Norma had made the effort to meet her two old friends in the city for lunch several times a year. When Lillian had married two years later and moved to Westchester, the three started meeting only once a year during the holidays. Norma hadn't even been sure if she should have invited the two to her baby shower, but her mother had insisted. After all, Mary had argued, Dorothy and Lillian had been Norma's best friends in high school, and the pair had been so supportive of Norma during and after her time in the hospital.

Upon reflection, Norma figured her two old friends assumed the tight-knit Strong Lane women were as close to Norma as they three had once been. Dorothy could have presumed Norma had confided in her new neighborhood friends, and, with the right prodding from gossipy Betty, mentioned Norma's past.

Betty! The name left a bad taste in Norma's mouth. It wasn't only the fact that Betty knew about Norma's past that angered her, although having her truth exposed was indeed bad enough! If Betty had come to her alone and specified what she knew, Norma would not have been happy, but she could have dealt with it. It was the fact that Betty went directly to Gordon, thinking about causing strife in her marriage, that infuriated Norma.

While Norma had stewed over the incident all weekend, Gordon's anger had slowly decreased. It had started to lessen shortly after the incident, when he had gone outside to speak with Bob as the neighbor made his way over with the pickaxe. Her mother had already departed for home, and Norma had been watching alone from her kitchen window. Seething, she had turned away as the two men had courteously worked together to remove the dead bush in the Lewises' yard.

After completing the chore with Bob, Gordon had returned to Norma indoors and said, "I was talking with Bob. He feels terrible about what happened with Betty and apologized on her behalf."

"I saw that. And what did you say?" Norma had snapped back. "Honestly Gor, I know you're probably the most congenial guy on the block, but don't tell me you've forgiven the Carters already?"

"Listen, sweetheart, I told Betty I wouldn't speak to her again, and I meant it. It's not right, though, to shun Bob and Robby in the future. They have nothing to do with Betty's vindictiveness. I think we still need to acknowledge the two of them."

Norma had started to soften and replied, "Sometimes, Gordon Lewis, you are just too nice, and it astounds me."

Although when they were first married, they'd made a pact to avoid the subject, she had added, "I wonder, who other than you could forgive a past such as mine and find it in his heart to still marry me? Now that all our friends will know about my mess, I truly regret that you will be embarrassed and part of the hearsay. I don't mind the discomfort for myself; God knows I deserve it. But you don't, and I wish I could change that."

"As I told you when I proposed and you made your confession, I fell in love with you, Norma, on our first date. The person you were before didn't matter to me, and it still doesn't matter. After serving in the war, I just wanted peace and contentment. I found both with you, sweetheart."

"Oh, Gor. I'm not worthy of you. All I bring is heartbreak."

"That's not true. You've brought only happiness to me." Gordon had slipped his arms around her hips and brought her close.

Norma had looked up at him. "I'm thankful I listened to my father and not my mother. Before I accepted your proposal, I asked my parents if they thought I should tell you about my past: the whole ugly thing." She had shuddered in his embrace as she remembered it all. "My mother advised me not to say anything. She hoped the surgeons would prove to be wrong about my infertility. She didn't want me to jeopardize the love of a good man like you. My father, however, had counseled me to be truthful and not start a marriage with lies."

"You never told me that you had asked your parents' opinion. I'm glad you took your father's advice."

"Yes, I knew I risked you retracting your proposal by telling you, but I had enough of life's deceptions. I swore to myself I would only be truthful with you, despite the possible consequences. I'm glad I was. Could you imagine hearing the truth about me today, for the first time, from Betty Carter?"

"Let's just be glad it didn't play out that way," a relieved Gordon had replied. "And now, don't let Betty ruin our happiness. After all, in another month, you'll be too busy with our new baby to worry about Betty."

Norma had smiled, yet obstinately finished with, "I still plan on avoiding all the Carters from now on."

"That will be a little difficult, my beautiful wife, considering they live right next door."

"You watch me," Norma had challenged.

This morning, Gordon had calmly left for work at seven as if the Saturday confrontation with Betty had never happened. He had kissed Norma goodbye and wished her a pleasant day. Sitting now at the table, and despite her best efforts to do otherwise, the jarring memories came flooding back. Since she had met Gordon in December of 1947, Norma had spent the last five years tenaciously willing herself not to let the time before she had met him creep back into her consciousness. The clash with Betty had weakened her resolve.

Now she cringed inwardly as she recalled the attractive, smooth-talking Larry Hall, the youngest partner at a New York City advertising agency. He had personally hired her fresh out of secretarial school in the spring of 1946. He had been seventeen years older than her; she had been a confident young lady of nineteen who thought she knew all the answers. *How wrong I was,* reflected Norma.

As Larry's secretary and eventual lover, she had believed everything that skunk had said, even when he had claimed he would leave his rich wife and newborn daughter to marry her. However, once Norma had confronted him with her own pregnancy, all he could do was laugh and explain his wife's money staked his claim in the advertising firm; he could never divorce her. The last thing he had given her was a small, printed business card of a Brooklyn "doctor" who specialized in "taking care of matters."

After the botched abortion and subsequent long recovery in a Manhattan hospital, Norma had returned to the advertising agency only once, after business hours. She had prearranged with the office manager, Emily Dunne, to retrieve her last paycheck and a box of personal items.

As if it were yesterday, Norma now remembered that meeting in the office building's lobby. It had been a cold mid-January weeknight. Norma, sad and remorseful, had felt like a lonely shell of the vivacious young woman she had been when first hired. Emily had been there waiting for her, and Norma recalled being surprised. She had thought the prudish spinster in her forties might send a lesser employee in her place. Emily had always seemed resentful of the young attractive secretaries she managed, and Norma had been no exception. As a result, Norma had been shocked when Emily had warmly embraced her.

"How are you, Norma? I hope you're feeling better," she'd said with genuine concern.

Norma knew no one at the firm had been told the real reason for her absence and consequential resignation. Upon Norma's hospitalization, Mary Wolf had called the office manager on her daughter's behalf and, without details, mentioned only a serious medical issue as the reason for departure.

"Yes, I'm almost fully recovered. Thank you for meeting me, Emily."

"Of course. I have everything of yours in this box. The last paycheck is on top, and I was also able to secure some extra severance pay for you in addition to the earnings from your last week of work."

"That was so kind of you," Norma had replied, although she was perplexed. *This woman never liked me.*

"I have to apologize to you, Norma," began Emily. "I never warned you, and I wish I had."

"Warned me of what?"

"Larry Hall. You were his third secretary to leave the firm."

This came as a shock to Norma. Since she had been so enamored with her handsome boss, she had never asked what had become of her predecessors.

Emily had continued, "The first was a newly engaged woman of twenty-two who resigned after two months with Larry. Upon her departure, the girl told me quite bluntly she was uncomfortable with Larry's constant harassment, and, if she stayed another day, her fiancé had threatened to punch Larry in the nose."

"That, I would have liked to see," Norma had chimed in.

"Yes, well, the second girl was a pretty twenty-year-old newly arrived from Virginia. She lasted longer but mysteriously returned to her home state after less than a year under Larry."

Most likely, literally under Larry, Norma had thought to herself. *I wonder if this girl from Virginia suffered the same fate as I had. Overall, I do feel somewhat vindicated learning I was not the only young, unassuming secretary to fall for this man's tricks.*

"However, after your resignation, Norma, I stood firm that the other two partners allow me to hire Larry's next secretary. All along, that man insisted on interviewing and hiring his own assistants. I'm not having it anymore! I want you to know a no-nonsense, fifty-year-old career executive secretary was just hired to answer to Larry. Although, I've observed, he's really almost answering to her! She's got him under control."

Norma had laughed aloud when she imagined Larry working with a straightforward professional woman that he could not manipulate.

"So, I apologize for not warning you when you took the job," Emily had concluded with regret.

Norma had just shaken her head. "I appreciate that Emily, but it wouldn't have deterred me from accepting what I thought of at the time as an outstanding opportunity."

"What will you do now, Norma? Despite everything, I always thought you were an excellent employee. If you need a reference to another New York advertising agency, I'd be glad to provide you with one."

"Thank you, Emily, but I've moved back to my family's home on Long Island. For now, at least, I'll be working at a company where my father is the chief accountant. He was able to secure a secretarial position for me. I start next week."

At the time, on some level, she had regretted leaving the excitement of life in New York City. Nevertheless, she had known she needed to return to her hometown to lick and heal her wounds. And it had been eleven months after that meeting with Emily when she had met Gordon, and her life had been renewed.

Norma, still sitting at her kitchen table, returned from her reverie to the present. She realized an hour had passed since Gordon's departure, and she decided she'd finally had enough contemplation. She was still wearing her pink chenille bathrobe and matching pink slippers. She hoped a quick shower would help wash away her negative thoughts before she dressed for the day ahead.

As she rose from her kitchen chair to make her way to the bathroom, she heard a tentative knock at the side door. Glancing to her left, she could see through the door's top half of glass that Betty was standing on the other side. Without waiting for a response from Norma, Betty hesitantly opened the door and stood on the kitchen threshold.

"May I come in, Nor?" asked Betty timidly. She was wearing a heavy pullover sweater, a plaid skirt, loafers, and a gloomy look on her face. "Bob is doing an afternoon shift today and is home with Robby."

"You can close the door and stand right there to say what you need to say. You're not welcome inside my house any longer," responded Norma icily. She was standing with her arms folded across her chest facing her neighbor squarely.

"I just came to apologize," started Betty and then nervously jabbered, "I never would have confronted Gordon if I knew he was already aware of your...umm...past. I never imagined you would have told him the whole sordid story! I mean, good for you for being honest and good for him for still accepting you."

Norma stood silently glaring as Betty blabbed on, "I just thought Gordon had a right to know, but since he did already know, there was no harm done. So, you can accept my apology, and we can get past this, right?"

"Wrong," snapped Norma, her green eyes blazing. "I can't get past this. I don't think you are sorry at all for upsetting me. I think you are only sorry that you couldn't ruin me. You were counting on breaking up my marriage. And when you found you couldn't, you now only regret that my husband, and probably your own, thinks less of you. You didn't think this all the way through before you rushed in and played your hand. You were in possession of a juicy story, Bets, and you couldn't wait to tell it at my expense."

"I *am* sorry the whole thing happened, Nor. Really I am," countered Betty with sincerity. "But you make it sound like I was spreading gossip. I was just speaking the truth! Your friend, Dorothy, didn't seem to think it was such a big secret. She assumed you told all of us on the block since we're all such good friends."

"If you were a *good* friend, you would have come to me with what you heard instead of playing God and going directly to my husband," fumed Norma. She paused and then added in a dead voice, "I have nothing left to say to you, Mrs. Carter. From now on, do not trespass on my property, or I will call the police."

"Oh, come on, Nor. Don't get your knickers in a twist! We live next door to each other. You must forgive me. And what are we going to do about our gatherings with the other gals?" implored Betty, apparently frightened that she would be the one ousted from the group.

"I'm going to be too busy with my little family for coffee klatch," declared a brusque Norma.

"If you're worried about me telling them about your past, I won't say a word if you ask me not to, Nor."

Norma let out a bitter humorless laugh before saying sarcastically, "That's mighty big of you, Bets! To think, my secrets are safe with the likes of you! Now, turn around, open the door, and get out of my house." And with that, Norma spun on her heel and walked out of her kitchen towards the bathroom at the back of the house.

A dejected Betty quietly opened the door and left.

The next day, Norma made the decision to telephone each of the remaining three women from coffee klatch and explain what had happened with Betty. She planned to tell Ella, Jane, and Anna the abridged, but honest, version of her past before Betty could spin a convoluted account. Norma didn't know how the three would judge her. After all, an affair with a married man and an illegal abortion were not even remotely typical occurrences in the lives of her neighbors. Nevertheless, at this point, Norma knew she had to explain the truth even if it meant being ostracized.

CHAPTER 15

Anna - 1952

Tuesday started out as a hectic mess for Anna. Sal's alarm clock didn't go off, and Anna was awakened by his frenzied attempts to get dressed and out the door in time. Shortly after he left, Susan decided to flush one of her small soft toys down into the toilet, requiring Anna to search frantically for their lone plunger before the overflowing water got out of control. Finally, as Anna was just finishing with that calamity, Susan, bouncing on the sofa while watching a cartoon on the television, fell and bumped her elbow on the coffee table. Howling with pain and grabbing her arm, Susan ran to her mother who was just exiting the bathroom, mop in hand. Anna gave her daughter a package of frozen peas to hold on her little elbow and dried the toddler's eyes.

It wasn't until eleven o'clock that Anna was finally able to prepare a much-needed pot of coffee. Susan was now calm and watching the television, safely sitting on the living room floor. While Anna waited for the percolator, her telephone started ringing. She silently pleaded with God for patience and picked up the receiver. She was grateful the phone had recently been relocated from the living room to her renovated kitchen so she could at least keep an eye on her vitally essential coffee pot.

It was Norma on the line. Although a famished Anna considered asking her neighbor if she could return the call after she ate some breakfast, she immediately deduced from Norma's serious tone that the conversation was important.

Norma started with, "I know this may shock you, Anna, but I need to tell you something personal from my past that also evolved into a situation between Betty and me this weekend." And then she launched into her tale.

Anna was silent as she listened intently. The coffee was done by the time Norma finished speaking. Anna mindlessly shut off the burner, leaving the untouched pot on the stovetop.

"Wow, Norma, I don't know what to say."

Anna was very upset over the blow-up between Norma and Betty. Despite her own best efforts, reconciliation between the two now seemed a gross impossibility. Even more disturbing to Anna, though, was the news Norma had shared about her decision to have an abortion as a younger woman. Anna was reverent in her Catholic upbringing; terminating a pregnancy was a sin. She asked herself if knowing this, could she still accept Norma as a friend? Did she still want to associate with someone who had chosen death over life?

"Yes, well, you are as speechless as Jane and Ella were when I telephoned each of them earlier. I wanted to speak with you three individually. I left your call for last because, quite honestly, out of all the neighbors, your opinion of me really matters. You're such a good person, Anna. I am so ashamed to tell you of my past. I was young and stupid, which is no excuse for what I did." Norma started to choke up at this point. Anna could hear the grief in her voice as she finally sobbed, "And it pains me terribly to have you disappointed in me."

Compassion instantly flowed through Anna. *This woman, who has steadily been a good friend to me, is agonizing over her past sins. Who am I to possibly criticize Norma over something that happened over five years ago, especially when Gordon lovingly married her without judgement?* And deep down, she felt again that jolt of involuntary envy over the devoted love Gordon and Norma shared. *Oh, to feel that kind of passionate commitment!*

Anna wanted to make this right, so she said consolingly, "I'm not disappointed in you, Nor. How can you think that? We all have things we're not proud of. It's human nature. But it's how we rise from our adversities that counts."

"I'm grateful for that, Anna. Truly, I am," said a clearly relieved Norma. "And as far as my not speaking to Betty, I'm not asking any of you to take sides. I'll just bow out of coffee klatch so there's no discomfort for you all. Besides, with the holidays quickly approaching followed immediately by the birth of my baby, I won't have time for the group's gatherings. Of course, as I told Jane and Ella, you three are always welcome to call on me at my house. Maybe we can do things together off of Strong Lane, you know, like shopping and meeting at parks with the kiddies."

"Yes, I'm sure we can work that all out," Anna said. "And, Nor... I'm glad you confided in us. That must have been a very heavy burden for you to carry over all these years."

"It was, but I still wish I never had to reveal it to each of you, even though you three are like sisters to me. Thank you so much for understanding."

"You're welcome," Anna said. She was disturbed that Norma already cut Betty out of the number of 'sisters.'

"Nor, would you do me a favor? I know the wounds are fresh now, but please consider forgiving Betty someday..."

Norma cut her off. "I love you, Anna, but that's not going to happen."

They said their good-byes, and Anna sat at her kitchen table, stunned. It saddened her to think the cohesiveness on this small street of neighbors was now fractured. She needed to know what Jane and Ella thought of all this. Would the two take sides? Personally, she knew she would stay neutral and try to stay friends with both Norma and Betty.

The telephone started ringing again, breaking into her thoughts. Before answering, Anna quickly glanced in on Susan, who was still occupied with the television and some toys. On the fifth ring, she picked up and immediately heard Jane's awestruck voice.

"Holy moly, Anna! Can you believe it? I'm sure you are as astonished as I am. And I just got off the phone with Ella. She's, of course, stunned too. An abortion! I've never known *anyone* who had one of those! And here I thought Norma was just born without a reproductive part or something."

Anna loved Jane but sometimes her bluntness was disconcerting.

"And now she and Betty aren't speaking, even though Nor admitted to me Betty did the right thing and apologized! How is that going to affect the rest of us?" Jane blurted out with exasperation.

"Calm down, Jane. First of all, are you saying you aren't going to associate with Norma any longer because of a decision she made before we knew her?"

"No, I'm not saying that. I'm flabbergasted by the drama of it all; it's like something from a soap opera, for crying out loud! But I truly like Norma; she's been a good friend and neighbor. And I also like Betty and feel sorry for her. I'm sure she knows what she did was wrong, and I'm sure she regrets her haste in pointing a finger. But, in Betty's defense, she didn't make up a nasty story; she just told the truth. Also, Betty did try to make amends, which Nor will not accept. It's a mess, Anna, a real mess. What are we going to do?"

"What did Ella think of Nor's past? Other than being surprised, did she indicate she would not want to see her any longer?"

"Ella took the attitude that what's done is done. She would never turn on Norma, especially since you and she delivered Nan. She says she won't judge Norma or Betty. She said she'll treat them each as she has before."

Anna had already guessed Ella would never give anyone the cold shoulder. Once, in a private discussion, Ella had admitted her dismay over the friction between Norma and Betty. Ella had said she had witnessed so much chaos in Germany, and now she just desired harmony among those around her. Anna assumed Ella, like herself, would feel hurt that the group was fragmented.

Jane was posing a question. "Anna, what do *you* think of the abortion? We're both Catholic, but you're definitely more devoted to the Church's teachings than I am. Will this news change your opinion or treatment of Norma?"

"No, it will not," Anna firmly replied. "I agree with Ella. I won't judge her. The only person who had the right to do that was Gordon, and he forgave her past. Love triumphed over hate; we should do the same."

"It was amazing that Gordon knew *everything* about her and still married her," marveled Jane. "I don't even think Danny would have done that for me. Do you think Sal could've forgiven you for something like that?"

"I don't know. I'm only glad I never had to test his love that way," Anna answered honestly. *Still,* she contemplated, *I've never doubted Sal's commitment to me; he has always loved me the best way he knows how. If Norma and Gordon's romance can teach me anything, it is that I should try harder to give Sal as much love as he gives me.*

"So, what about coffee klatch?" fretted Jane, interrupting Anna's thoughts. "Nor says she'll be too busy to attend. I'll feel terrible not having all five of us."

Anna reasoned, "We should carry on. Each time one of us hosts, we will invite Betty and Norma. We know Nor will refuse, unless Betty does not attend for some reason, and that is her prerogative. I'll just pray that at some point Norma will accept Betty's apology, and we can reunite. Until that time, we'll stop in on Nor and encourage her to pop into our homes. And most of us have cars to use now, so we don't have to socialize exclusively with either Norma or Betty only in the confines of this block. Have faith it will all work out, Jane."

"I'll try," Jane said with uncertainty, "But it's going to be really awkward until it does."

CHAPTER 16

Norma – 1952-1953

By Christmas, Norma was happier than she had been in a long time. There was something wonderful and liberating in not worrying that the people she loved would discover her old indiscretions. She had been accepted by her husband, family, and friends for who she was as a person and not judged harshly for her actions in the past.

True to their words, Ella, Jane, and Anna separately stopped by to see her throughout December. Each had a pretext of borrowing an item such as a cup of sugar or an egg, but Norma saw through their ploys. She realized they just wanted her to know she was still one of them. How much they socialized with Betty, Norma did not know, since none would mention Betty's name in her presence.

On the morning of January second, Norma was blissfully survey-ing the completed and fully stocked yellow and white nursery, situated in the smaller bedroom of her house, when the telephone started ringing. The caller was the caseworker from the adoption agency.

"Good morning, Norma, and happy new year," she greeted. "I wanted to let you know I just got word from the hospital that Amy was admitted. She was sent directly there by her doctor from his office. Apparently, she is in labor."

"That's unusual," responded a puzzled Norma. "Her due date isn't for another two weeks."

"Well, I guess she's early. We'd all previously agreed you and Gordon are permitted to wait at the hospital for the birth. You can make your way over there, if you still want to."

"Oh, yes, we definitely planned on waiting together," replied an excited Norma. "Gor's at work, but I'll telephone him so he can meet me there. I can't believe this is actually happening!"

"You can believe it. If her labor isn't too long, you two should be parents by the end of the day. Congratulations! What a wonderful way to start off a new year. I'll let the lawyer's office know too so the papers can be finalized after the birth. Good-bye, Norma."

"Good-bye and thank you so much!" After hanging up, Norma telephoned Gordon's office, and they made plans to drive their own cars and meet at the hospital. Next, she telephoned her mother to share the news, but both women agreed Norma's parents would not join the couple at the hospital. Norma promised to call as soon as the baby was born. Mary Wolf offered to call Gordon's mother, Louise, to keep all the family in the loop.

Norma had just finished her brief conversation with her mother when there was a knock at the door. She hurriedly grabbed her purse, coat and car keys, planning to tell whoever was on the doorstep to go away. She opened her front door to find Jane.

"Are you ready for our professional manicures, Nor? I'm so excited Danny agreed to watch the kids for the whole morning so we can go. I think his gift certificate to the beauty salon was the best present I received this Christmas," said Jane in a rush. "Even though it will only take an hour, I'll feel like a queen for the day......hey, wait a minute. You're putting on your coat backwards. What's the matter with you?"

"I'm sorry, Jane. I forgot all about our appointments. I'm on my way to meet Gor at the hospital. The baby's coming!" exclaimed Norma as she tried to put her correct arm in the proper sleeve of her coat, dropping her ring of keys in the process.

"Gee whiz! I thought you had more time," Jane said while Norma's shaking hands picked up her keys and started to fumble with them in an attempt to lock her door.

"Look, Norma. I'll drive you to the hospital," offered Jane. "This way, you and Gor can travel home together in his car later. And besides, you're shaking so much, I don't think you should be driving yourself. You're like one of those crazed expectant fathers!"

"Well, now I know how they feel! Thanks so much. I'd really appreciate the ride, and, more importantly, your company on the way over there. I'm so nervous all of a sudden."

"Happy to be of service," Jane said, then added in her best take-charge voice, "Now, let me lock your door and help you with your coat before we try to walk calmly across the street to my car."

Once the two were seated in the station wagon, Jane started to maneuver it down the block, passing Ella's house on the left before exiting Strong Lane. By chance, Anna, holding Susan's hand, was standing on the Schmidts' front step talking to Ella at the open door. Jane slowed the car, rolled down her window and shouted out to them, "Hey girls! Good news...we got a baby on the way. I'm taking the mother-to-be to the hospital!"

Ella and Anna waved and shouted, "Good luck!" in unison, as Jane resumed her speed and drove away. Norma started to laugh, and Jane frowned.

"I'm sorry, Nor. I probably shouldn't have told your news, but I'm just so gosh-darned excited for you."

"It's okay, Jane," replied Norma with a big grin on her face. "You're just being our typical Jane, the cheerleader, and I love you for it."

They made it to the hospital in record time. Jane dropped Norma at the front doors. "Now swear to me, Nor, that you will telephone as soon as the little one is born. I don't care how late it is. I'll be on pins and needles until you let me know if it's a boy or a girl. Promise?"

"I promise, Jane. And thank you so much for driving me here," answered Norma, and she trotted off to meet Gordon at the maternity ward.

It became a long day for the Lewises. They waited hours in the waiting room with the pacing expectant fathers. The men in the room looked curiously at Norma. The attractive young woman was definitely not an expectant grandmother, the only woman they thought they might encounter in a maternity ward's waiting room, other than a nurse. Norma didn't acknowledge their collective stares. She sat happily with Gordon, holding his hand and discussing baby names. They still had several favorites for each sex, and eventually decided they would make the final choice when they saw what the baby looked like. Much to Gordon's amusement, Norma had a silly notion that some of the names were only suitable depending on the baby's hair color.

A friendly labor and delivery nurse named Wilma Borden came in occasionally to inform the couple of the teen-aged Amy's progress. Most of the staff knew Norma from the year she'd worked in this very wing at the hospital. They all liked their co-worker immensely, even throwing a small baby shower on Norma's last day of work the afternoon before Christmas Eve.

Amy's maiden aunt was kept informed of her niece's progress, too. However, the older woman was sitting alone, by choice, in the hospital's main waiting room off the lobby by the front doors. Although Norma and Gordon had offered to sit with her, the woman declined stating she did not want to share in their joy. She was there solely for Amy's well-being. Once the baby was delivered, she would join her niece in the recovery room. Neither Amy nor her aunt wanted to see the baby that would be brought to the Lewises.

At eight o'clock in the evening, Norma and Gordon were the last two people left in the waiting room. They were tired and anxious, wondering if there were any problems. The last time Nurse Borden had checked in with them was before six when she declared the baby should be born within the hour. Just as Gordon was about to go to the nurse's station to see what he could learn, a man in surgical scrubs walked in. The couple immediately recognized him as Dr. Stern, Amy's obstetrician. He had a strange look on his face as he greeted the fretful pair.

"Well....we are finally done. Everyone came through with flying colors. All are healthy. Norma and Gordon, you are the parents of a baby girl...."

Norma collapsed in Gordon's arms in happy tears. Her husband put his arms around her and kissed the top of her head. In their excitement, they almost didn't hear Dr. Stern's next words.

"...AND another baby girl. You have identical twins. Congratulations!"

"What...wait a minute," began Gordon. "Why did no one know this before?"

"It was a little shock to us, too. In all of Amy's examinations, we only heard one heartbeat. The second twin was hiding behind the first. The girls are a little small, just over five pounds each, but both are perfect. We'll get you two in to see them shortly."

Norma was still speechless, so Gordon asked about Amy's health. The doctor assured them she was fine and in recovery with her aunt by her side. He turned to leave telling the couple he would send a nurse to let them know when they could see their daughters.

"Our daughters.... golly, can you believe it, Nor?" wondered Gordon, with a look of awe on his face.

"Oh, Gordon. It's so wonderful, isn't it? We couldn't have any children and now we have two. Are you as amazed as I am?" asked Norma looking up at her husband with tears of bliss streaming down her face.

"Yes, I'm surprised, but thrilled. It's going to be a lot of work but so worth it to have a ready-made little family. I'm a lucky man!"

Norma had a thought and stopped smiling. In a serious tone, she asked, "Gor, do you mind much that they aren't boys or even that we don't have one of each?"

"Are you crazy, Norma? Who wants a boy! I'll be surrounded by gorgeous girls. Yet, no matter how beautiful our daughters are, they will never be as lovely as their mommy is to me. I love you, sweetheart."

They embraced with Norma's ear close to Gordon's beating heart and a huge smile on her face. Gordon had called her a mommy. She, Norma June Wolf Lewis, was finally a mother.

Since the babies were small at birth, they remained in the hospital for two and a half weeks. They thrived during that time and had a constant stream of visitors observing them through the glass window of the hospital's nursery. Both sets of first-time grandparents marveled with pride at the new granddaughters. Norma's father, George, would pull over anyone walking down the nursery hallway to see the twins through the glass. Mary had to laughingly plead with her husband to stop accosting total strangers. Norma's twenty-two-year-old brother, Stewart, claimed he could not believe he was an uncle, but he happily told anyone who would listen that he was. On a Sunday afternoon, Ella, Jane, and Anna left their children with their husbands to visit the newest members of the Lewis family.

Norma went to the hospital every day and convinced the nursing staff to allow her to diaper and feed her girls. Gordon met his wife there each night. After much deliberation, they decided to name the older twin Joy Louise and the younger Janet Mary. The girls' middle names were in honor of Gordon's and Norma's mothers.

On Tuesday, the twentieth of January, the babies were finally discharged from the hospital. It was the same day that Dwight D. Eisenhower took an oath in Washington D.C. to become the thirty-fourth president of the United States. As Gordon drove his little family home from the hospital, Norma thought to herself that the inauguration was a good sign. A new era in America was starting as a new chapter in her life was beginning.

CHAPTER 17

Ella - 1953

Acrouching Ella finished buttoning Nan's ruby colored coat and proceeded to tie its matching winter hat's ribbons under her daughter's chin. She stood to her full petite height of five feet and picked up her own wool coat from the living room chair. She started to pull it on when Nan began to tug at her hat's ribbons and proclaimed, "Tight, Mommy! No want it!"

Ella laughed and stooped back down saying, "I will loosen it, Nan, but you have to keep the hat on. It is very windy and cold outside this morning."

"No hat. Me big girl. Me's two," sulked Nan.

"I know you are now a big girl, but you still need a hat on such a windy day. Look, Mommy is putting on a hat, too," reasoned Ella, and she placed a knit cap on her own head.

The fair-haired toddler crossed her short arms over her tiny chest and produced a disdainful pout on her cherub face. Ella rolled her eyes as she finished securing her own garments. Her daughter had celebrated her second birthday a few weeks ago, and Ella started to fear the 'terrible twos' stage was beginning for her bright first-born.

Ella took Nan's hand and walked out her front door. She shortened her stride to match her daughter's small steps as they walked down the path to the street. It was colder than it should have been for the last day of March, and Ella would have preferred to pick up the toddler to run the short distance to Norma's warm house across the road. However, Ella didn't want her independent daughter to throw a tantrum at being picked up like a baby, so they continued at a snail's pace.

Norma greeted the two at her front door. She had one of the twins in the crook of her right arm. Ella didn't know which one it was, and she wondered how Norma could tell the babies apart. When the Lewises had first brought the infants home, Norma had painted Joy's big toenail pink and Janet's red. Recently, however, Norma claimed she could see the differences in her daughters, both in looks and personality, and didn't need to differentiate with nail polish any longer. Ella and the rest of the neighbors still could not distinguish one twin from the other.

"Hello, Ella. Do me a favor and take Janet from me. I hear Joy fussing in her bassinet," requested Norma as she placed the baby in Ella's arms and rushed to the back of the house.

So, this one is Janet, thought Ella. She started to coo to the baby while unbuttoning her own coat. She then bent down and, with her free hand, helped Nan wiggle out of her little matching coat and hat.

The toddler was gleeful when she discovered a large empty cardboard box and proceeded to climb into it. Norma's living room was filled with such boxes of assorted sizes in various stages of packing.

The Lewis family was moving from Strong Lane, and the idea of losing good friends was upsetting to Ella and John. They, with the Marinos and Flynns, learned the surprising news two weeks ago. After three years together on the same street, Ella found it heartbreaking to see one of the original families depart.

Ella thought that Norma and Gordon's decision to move to Long Island's north shore town of Huntington had been swift. The reason for moving was slightly different depending on which of the two was being asked. Gordon had claimed to John the change was because of the lucrative job offer he had received in early February from the huge aircraft engineering corporation, Grumman. Located in Bethpage, it was considered the largest corporate employer on Long Island. Gordon reasoned that the increase in salary permitted Norma and him to either expand their current home or shop for new real estate.

Norma had told Ella, Jane, and Anna that the move was solely due to the jam-packed status of their Strong Lane house. Gordon's promotion and raise had just made the decision easier. The nursery Norma had so carefully planned for one baby now had two matching cribs squeezed into its small dimensions, forcing her rocking chair to be relocated to the living room. There were also two bassinets pressed into the master bedroom, and Norma anticipated the eventual necessity of a pair of highchairs in her cramped ten-by-ten kitchen. In addition, there were innumerable diapers and clothes for two. They were running out of space, and the girls weren't even mobile yet. The situation would only grow worse with time. As much as Norma wanted to stay on Strong Lane and raise her twins with Ella, Jane, and Anna nearby, she knew Gordon's suggestion to expand their current home was not the answer. It would be impossible to take care of her newborns with messy construction going on around her. Moving to a bigger home had been the only answer.

"I really appreciate you being here today, Ella," said Norma as she returned to the living room with little Joy over her shoulder. "With Gor having just started the new job a few weeks ago and working late trying to get up to speed, he hasn't been as much help as he'd like to be. You, Jane, and Anna have been angels taking the time to come over here and help me pack. I can only pray I have such wonderful neighbors in my new neighborhood."

"I know it is so selfish of me to say this," said Ella sadly. "But I wish you and Gordon were not going. John and I will miss you both so much."

"Oh, darling, we will miss you too! But we'll see you often. It's not a long car ride from here to Huntington. And now that you passed your driving test and have a license, you and Nan can drive up to my house and spend an entire day with me and the girls. Did I tell you there is a true Main Street shopping area just south of our house? It's within walking distance, and there's a cute soda fountain where we can have lunch. In the summer, we can go to the beautiful park on Main Street with its adorable stone gazebo and children's wading pool. You and little Nan will love it," gushed Norma with enthusiasm.

"It does sound wonderful, Nor. I hope you will be very happy there," conceded Ella sincerely.

Norma continued, clearly excited, "Thanks, sweetie. Did I tell you my parents asked us to shop for a larger home in their neighborhood? Although I wanted a house like my parents' colonial with a basement and garage, I just felt Gor and I needed to discover a new locale, all our own. And we found one! That new co-worker of Gordon's who suggested Huntington did us such a favor. It's only ten miles north of Gor's new job. And the Dutch colonial we bought is just adorable! It's blue with white shutters, and I instantly fell in love with the rear porch off the kitchen. Best of all, it has three bedrooms and two bathrooms!"

"I cannot wait to see it," Ella said. She was happy for Norma, but she would miss the daily contact with her friend immensely. "Little Janet fell asleep in my arms. Shall I put her down?"

"Yes, thank you. I think Joy is almost out, too. Let's put them in their bassinets and close my bedroom door. With any luck, we'll get an hour or two of quiet from them while we get some packing done," said Norma. With a quiet laugh, she added, "It looks like Nan is having a fun time crawling in and out of that box."

"I also brought a bag of toys and books to occupy her. She will be fine as we work," replied Ella.

Thirty minutes later, Norma and Ella were making true progress in packing kitchen items. Ella asked when the moving day was scheduled, and Norma said they were hoping to meet with the lawyers within the next few weeks to finalize the sale. The move would be shortly after.

"And, I almost forgot to tell you, we had an offer last weekend for this house!" announced Norma. "I must admit, I was a little worried we would have a tough time selling with the town sump next to us. Although its fence and straggly shrubs block the view from our side windows, I thought a big old hole in the ground still might be a negative selling point."

As she reached for more newspaper to wrap a large platter, Norma continued, "I'm so excited to say that you'll love the couple who will be the block's new neighbors. It's a nurse friend of mine from the hospital. Her name is Wilma Borden, and her husband is Roger. In fact, she was the labor and delivery nurse on duty the day the twins were born. I had brought the babies into the hospital for a promised visit a few weeks ago. When Wilma heard we were selling our house, she asked if she and Roger could take a look. They've been searching for a small house to purchase."

"Are they young newlyweds as we all were when we first moved here?" inquired Ella.

"No, they're in their mid-forties, no children, and they've rented apartments since they married eight years ago. Roger works in the administrative offices of the hospital. I think that's how they met, both working at the same place. Well, anyway, they really are an extremely sweet couple. I don't think Wilma will be part of coffee klatch, though, since she works full-time and has all crazy hours in the maternity ward."

"They sound very nice," said Ella. "However, I am not so sure we will have our coffee klatches as often as we did in the past. We are all getting so busy."

"Anna said the same thing when I told her about the Bordens. She doesn't think you gals will continue to get together for the gatherings, at least not on a weekly basis." Norma then coyly added, "I understand Anna will be getting *much* busier in six months. Did she tell you her news, Ella?"

"Yes, she did. I am very happy for her and Sal. A new baby in early September," said Ella. She hesitated before adding softly, "Nor, I went to my doctor's office last Friday. I am also expecting a second child in September, but closer to the end of that month. You are the first neighbor I am telling."

"Oh, Ella! I'm so very thrilled for you and John… and little Nan, too! She'll be a big sister. How are you feeling?"

"I am very well now. I only had a little of the morning sickness. It is now gone. I am just very tired some of the time."

"Well, put down those dishes of mine. I don't want you lifting a thing," insisted Norma. "Please just sit and keep me company."

"No, I will help you. I like to keep busy. I have a lot of energy today." Ella picked up another plate and wrapped it in newspaper. "I will tell the other ladies about my happy news as I see them."

"I'm glad your second baby is not due in the winter like your first-born," said Norma with a chuckle. "Although now you'll have a certified maternity nurse living right here to deliver any unexpected babies. Gosh, we could have used Wilma that day Nan entered the world!"

"I did not need a certified nurse that day. I had you and Anna. You both did just as well as any hospital," said Ella matter-of-factly before calmly picking up an additional piece from Norma's dinnerware.

"I'm glad it all worked out, but I was so nervous for you. Anna was as cool as a cucumber. But not me; I was inwardly shaking all day. I even get goose bumps now just thinking about it."

Ella put down the dish she was wrapping, touched Norma's arm and looked her friend directly in the eyes before stating in her serious manner, "I never felt alarmed with you and Anna. You were both very reassuring that day. I am forever grateful to the two of you. I will never forget what you did for me, a foreign woman you had known for less than a year."

Norma blushed. "I've never felt like I did anything extraordinary that day. Anna and you were the amazing ones. I did what I assumed anyone would have done: appear calm and carry on."

"I do not think Jane or Betty could have been as composed as you were. You should be very proud of yourself, Norma," Ella said, then resumed wrapping the dish in front of her.

"Thank you for saying that, Ella. I appreciate it." Norma seemed pleased with herself and stood a little taller. She continued wrapping dishes, then added, "The ladies will be thrilled with your announcement, especially Anna. You two will be raising infants together. Other than my twins, we haven't had two babies born at the same time since Robby and Susan were born two months apart in 1950."

"Yes, and everyone will have two children except for Betty," Ella said sadly. "I will feel a little unhappy when I tell Betty I am expecting a second child. I know she wants another one, but she has not had any luck since her miscarriage."

"Don't let her problems make you feel anything but joyful for your good fortune," replied Norma with an edge to her voice.

"Yes, I know," sighed Ella.

For a while, the two worked silently side by side, each lost in her own thoughts. Then Ella said quietly, "Nor, do you think you can forgive Betty before you move away?"

"I don't think so," stated Norma adamantly. "Frankly, Ella, Betty is one of my reasons for moving. It's been very awkward living right next door to her since 'the incident,' as I call it. She has never acknowledged the twins. She doesn't even give me a wave if we are outside at the same time. Not that I have been out too much with this frosty winter, but I've carried the girls to my car while she was entering or exiting her house and she doesn't look up. No, I'm done with her. She's the only reason I'm happy I'm leaving this block."

"But, Nor, if I can be so bold as to say so, she asked your forgiveness, and you did not grant it. She may be waiting for you to make the next move. Can you two not agree to put the matter behind and make amends before you leave?" pleaded Ella timidly.

"You sound like Anna. She was always the peacemaker of our little group. But, no, I can't do it," answered Norma firmly. "Betty was never sorry for attempting to ruin my life. She was just sorry it blew up in her face."

"Then do it for yourself, Nor. There is a Buddhist quote, 'Holding on to anger is like grasping a hot coal with the intent of throwing it at someone else; you are the one who gets burned.'"

"I admire your intellect, Ella. I really do. You're the most widely read of all of us. Yet that quote will not change my mind," a stubborn Norma responded. "Now, let's change the subject. Do you have any ideas of names for the new baby?"

Ella, realizing the subject of Betty was undeniably closed, replied, "If it is a boy, we will name him after John. And I had an idea for a girl's name the first time that I did not use because I wanted to honor you and Anna. So, I will use it if this baby is a girl. The name is Natalie. It is in honor of John's grandmother who taught him how to speak, read and write the German language. If she had not tutored him, John and I never would have met."

"That's a lovely name, Ella. But you should have a spare name for each gender just in case you get surprised and have twins, like we did! Could you imagine?"

Before the expectant mother could reply, they heard from the rear of the house the start of a baby's wail. Nan trotted into the kitchen and announced, "Mommy, baby cwying!"

"Let me dash and see if I can pick up the fussy one before she wakes her sister. God knows I love them, but, honestly Ella, I wouldn't wish the double trouble of twins on you," Norma said hurriedly with a smile.

Ella learned that by the end of April, paperwork had been completed on both the sale of the Lewises Levittown house and the purchase of the Huntington one. The closings were then scheduled back-to-back on the first Thursday in May. The moving day was scheduled for the day after.

That Friday morning, Norma's parents drove to Levittown bright and early to gather the twins to take to their home, just as a moving van pulled in front of Number Two Strong Lane. Gordon directed the workers with the emptying of the Cape Cod, strategizing with the lead man as to the most efficient way to pack the truck. Norma loaded their more personal belongings into their two cars, which they would each drive to the new house after the movers completed their tasks.

Together, Ella, Jane, and Anna, each with their respective children, walked over to Norma's yard to give their friend a final goodbye hug. The night before, John, Danny and Sal had each stopped at the Lewises' house to offer their farewells and best wishes. Today, all the husbands were at work, except for Bob Carter. Alone, Bob came over to shake Gordon's hand and wish Norma good luck.

As Ella stood with the others in the yard outside Norma's kitchen door, she noticed a frowning Betty, inside her own home, observing the scene through her side living room window. Ella looked directly at her, silently willing Betty to come outside and join them. She knew Betty saw the pleading look in her eyes. Nevertheless, Betty turned from the window and walked away.

PART II

1969 – 1971

CHAPTER 18

Ella - 1969

Ella, sipping a warm mug of coffee, watched from her kitchen window as the four teenagers boarded the school bus that had just stopped at the corner of Strong Lane. Fair-haired Nan, the oldest of the group, confidently stepped onto the vehicle first. Ella's first-born looked more like her each day, although Ella was grateful Nan had also inherited some of John's height. Ella's younger daughter, Natalie, had roughly the same stature as her sister but instead possessed John's same light-brown hair and large hazel eyes flecked with gold. *Sometimes,* Ella mused as her only two children disappeared onto the bus, *it's so very difficult to fathom that Nan is graduating from high school next month, and Natalie is finishing her sophomore year there. Where has the time gone?*

From her vantage point, Ella also observed the dark-haired Christina Marino following closely behind Natalie. Since the two had been toddlers, they were inseparable. Ella smiled at the familiar happy notion of her and Anna raising their younger daughters together over the past years. The friendship between the two girls closely mirrored that of their mothers.

Lagging a short distance behind the three girls was Jane's handsome middle child, Mark. At seventeen, he was the lone dark-haired member of the red-headed Flynn family. He was in the grade between Ella's two daughters. The only other child on the street who still attended public school was Mark's younger brother, Matthew. The twelve-year-old would be taking the later bus to the junior high school.

It was on mornings like this when a pensive Ella deeply missed the old days of frequent, organized coffee klatches. Life had evolved frantically from those early years when the children were babies. Now the women caught each other rarely, only when they managed to carve out mutual free time, such as this morning's much anticipated gathering at Jane's house.

Ella hurried to finish her coffee so she could change into her black leotard before heading out. Jane insisted on a prompt start when following along with Jack LaLanne's television exercise program. Ella admired Jane's dedication to stretching, bending, and jumping with Jack during his half hour show on any weekday morning she wasn't otherwise engaged. Jane was on a constant mission to stay in shape since the birth of her third and, she swore, *final* child, Matthew. She had convinced Ella, Anna, and Betty to join her when their schedules permitted.

At fifteen minutes after nine o'clock, Ella arrived at Jane's kitchen door at the same time as Anna. When the two entered Jane's living room, they discovered Betty perched reluctantly on the sofa, removing the plaid slacks she wore over her own tight black leotard. Jane was adjusting the television opposite the sofa. She had already pushed aside the room's coffee table and upholstered chairs to create more space for the four women to exercise. Jane's expanded living room had a good-sized area for this morning's purpose. Years ago, Danny and his construction crew had removed the wall that had separated the front living room and the original back master bedroom. The larger living room, along with Jane's newly expanded and remodeled kitchen, made the Flynns' home a spacious haven for the family of five.

"Can't we skip the show today, Jane?" grumbled Betty. "I don't feel like exercising. Let's just have coffee now and then watch *Girl Talk*. I love that program. Virginia Graham always has such interesting guests."

"We can watch Virginia after Jack's program. Don't you all think his show is a groovy way to stay in shape?" questioned an impatient Jane and then, without waiting for an answer, demanded, "Now, let's get into our spots, girls. It's starting."

The four exercised for the next thirty minutes with Jane making the best effort, and Betty displaying the most lackluster attempt. Anna and Ella did their best to keep up with their energetic hostess.

When the television show finished, a perspiring Jane said, "Thanks, ladies. It's always a gas to do the program with others. I know our get-togethers are rare these days, and I appreciate your willingness to combine it with a half hour of exercise. It's important now that we're all in our forties. Don't you agree?"

"I don't mind," replied Ella. "I sit too much at the library. Being active on a day off is good for me."

As they made their way into Jane's kitchen, Betty asked, "How are you doing at the library, Ella? Do you like working there?"

Ella had recently been hired as a professional librarian at the town's public library: a modern building that had opened in 1963. She was extremely proud of the diploma she had received from a local college five months ago. Commencing her studies after her younger daughter had started public school, Ella had taken years of daytime classes as a part-time undergraduate student to achieve her goal. Additionally, while pursuing a higher education, she had found her confidence, evolving from a shy young war bride into a self-assured modern woman.

"I like it very much. I've loved books my whole life, so it's not like work to me," Ella answered with genuine enthusiasm.

Anna, plopping down on a chair at Jane's new dinette table, added, "That's terrific! It's important to enjoy your work. I find constant delight in my job at the hospital, helping to deliver babies."

Ella sat in the chair next to Anna and offered praise to her friend. "I owe a great part of my career inspiration to you, Anna. When you returned to school before me to become a nurse, it encouraged me to pursue a degree, too. And now, my Nan has enrolled in a librarian course of study in college when she starts attending this September. I'm so thrilled she wants to follow in my footsteps!"

"I motivated you, and, in turn, you inspired your daughter. And if Wilma Borden hadn't guided me as to which program of study I should pursue, I never would've become a labor and delivery nurse at her hospital," noted Anna as she helped herself to a slice of pound cake Jane had just placed on the table. "We women must stick together and spur each other on!"

"Here, here!" proclaimed Jane, the last of the four to take a seat.

"But you had prior experience with midwifery, Anna," began Betty, pouring herself a cup of coffee. "There wasn't much you had to learn after delivering Ella's Nan all those years ago."

"Believe me, Betty, there was plenty I needed to learn! And I did, with Sal and my girls cheering me on."

"So... Ella is a librarian. I'm a Tupperware regional rep, and Anna is a maternity nurse. We must find a career for you, Betty. What about a professional baker?" suggested Jane. "You always make the most wonderful cakes."

"Crikey, Jane, you are a nutter! Why would I want to exhaust myself with more work at a job outside of my home?" asked Betty incredulously. "I give you gals credit, but I have enough to do caring for Bob, Robby, and my house. And I bake for enjoyment. I have no desire to turn it into a career."

"Betty, just think about it. You make the best fancy birthday cakes. You could bake them in your own kitchen and sell them to mothers for children's birthday parties," continued the business-minded Jane eagerly. "I could give your name to some of the homemakers who run the Tupperware parties and ask them to pass on the info to their guests. We could have some business cards made for you with your telephone number and cake prices. Then you could..."

Betty raised her palm in a stop signal, interrupting Jane's enthusiastic plan, "Slow down there, Jane. I just said I'm not looking for a job."

"It's not a bad idea, Betty, if you want to make some extra money," added Anna.

"I don't need to. Bob is the provider in our household, and I've always kept a very tidy budget. We even own a second car now. And Robby has his own salary to spend. He also insists on giving us a small token amount for rent while he still lives at home. So, I have no need for a job," replied Betty with a firm finality.

Since academics had never been his strong suit, Robby had not been interested in furthering his education after high school, as Pamela Flynn and Susan Marino were currently doing. Despite Betty vehemently urging her son to try at least one college course, Robby, like his father, had refused. He was happily working full-time as a conductor on the Long Island Rail Road, a position Bob had helped him acquire after graduating from high school.

Rising from her chair at the table, Betty asked, "Jane, may I bring my coffee into your living room and turn on *Girl Talk?*"

"Sure, go ahead," said Jane, and, after Betty left the room, she added quietly to the two others, "Boy, she is so prickly! We were just trying to help. I thought she might feel left out with all of us discovering careers for ourselves. With Wilma working full-time and the three of us doing our gigs, Betty is the only exclusive housewife remaining on Strong Lane."

"Betty is Betty. It makes me sad to think she's not open to change," observed Anna tactfully. There was a long pause as the women sipped their coffee.

"What do you ladies hear from Norma these days?" Jane asked. "I haven't talked to her in a while. You two see her more than I ever do, with her twins and your younger girls all the same age."

"I spoke to her on the telephone last week," shared Ella, keeping her voice low. She didn't want Betty to hear her from the living room. It was an unspoken agreement among the three neighbors not to mention Norma in front of Betty. Although Anna, Jane, and Ella had remained friends with the Lewises over the years, Betty and Norma had never reconciled.

Ella continued, "Nor told me she recently stopped volunteering with the school's PTA and the town's historical society. She says she's ready to get a 'real job;' her words, not mine. She's toying with the idea of a career in real estate. She said since her twins did so well in their sophomore year at Huntington High, she no longer feels the need to be home every afternoon after school."

"That sounds like a good plan," said Jane.

"It's funny, Christina sort of idolizes Janet and Joy, mainly because they're identical. My daughter has been envious of those two ever since she was eight and saw that cute Disney movie about the twins," said Anna, rolling her dark eyes and smiling. "What was the name of that film?"

"It was *The Parent Trap*," replied Ella. "And I know what you mean about Christina's view of the twins. When Natalie was younger, she asked me why I couldn't have had a twin for her instead of an older sister. She doesn't always appreciate Nan. I tell her she will value her sister when they are adults."

"My sisters and I fought like cats when we were young, but we like each other now that we don't all live in the same cramped house," Jane said with an impish grin before continuing. "Seriously, I think it's great that Nor's twins, and Christina and Natalie, are all turning sweet sixteen in the same year and still get along when they're together. Especially since they grew up in different towns."

"Yes," agreed Ella. "The friendship among the four girls started with toddler playdates and then evolved into pen pals and sleepovers."

"Christina thinks it's so cool, as she says, having friends attending a different school in another town," added Anna.

"Well, it's a credit to the both of you that you remain close to Norma, too. I guess the common bond of all your daughters helps," observed Jane. Then, with a furrowed brow, she added, "When Norma and Gordon first moved, it was lots of fun when they'd invite the three of us and our hubbies and kids to their home for bar-b-ques. We were all still tight then. But over the years, everyone got so busy, and we didn't socialize as much. Now, I only speak on the phone with Nor periodically, and I haven't seen her in person since she, Gordon, and their girls came to my Independence Day extravaganza last year. Remember? We all had a super time, as if they had never left Strong Lane. But they only came to that because Betty and Bob took Robby to England as a high school graduation gift that same week in July."

"Yes, as Norma has said for way too many years, her rule is if Betty is at a function, she is not," lamented Anna. "It's sad those two have never reconciled. Sixteen years is a long time to hold a grudge. I really don't see any way they can ever be friends again."

"Just this morning," began Ella. "I was reminiscing about those old days, before their altercation, when we had coffee klatch at least once a week. Life seemed simpler then."

"Oh, I miss those days," Anna mused, a dreamy look on her face.

Jane, looking melancholy, nodded in agreement. "Despite Betty's and Norma's minor squabbles back then, all five of us used to have a grand time, even when we felt marooned on this little street. Now things have gotten... I don't know... so big and complex, both in our group and the world in general."

Ella was meditative for a moment before adding, "We lived in such an insular little world back then, but it was truly wonderful in its own limited way."

"What was wonderful?" asked Betty as she reentered the kitchen, empty coffee mug in hand. She sat down at the table and poured another cup.

"The old days when we first moved here. Before the world got so crazy," groaned Jane with a frown.

"Yes, I miss when the kids were babies," agreed Betty wistfully.

There were a few moments of quiet contemplation. Still the most altruistic of the group, Anna's kind eyes sought Jane's distraught ones and asked, "Jane, why do you feel things have gotten so complex and crazy? Is everything okay with you?"

"I'm fine, but it's the war that really worries me. Pam's boyfriend, Paul, just graduated from their university last week. Therefore, he's no longer considered 2-S status— you know, deferred from military service. Pam told me that he's thinking about going up to Canada. If he emigrates before the army calls him up, he won't be breaking any law by moving to Canada. He doesn't believe in this war in Vietnam and says he won't fight in it. Pam has another year to go to graduate with her degree in elementary education. I really want her to finish, especially since Danny and I don't have college diplomas. We are so enormously proud of her. But I'm afraid she'll possibly follow Paul if he moves out of the country."

"Robby registered for Selective Service when he turned eighteen last year," said Betty quietly. "It's very upsetting to me, but I know he had no choice."

"Paul is registered too, but, as a college student, he was entitled to the deferment. Now that he's graduated, he could get a notice to serve any day," mourned Jane.

"What was Paul's course of study?" asked Ella.

"He had a double major of Philosophy and English. He's an outstanding writer and did a lot of work for the campus newspaper and magazine," replied Jane. "God knows, he had plenty of opportunities during college to write articles protesting this war, in addition to actively taking part in anti-war marches. Although I wasn't happy about it, Pam marched with him, along with most of their friends."

"That's what you get, Jane, when you send your daughter to a liberal university in New York City," commented Betty.

"It doesn't matter if your child goes to a college in the city or the country," reflected Anna. "Susan is at a fairly rural upstate university, and there are protests on her campus, too. It doesn't make the evening news like the big schools, but it still happens."

"This stupid controversial war is going to cause the loss of my only daughter to Canada. I just know she'll want to follow Paul," Jane fretted.

"Maybe Pam and Paul aren't as serious with each other as you think," soothed Betty. "Girls break up with blokes all the time."

"Those two have been dating for three years. I'm almost sure he is 'the one' for Pam. Overall, Paul's a good guy; Danny and I like him. But I won't be happy if he takes our baby girl out of the country!"

"What does Danny think of all this?" asked Ella.

"He doesn't know. Pam told me about Canada in confidence. Danny will just about flip his lid if he finds out. I'm just praying some miracle happens, like the war ending or at least the draft stopping. And I worry about my Mark, too. He's seventeen, and he'll have to register soon enough."

"As a mother of a boy too, I hear you loud and clear, Jane," Betty said with empathy. "I'm hoping for the same miracle."

Ella looked over at Anna. They exchanged a look of great concern for the two others, but also one of some relief. Ella knew Anna, like her, was glad to be a mother to daughters only.

CHAPTER 19

Jane - 1969

July twentieth was not a day anyone on Strong Lane would ever forget. Along with most of the world, the eyes of all the neighbors, both children and parents, were glued to their televisions. In the early afternoon of that historic day, the Apollo Eleven lunar module named Eagle, with astronauts Neil Armstrong and Edwin (Buzz) Aldrin Junior aboard, separated from the command module and its pilot Michael Collins. The lunar module was the pride of Long Island since it had been designed and manufactured at the Grumman Aerospace Corporation in Bethpage by the team of engineers and technicians with whom Gordon Lewis worked.

As the Eagle made its descent to the moon's surface, all five Flynns, along with Pamela's boyfriend, Paul, were perched on the living room furniture watching the drama unfold. When the craft finally touched down on the edge of the moon's Sea of Tranquility, and Armstrong subsequently radioed Mission Control in Texas that "the Eagle has landed," Jane jumped up and declared, "That's it. This calls for a party. I'm phoning the neighbors!"

"That's a fine idea, babe, but it's already after four o'clock.... getting close to dinnertime. We don't have enough grub for a party," Danny countered.

"We'll just do a potluck dinner. Pam helped me make that big tray of macaroni and cheese earlier. We have plenty of beer and soda leftovers from July Fourth in the spare fridge in the garage. And Anna always has a slew of cold cuts in her house from Sal's store. I'm going to phone them all and see what they have at home to bring. This is history! We've got to watch it all unfold with the rest of the block," babbled Jane before pausing and asking, "What do you kids think? Is it okay to invite in the neighborhood?"

Mark and Matthew thought it was a good idea. Pamela said she didn't care as long as Paul could stay until the astronauts walked on the moon. Danny added that he knew Wilma and Roger Borden from across the street were away on vacation, so there was no need for Jane to contact them. Jane trotted to the kitchen to telephone Ella, Anna, and Betty.

Twenty minutes later, she came back into the living room asking if she had missed anything exciting on the television. "Did they step onto the moon yet?"

"No, Mom. The guy on the TV said it would take a long time until they're ready to get out of the Eagle," explained twelve-year-old Matthew. "I can stay up late until they do, right? I don't want to miss any of the cool stuff."

"Yes, it's summer school break so of course you can stay up as long as it takes to see them walk on the moon," answered Jane. "And you'll have plenty of company to witness it with. The Carters, Schmidts, and Marinos are all coming over, and everyone has food to share. Betty Carter has even baked a festive cake with an Apollo theme."

"Are all the kids coming?" asked Mark hopefully. Mark, who had just completed his junior year in high school, had recently parted ways with his girlfriend. Jane knew her son had just started a little summer crush on pretty Natalie Schmidt, although she was a year and a half younger than him and didn't seem to share his captivation, at least not yet.

"Natalie Schmidt and Christina Marino are both at a sleepover party at the Lewises' house in Huntington," Jane reported to her crestfallen son. "And Nan Schmidt is away with a group of friends on a post high school graduation vacation. But Mr. and Mrs. Schmidt will come on their own. The Marinos will come with just Susan, and all three Carters will be here."

"Janie, do you know if Gordon is on duty today at Grumman?" asked Danny as he rose from his club chair to start helping Jane get the house ready for their guests.

"Anna said that Norma told her Gordon, with the rest of the engineers, must man a mission support room in case there are any problems with the lunar module. That's why Norma invited over Natalie and Christina to watch it on television with the twins. Since their dad isn't home to share it with them, Norma wanted to throw a little party for her girls. Anna said the twins invited some other classmates too, so Norma is monitoring quite a large group of sixteen-year-olds in her home today. Better her than me!"

It was after eight o'clock that evening, and Anna, Betty, and Ella were seated at Jane's kitchen table. The potluck buffet dinner and dessert had been a success. They had just finished helping Jane clean up the paper goods and pans that had been used.

Before Jane joined the ladies, she glanced into the living room at the rest of the group watching the television. Pamela and Paul sat gazing into each other's eyes on the small loveseat. The rest of the young people were lounging on the floor. Sal and Bob, the closest friends among the husbands, were sitting on the sofa discussing their bowling league. Danny, trying to be a good host, was listening to Ella's husband, John, describe in minute detail why Astronauts Armstrong and Aldrin were still inside the Eagle. Danny looked back at Jane, and without anyone else noticing, rolled his eyes and grimaced. Jane smiled back, knowing her husband thought John was a pleasant enough guy, but too much of an egghead for his taste. Danny would rather discuss sports, but since Gordon Lewis had moved away, he'd lost his best chance at it, as none of the other men were particularly interested in the local teams.

A thought suddenly occurred to Jane. *Back in the early days of Strong Lane, Gordon was the spoon who stirred the pot of men. He had the talent of engaging all the men as a group. It's maddening that the husbands haven't really meshed since his departure. They gather for the sake of us wives and their children, but apart from Sal and Bob, they don't particularly enjoy each other's company.*

"Danny, we girls will be in the kitchen gossiping," said Jane, shooting her husband one last look of empathy. "Call us when those guys get out of the module and walk on the moon. All that sub-reporting is boring!"

"Will do, Janie," said a resigned Danny, as John launched into another scientific discussion.

Jane returned to the kitchen table, opened the window near her chair, plopped down, and lit a cigarette. She inhaled and then blew smoke toward the open window. She wore her strawberry blonde hair straight and long, like her twenty-one-year-old daughter. Since both were about the same height, a person walking behind the pair might mistake one for the other. Devoted to her exercise regime, Jane remained a trim woman. She also claimed that her recently adopted habit of cigarette smoking helped keep her weight down.

"Blimey, Jane! Do you have to smoke your fags in front of us?" bristled Betty, waving her hand in front of her nose. Although she was a year younger than her hostess, Betty would not be mistaken for a young woman from behind. Unlike her friends, she had never really updated the style of her soft brown hair, and she still wore it in a short permanent wave of curls, à la 1950. Her best feature was her still flawless, fair, peaches-and-cream English complexion, which she now scrunched up in distaste.

"I agreed not to smoke in your homes, but in mine, I get to do what I want to do," Jane snapped, but then she reconsidered. "I'm sorry, girls. I know none of you smoke, and it used to drive me batty when Danny smoked around me before I picked up his habit. But it's the only thing that calms me down these days. And your husbands smoke, too."

"Bob, like John, only smokes an occasional pipe," Betty shot back. "And I've only seen Sal with cigars. I think you two Flynns are the only ones smoking fags. And after the Surgeon General warned the American people about the dangers of cigarette smoking, I can't believe you'd..."

"Oh, put a sock in it, Betty! I'll stub it out already," Jane countered with obvious annoyance, and she reached for the ceramic ashtray in the center of the table to extinguish her partially smoked cigarette.

She closed the open window since Danny had the air conditioner still running on this humid evening.

"Why are you so anxious these days, Jane?" inquired Ella.

"It's just everything," began Jane. "Other than the wonder of the Apollo landing, the nightly news programs are full of depressing stories. I'm not wild about any of the politicians out there. I never liked Nixon when he was Eisenhower's vice-president, and now he's our leader. And that Senator Ted Kennedy let that poor secretary drown in a creek in Martha's Vineyard. Who can you trust these days? No wonder Pam and her college classmates want to drop out of society."

"You've been very down this whole summer, Jane. It's surprising. You have always been the can-do, never-say-die gal in our group," observed Betty.

"It's difficult to be upbeat these days," Jane replied in a depressed monotone.

"And what do you mean by drop out?" asked Ella nervously as she tucked a stray piece of her shoulder-length pale blonde hair behind her right ear.

"You know, like drop out of conformity... social change... all that stuff the kids are talking about now," Jane explained.

"I blame it on the movies our kids see today," said Betty. "I read in the newspaper that there's a major motion picture being released with an X rating! Now, I ask you ladies, why must a film be that graphic? I think these sordid themes started last year with that movie based on the idea of a middle-aged woman, like us, having an affair with a college student."

"That movie's music was really good, though. I listen to the original soundtrack album with my girls all the time," Anna said optimistically. "It's all about how you look at things, girls. It doesn't necessarily have to be depressing."

"And our space program is amazing. So many wonderful discoveries will happen in our lifetime," added Ella. "It's wonderful to see children come into the library and ask me for books about space exploration."

"Yes, they're all positive things, but there's still so much tension in this country right now," insisted Jane. "People don't seem to agree on anything."

Ella cringed a little with Jane's words. "As a girl growing up in Germany, I witnessed all the social unrest I ever want to experience during my lifetime. The turmoil over this controversial war makes me very uneasy. I'll admit, I'm a little worried about the things Nan will observe during her upcoming freshman year in college."

As if on cue, Susan walked into the kitchen with Robby directly behind her. She had apparently overheard the last of Ella's remarks and soothed, "Don't worry, Mrs. Schmidt. Nan will be fine. She signed up for the same dorm I'll be living in. Freshmen are on a different floor than we sophomores, but I'll be happy to keep an eye out for her."

"I know you will, Susan, and I thank you. I'm glad she'll be attending the same college. Nan looks up to you. You have always been so kind to her," Ella answered sincerely.

"Now, if you would only be as kind to your little sister," teased Anna with jollity and reached her hand up from her seated position to tousle her daughter's long, wavy black hair.

With an equal display of amusement in her dark eyes, Susan, without missing a beat, replied, "Well, if Christina wasn't such a drama queen all the time, maybe I *would* be kinder to the little pest."

"Yes, Christina is definitely the actress of our family. Where are you two headed?" asked Anna as Robby opened the kitchen door and held it for Susan.

"We're going to go out and look up at the moon," began Robby. "I know we won't see the spaceship up there, but it's getting a little boring on the TV. The announcer says it'll be at least another hour before Armstrong unlocks the hatch."

"Please close the door tightly, Robby, on your way out. The air conditioner is on," requested Jane.

"Will do, Mrs. Flynn," responded the affable Robby. Just as kind, truthful, and mild-mannered as his father, Robby Carter had always been a favorite among the mothers on Strong Lane.

After the two young people exited, Jane commented, "He's such a nice guy, Betty. You must be so proud of him. Although, I do wish he would call me Jane. I always look for my mother-in-law when I hear Mrs. Flynn."

"He is a very fine young man," agreed Anna with a pleasant smile.

"Well, I hope Susan thinks so, too," responded Betty with an optimistic look on her face. "My Robby has had a crush on her for ages, and I think now that she's between boyfriends, he might finally have the nerve to ask her out."

Anna's eyes opened wide with surprise. "Susan certainly thinks the world of Robby. She always has."

"And they grew up together, and are only a few months apart in age," added Betty warming to the idea. "Wouldn't it be brilliant, Anna, if our two kiddies got married someday? Imagine it, we would be in-laws then. And you, me, Sal, and Bob would make the best grandparents since we were friends first."

Jane and Ella both sat very still, darting their eyes back and forth between Anna and Betty as if watching a ping pong match. Jane was particularly interested in the conversation because she secretly knew her Mark was attracted to Ella's Natalie. Up to this point, none of the children on the street had ever dated one another. All of them got along amicably and watched out for each other since their respective families had always been close-knit, but there had never been any romantic attachments.

Anna, clearly flabbergasted, warned, "Whoa, Betty! Let's not get ahead of ourselves. Those two will have to figure out things for themselves first. We don't even know if the affection is mutual."

Betty looked a bit deflated. "You just said he's a fine young man."

"And he is, but I have no idea what my daughter's thoughts are except that she thinks Robby is a good guy."

Jane was not going to say aloud what she was thinking. *As far as husband material is concerned, intelligent and outgoing Susan can do a lot better than sweet, puppy-dog faithful Robby.*

In what almost seemed like an immediate response to the women's imagined scenarios, Susan slipped back into the kitchen. She looked quite forlorn. The mothers could tell she was holding back some tears.

"Where's Robby?" Betty asked fretfully.

"He went home, Mrs. Carter. I'm so sorry. I think I disappointed him."

"What happened?" asked Anna gently as she rose from her chair to put her arm around her daughter's shoulders.

"Oh, Mom," began Susan. "I'm so upset that I let him down. He wanted us to go steady, and I told him I've never thought of him in that way. I was sort of shocked he thought of me as anything more than a sisterly friend. He's always been like the brother I never had."

"Robby has such a sensitive soul," Betty said in a worried tone. She continued without anger, only empathy for her son. "You may have broken his heart."

Staring at Betty with fury, Anna stated defiantly, "You know my Susan doesn't have a mean bone in her body. I'm sure she did her best to let him down easy."

Jane had never witnessed Anna being anything but cool and calm. *However, when a mother bear must rise and defend her cub, even a peacemaker like Anna can get riled.*

"I apologize, Susan. I certainly wasn't blaming you, and I don't want you to feel badly," said a sheepish Betty, reaching out and patting Susan's arm. "I was just stating what I know is true of my son." She let out a deep, sorrowful sigh and added, "I'll go over to my house and speak with him. Jane, would you tell Bob where Robby and I went and ask him to join us?"

"Yes, of course, Betty," Jane replied.

After Betty left the house, Susan's tears started to fall as she said, "I was as kind as I could be, Mom, but I know I made him so unhappy."

"I know, honey," acknowledged Anna with a profound look of sorrow. "Take it from me, one of the saddest things in life is when a man has true feelings for a woman, and it's not reciprocated."

Ella nudged Jane, indicating they should leave mother and daughter alone. Jane made her way into the living room where she quietly told Bob he should head home.

After the Carters left, the remaining eleven neighbors gathered around the Flynns' television finally to witness Armstrong's first step on the moon at 10:56 that evening. They watched with trepidation as the astronaut collected a sample of soil. When Aldrin joined Armstrong to plant the American flag, there was a unified shout of approval from the group in the living room. At one point, President Nixon placed a telephone call to the men on the moon. Around the same time as this historic call, Natalie and Christina telephoned from the Lewises' home to share with their families the monumental event.

It was after one o'clock in the morning when the astronauts returned to the Eagle. The men had been outside the lunar module for just over two hours. Shortly after, the party at the Flynns' finally broke up. The neighbors returned to their homes, and Pamela kissed her boyfriend goodnight before he got in his old car to drive to his mother's home in Brooklyn.

After Danny and the boys retreated to the bedrooms upstairs, Jane carried the last of the glassware from the living room to her kitchen sink. Pamela had just closed the side door after Paul's departure. She turned and stammered, "Mom, may I... may I speak with you?"

Standing at the sink with her back towards her daughter, Jane's shoulders tensed. She knew this had to be a matter of significant importance for Pamela to corner her alone this late in the evening. She tried to put a smile on her face as she turned around to answer. "Of course, sweetheart. What's up?"

Pamela took a deep breath before blurting out, "Paul has asked me to marry him and move with him to Canada."

Although Jane knew this day had been coming, she was still not prepared for it. "I need to sit down and have a cigarette," she mumbled and dropped into a kitchen chair. "Join me at the table, Pammy, and tell me everything."

Pamela, who for once did not bristle at the use of her childhood nickname, sat down in the chair next to her mother.

"He wants to get married quickly, at a town hall or something. Of course, our immediate families can be there, but we don't want a big party. Paul has already investigated moving to the Toronto area. He's been in touch with a locally based anti-draft program up there who aid Americans dodging the draft and wanting to start over. Toronto isn't that far. It's just across Lake Ontario from Niagara Falls. We'd practically still be in New York State," Pamela explained in a rush.

"I hear what Paul wants, Pam, but what do you want?" asked Jane before she lit her cigarette.

"I love him, Mom," Pamela replied plainly. "He's everything I've ever wanted in a guy. I'd follow him anywhere."

Jane took a long first drag on her cigarette and exhaled the smoke upwards. "Yes, I know that feeling; I felt that same way about your father when I was young, and I still do." She chose her next words carefully. "And you know Daddy and I love Paul. He's always been respectful and kind to you and us. But, what about your schooling, Pam? Your dad and I will be so disappointed if you don't complete it. I understand it's important for Paul to leave immediately. Do you think you can wait, finish your degree, and maybe join him next May?"

"No, Mom. I know I can't be without him for that long," admitted Pamela. "And Paul and I talked about my degree. We have it all figured out. He'll get a full-time job. I'll transfer my college credits to a school up there and get my diploma. And, after all, it's better I complete my teaching certificate in Canada if that's where I'll be teaching. The Canadian education system probably has different requirements than New York State."

"Sounds like you think you have it all figured out," noted an annoyed Jane. She puffed on her cigarette and then sadly added, "I'm not sure if I can accept this, Pam. And your father is going to explode."

"You can convince Daddy to get on board with it. I know you can. You can talk Daddy into anything!"

"I'm not sure if *I'm* on board with it, Pam," argued Jane becoming frustrated. "It's such a big decision. Won't you at least think about joining Paul next spring? I might be able to convince your dad with that plan, and it would give *me* more time to adjust to the idea of you leaving."

Pamela whined, "But, Mom, you've had time to adjust. I told you about this idea two months ago when Paul graduated."

"That's not fair, Pam! You never told me it was definite. And I kept your confidence, never telling your dad. I've been carrying this anxiety on my shoulders alone since then."

Pamela, seeing the hurt in her mother's eyes, relented. "I'm sorry, Mom. I know it's not how you and Daddy thought my future would evolve. I know you two wanted me to marry and stay close by. But you all can visit. Toronto's not that far away."

"It's another country, Pam. You'll be giving up everything that's familiar to you: family, friends...."

A calm determination came over Pamela's face before she quietly interrupted, "Mom, I turned twenty-one in April. I'm a legal adult and can do as I please. I just want my family's blessing. Please, don't make me choose. I can't imagine living my life without Paul."

Jane continued smoking her cigarette. *When did my little girl turn into a woman? And one who knows her own mind. She's as determined and willful as me,* Jane reflected wryly.

Jane reminisced to herself about how their similarities had led to many altercations over the years. When Pamela was a teenager, she had tested and argued all of Jane's rules. Jane had demanded Pamela wait until junior high school to start wearing makeup… and then found mascara in her daughter's fifth-grade knapsack. She had asked Pamela to wait until sixteen to pierce her ears… but Pamela did it a year earlier. When Jane complained to Danny, he always took Pamela's side. He had argued that mascara and piercings were minor issues. It was more important that their girl was a good student who loved her family and made them proud. Jane had reluctantly agreed with him, and as Pamela matured, mother and daughter had become friends. Jane did not want to lose their close relationship.

However, Jane also knew that despite his usual role as Pamela's champion, Danny was the type of father who liked his family close and happy. He would need a lot of convincing to accept his only daughter, his 'baby girl,' moving out of the country. She looked into Pamela's pleading eyes and knew she would have to try.

Jane stubbed out her cigarette and then reached for her daughter's hand. "We'll work on your father together. I don't want our family to fracture over a decision that will ultimately make you happy."

The next afternoon, Jane and Pamela waited until Danny was alone in the living room. Pamela's brothers had just left the house for a neighborhood baseball game. Jane let Pamela tell Danny her news. To his credit, Danny remained quiet and listened, although Jane witnessed his complexion growing redder. When Pamela finished, he had two words to say: "No way."

"What?" asked Pamela.

Danny very calmly pronounced, "No way are you going to Canada. No way are you leaving school, especially when you are almost done. And no way are you splitting this family apart."

"Daddy don't be ridiculous. I've explained everything to you. I'm not asking your permission. I'm twenty-one. What I'm asking for is your blessing. I want you, Mom, Mark and Matty to be at my wedding. I want you to give me away willingly," said Pamela. And, with a few tears in her eyes, she softly concluded, "I want you to be happy for me."

"Sorry, baby girl, I can't bless this. You'll be on the lam with Paul. He may never be allowed to return to the U.S. Are you willing to turn your back on the country you were born in? And why can't he fight if his number is called? I volunteered to fight in the World War."

Jane interjected, "Danny, she just told you—if Paul leaves before the army calls him up, he won't be breaking any law by moving to Canada. He won't be on the lam because he won't be a deserter."

"And Daddy, you and I have discussed this war versus your war, a good war as you called it. America was attacked and threatened during the second World War. Of course, you fought, and Paul would have too if he were a man then. But you've told me many times you think young men's lives are being wasted in Vietnam."

Jane knew this last part was true. Danny was angry and frustrated when he saw film footage of Vietnam on the evening news. He called it a bad war, and a conflict the U.S. shouldn't have become involved in. Jane also knew that the root of his anger was his fear for their son, Mark, eventually being drafted into the mess in Asia.

Danny was unusually silent. His anguish was obvious to his wife. Jane took that as her cue to speak to him on her own. She told Pamela to go for a walk and give them some privacy.

Once Pamela left, Jane sat next to the immobile Danny and took his hand. She quietly stated, "We have to let her go. And we must give her our blessing."

"I can't be happy about it, Janie. She's my only little girl. Our family will never be the same."

"We can visit her, and nothing will prevent her from visiting us, even if Paul feels uncomfortable coming back. And she's already investigated a university up there that will work with her college credits so she can complete her degree. She's handling this intelligently, Danny. Deep down, you know we must agree with this marriage and relocation, or..." Jane trailed off with panic in her eyes.

"Or what?"

"Or we'll lose her completely. I can't live with that, and neither can you."

Within a month, Pamela Jane Flynn became Mrs. Paul Gergen. As a tribute to the city where the couple first met in college, they chose to be married at the Office of the City Clerk in Manhattan. Paul's widowed mother and his only sibling, an older sister, with her husband, attended. Jane, Mark, Matthew, and a resigned Danny were there too. At the request of the wedding couple, no other extended family members or neighbors were invited. Much to Jane's dismay, there would be no party following the ceremony. However, Danny insisted he treat all the attendees to a luncheon at a nearby establishment.

At the restaurant, the nine gathered around a large table. Seated at the table's head, Pamela looked lovely in a floor-length, white cotton eyelet, peasant-style dress with a ring of silk daisies perched on the crown of her long, straight hair. With her right hand, she held her husband's left one, and she kept glancing, with a dreamy smile curling her lips, at the simple gold band on her left ring finger. She laughed when her brothers playfully teased her and entertained their new brother-in-law with tales from their sister's childhood.

Jane sat stoically across from her only daughter, a forced smile on her face. Inside, she was still distraught at the idea of losing her first-born. However, she was determined not to cry, as Paul's mother was openly doing, and ruin their short remaining time together.

After the luncheon, Pamela and Paul would be getting in his already packed car and making their way north. The two would spend their wedding night at an upstate inn before crossing the border tomorrow. With them would be a generous monetary gift to start their new marriage. Jane had convinced Danny to give their daughter the money they had saved for the opulent wedding reception they had always planned to throw for their only girl.

When the celebration ended, everyone stood in line to kiss and hug the newlyweds as a final farewell. The bride's parents were the last two well-wishers. The usually unflappable Danny had watery eyes and one tear running down his cheek as he silently encircled Pamela into a huge bear hug. He clapped an arm around the shoulders of his new son-in-law, and the two men followed the others to the sidewalk. Jane was proud of her husband. She knew it took every ounce of his goodwill to appear magnanimous while his heart was breaking.

Jane was finally left alone with her daughter. After the emotional embrace from her father, Pamela was left with tears streaming down her own face. She took one look at Jane and ran into her mother's outstretched arms.

"Oh, Mom," sobbed Pamela. "I'll miss you most of all!"

Still surprisingly dry-eyed, Jane had dozens of things she wanted to say to Pamela. Since the wedding had been planned so hurriedly, she had never had the time to advise her daughter tenderly on the big and little factors that make a marriage, at least in Jane's mind, successful. To a lesser degree, she wished there had been more time to share with Pamela some of her favorite recipes and housekeeping shortcuts. She had always believed that when Pamela married, her daughter would settle nearby where Jane could have periodically dispensed maternal words of wisdom to the newlyweds. Now she felt as if she were sending her baby bird out into the world unprepared.

As she stood holding her daughter in her arms, her lips close to Pamela's ear, the only words Jane could muster were, "Just be happy, my darling Pammy!"

CHAPTER 20

Betty - 1970

There is something very wrong with this world, a distraught Betty contemplated, *when a young man is sent halfway around it to fight a war for someone else.*

Alone, she was sitting at her kitchen table with her hands wrapped around an avocado-green ceramic mug of coffee, now cold. Staring out her window at the brilliant May morning sunshine enveloping Strong Lane, she did not take note of any of the telltale signs of spring: the light green leaves sprouting on her front yard's tree; the lawn's emerald color recently transformed from a winter of brown; the abundance of daffodils gracing Anna's front garden directly across the street. No, she could not take any joy in what she was blindly staring at. She kept returning her gaze to the letter that lay open on the table next to her mug.

It arrived yesterday. She picked up the one thin page and reread the words she already had memorized.

Dear Mom and Dad,

As you know, all my training is now done. I had eight weeks of basic and then eight more of infantry. I found out today that my unit will be leaving New Jersey soon for deployment to Nam. I don't really mind. After all this training, I just want to use what I learned. And believe it or not, I was one of the best marksmen during our weapons training sessions. Who knew I had the talent to be an accurate shooter? I also have a great group of guys in my division. There are two others from Long Island too.

Sometimes I wonder if I should have enlisted in the Air Force like Dad did during WWII instead of getting drafted like I did. But I can't change that now, so I'll just make the best of it. Anyway, someone told me if you enlisted, you must serve three years but if drafted, it's two. I don't know if that's true, but the time is already going fast. I can't believe I left home four months ago. Hope to see you before I go.

Your loving son,

Robby

Betty carefully folded the letter to save it with the others her son had sent to them. She did not share Robby's assessment of the last four months passing quickly. For her, time had stood still since the first draft lottery had been held on December 1, 1969. On that date, the United States military had determined the order of call for induction during the calendar year of 1970 for registrants born between the beginning of 1944 and the end of 1950. Robby had been called up for induction into the army shortly after his twentieth birthday this past January. Betty had not had a carefree day since. She still felt as if she was in a constant state of holding her breath.

When the notice had come, she had refused to accept the possibility of sending her only child into her adopted land's armed services. She recalled her confrontation with Bob.

"It's Robby's duty to serve his country, just as I did after Pearl Harbor," Bob had pointed out to her.

Betty argued, "Our son is half British! Why can't we send him to live with my mother in England?"

Bob calmly countered, "Robby is an American citizen, born in the USA. And be reasonable, Betty. As a young man, he wouldn't want to go live with your elderly widowed mother."

Betty, as a last-ditch effort, suggested, "Then why can't the three of us run away to Canada, as Pamela and Paul did?"

Bob reminded his wife, "Betty, you know as well as I do that is not a solution. Paul emigrated before he had been called up by the draft, and, therefore, he didn't break the law by moving to Canada. Robby has already been conscripted. Our son would be a deserter if he moved north."

It was Robby who had finally ended his parents' argument when, upon walking in at the tail end of the heated words, he announced he was more than willing to go. He was going to fight for his country, just as Bob and the rest of the fathers on Strong Lane had done thirty years ago.

And now, lamented Betty to herself, *my gentle son will be risking his life on foreign soil, and my world will never be the same.* She was startled from her reverie by a loud knock on the door.

"Hey there," shouted Jane as she walked into the kitchen. "I brought you and Bob some of my Irish soda bread. I made three loaves yesterday so I could mail one up to Pam and Paul, and my guys and I had one with dinner last night. But I know Bob really digs it, so I'm giving you two the third loaf." She placed a tin-foil-wrapped package on the table next to the folded letter and then asked, "Oh, is that a new letter from Robby?"

"Yes, it is," replied Betty flatly. "And thanks for the bread. Bob will love it."

"That's okay. I hope you'll enjoy it, too. Mind if I sit down and rap for a while?" said Jane, and without waiting for an answer, she pulled a chair out and plopped down at the table.

"There's some leftover coffee on the stovetop that you can reheat, if you want it," Betty stated unenthusiastically.

"Don't mind if I do," replied Jane, and she popped back up and went to turn on the burner under the percolator. "You'll have some more, Betty? What's in your mug looks like it's gone cold. Here, let me take that from you and get you a fresh cup." She reached over to Betty and took the mug.

Jane stood at the stove and chatted about the weather and other nonsensical topics. Betty didn't say a word. After the coffee was reheated and Jane brought two steaming mugs to the table, she sat back down and observed, "I'm worried about you, Betty."

"Why?" questioned Betty wrapping her hands around the new warm mug and not making any effort to add her usual milk and sugar.

"You've seemed sort of low over the past few months," started Jane after taking a sip of her coffee. "I mean, I know how hard it is to have your child far from home. When Pam and Paul split to Canada, I was a little depressed, but I told myself..."

Betty interrupted her and barked, "*You*, Jane Flynn, have no idea what it feels like to have a child far from home. You can NOT compare Pam living safely in Canada to my Robby leaving to serve in a dangerous war halfway around the world!"

"Look, Betty, I'll pretend I didn't hear that because I know you are upset," replied Jane tersely. "All of us neighbors feel down about Robby. But you must remember, I have an eighteen-year-old son who graduates high school next month. I am just as worried about him as you are about Robby."

"I'm sorry I snapped at you, Jane," a deflated Betty apologized. "All of us mothers of sons are on edge." She finally added the milk and sugar to her coffee. As she stirred, she looked up and asked, "What will Mark do after graduation?"

"He wants to get into the construction business with Danny. He's really good with his hands and has always trailed after Danny and his crew at any opportunity, even when he was a little boy. And Danny would love to rename the business Daniel Flynn and Son Construction. But the prospect of the draft is putting a kink in their plans. Mark says he's a conscientious objector based on moral grounds and his Catholic upbringing. He would refuse to shoot anybody if he had to serve. He sincerely believes in the commandment, 'thou shall not kill.'"

"So, what are you going to do? Did he register when he turned eighteen?"

"Yes, he did, because he didn't know what else to do," answered Jane. "But he decided he'd also put in for a student deferment if it comes to that. Mark is registered to attend full-time community college this fall. He's going to take business classes, which Danny and I agree will help him with co-running the business someday. Mark would rather have gone straight to work and skip the college route, but he sees the advantages of putting in two years of additional schooling. I just hope Congress doesn't change the deferment rule. I read somewhere they might amend it so that a guy in college can have his induction postponed only until the end of the current semester, not until he finishes his degree, like it was for Paul."

"Well, at least he'll be temporarily safe at college," observed Betty and then added wistfully, "I wish Robby had considered continuing his education."

"I'm not so sure the kids are safe at college either," declared Jane. "Did you read in the newspaper two weeks ago that horrific Kent State story? Can you believe Ohio National Guardsmen opened fire on students during an anti-war protest? What is wrong with this country when four innocent kids get killed by our own forces? That could have been Pam or Paul a year ago! They participated in lots of rallies."

Betty just nodded. She never condoned the college demonstrations she saw on television. Disagreeing with the government was all just useless effort, she had always thought. However, she said nothing while Jane ranted about the injustice of the incident. Betty didn't want to argue with her neighbor because, of all the women on Strong Lane, Jane was the least likely to consider both sides of a story. Betty remembered how in the old days of coffee klatch, Norma, Ella, and Anna had sensibly debated current events while she and Jane had both been indifferent. Now that the latest news affected Jane's family personally, she was committed to her beliefs like a dog was committed to a good bone. Betty knew expressing her own opinion would be pointless.

"Well, listen to me carrying on," stated Jane. "I'm sorry, Betty. You were going to tell me what Robby had to say in his letter."

With a start, Betty was immediately brought back to her present dilemma. The lump in her throat was growing, and she croaked, "He and his unit are being sent to Vietnam."

"I'm so sorry to hear that," sympathized Jane. "I was praying he would be assigned a desk job or something here in the States."

"So was I..." bawled Betty, and her tears started flowing as she reached for the handkerchief in her house-dress pocket.

"Oh, you poor thing," said Jane, wringing her hands. She reached out, patted the sobbing Betty, and offered, "Try not to despair. He'll be okay. All the men on this block served in the last war and came home safely. Your Robby will too."

Robby did come home to Strong Lane, in the autumn of that year. However, he did not come home unscathed. In August, during an exchange of gunfire on one of his first patrols into enemy territory, Private Robert Edward Carter, Junior had been severely wounded.

Betty was preparing dinner while Bob read the evening newspaper when she learned of her son's injury. Although Bob was the one who accepted the telegram, Betty took one look at the envelope, assumed it was a death notice, and fainted on the kitchen's linoleum. Once Bob revived his wife and read her the brief statement that their son had been wounded in action, Betty had hope. However, the telegram lacked details about his injury. It wasn't until days later that the Carters learned more.

During that fateful patrol, Robby, attempting to lift a fallen comrade, had been shot in his back. He had suffered a spinal cord injury, leaving him paralyzed from the waist down. A medic from the unit had been able eventually to drag both men to safety. The first soldier had died at the scene, but Robby had been air-lifted out of the jungle by a helicopter. He had then spent some time in an intensive care unit in South Vietnam before being transferred to the States for rehabilitation.

For weeks, Robby resided at a New York City veteran's hospital, learning how to live his new life in a wheelchair. To facilitate visiting their son, the Carters lived temporarily at Bob's elderly parents' house in nearby Queens. Betty visited Robby in the hospital daily, for hours at a time. Bob visited the hospital between his shifts at the railroad, saving time for a leave of absence when Robby would return to Strong Lane.

As devastated as she was, Betty was grateful her only child had returned home alive. She felt like she could finally breathe again. Her past all-consuming distress over her son's unknown fate was replaced by a compelling new mission to rehabilitate him. She made a point of speaking with every doctor, nurse, and therapist concerning Robby's progress. She willed herself to appear upbeat and cheerful anytime she was in the presence of her noticeably quiet son. She disagreed with the medical personnel who told her Robby needed to heal mentally as well as physically. She knew once she had him home again, his formerly affable personality would reemerge.

Before the Carters returned with Robby to Strong Lane, the neighbors banded together to prepare their house. With approval from Bob and Betty, Danny and Mark Flynn had constructed a wooden ramp outside the front door to simplify Robby's wheeled path into his home. Danny's crew had widened the downstairs interior doorways to accommodate the wheelchair's width. Borrowing space from the smallest ground floor bedroom, the bathroom was then enlarged and modified. The nurses of the block, Anna Marino and Wilma Borden, had researched and ordered a special hospital bed to be used in the larger downstairs master bedroom, which would now be Robby's. Furthermore, Bob's and Betty's master bedroom furniture had then been relocated to a bedroom upstairs. Jane and Ella had prepared meals for the Carters' freezer. And during the Carters' absence, John and Sal had made sure the Carters' lawn was tended and the fall leaves were raked.

Robby returned to his boyhood home on an overcast, unusually raw Saturday in mid-October. Half-sitting and half-laying on the car's rear bench seat, Robby was silent and surly. Betty sat in the front passenger seat, and, since leaving the rehabilitation center, she was fully aware she had been talking nonstop nonsense to fill the hushed vehicle. Bob occasionally made a brief reply to her gibberish, but he was abnormally quiet. Betty had observed weeks ago that Bob appeared perpetually grim, looking like he had aged twenty years overnight. Only in their mid-forties, Betty had also noticed she and Bob each now had substantial amounts of gray laced throughout the hair on their heads.

After Bob turned the car onto Strong Lane and proceeded to their property's driveway, Betty exclaimed, "Oh Robby, look! The neighbors made you a 'welcome home' banner! How thoughtful. Don't you think so?"

Robby observed the pristine white bed sheet tacked onto their garage door. The blue spray-painted letters were each about two feet high and were surrounded by red and gold stars. *WELCOME HOME ROBBY - THE HERO OF STRONG LANE*

In response, Robby grunted, "I wish everyone would call me Rob. I'm not eight years old anymore."

Betty felt as deflated as a punctured balloon. She looked at the banner and remembered with tenderness a welcome-home sign a much younger Robby had once made her, upon her own return home from a hospital stay after her miscarriage. *Where is that sweet boy of mine from eighteen years ago*, lamented Betty.

Bob parked the car. Just as he went around to the car's rear to take the wheelchair out of the trunk, Anna, Sal, and seventeen-year-old Christina started to cross the street from their house. Sal offered Bob a hand with the wheelchair and the other items in the trunk, and Anna hugged Betty after handing her an autumnal bouquet of chrysanthemums. The men maneuvered a wordless Robby into his chair, and Bob started to push his son up the path to the front door.

Christina walked next to Robby and said enthusiastically, "Susan would have liked to be here today to welcome you home, Robby. But she's at school. She said to tell you she'll visit you when she's home from college during Thanksgiving weekend."

"Why would she want to? Hasn't she ever seen a gimp in a wheel-chair before?" asked Robby bitterly.

The usually bubbly and garrulous Christina clamped her lips tightly shut and stared at Robby. Betty, who had overheard the exchange, scolded, "Robby, I mean Rob, that wasn't very nice. Susan wants to see you because she's one of your oldest friends. You should apologize for being rude to Christina."

Robby remained silent and unsmiling with a dark look in his eyes. A tactful Anna said, "Christina, see if there's anything left in the car's trunk that you can carry in. Once we help you get everything in the house, Betty, we three will leave you alone to get settled."

Betty panicked. She would have liked the Marinos to stay and take some of the awkward pressure off her own family. The staff at the rehab center had warned her and Bob of the huge adjustment their son would need to make upon returning home. Betty, thinking she knew her only child better than anyone, had thought Robby would perk up considerably at the prospect of coming home to familiar surroundings. *However, if the tense car ride home was any indication, this is going to be much more difficult than I anticipated.*

Whenever she became anxious, Betty always resorted to excessive babbling. When they were all inside the house, she fervently pointed out each wonderful change that had been made and kept asking the with-drawn Robby his opinion on the improvements. Bob made appropriate comments praising the work done on his son's behalf and stated he would later personally thank Danny and Mark. Anna told the Carters about the meals in the freezer provided by Ella and Jane. She informed Betty that she had stocked the refrigerator with fresh produce, milk, and eggs this morning.

"I can't thank you all enough," enthused Betty with tears in her eyes. "We really appreciate it, don't we, Rob?"

"I'm going to my room," mumbled Robby as he navigated his wheelchair to the rear of the house.

When her son closed his bedroom door, an embarrassed Betty turned to the Marinos and apologized. "I'm so sorry for his behavior. I'm sure he appreciates everything that was done and will thank you all in the future. It's just that..." and a dejected Betty trailed off.

Anna reached her hand out to touch Betty's shoulder and said, "Not to worry, Betty. Everything can be improved with time. Each of you have big adjustments to make. It'll all work out. I know it will."

"I hope so, Anna. I truly hope so," replied a skeptical Betty.

A routine was established in the Carters' home. Upon Robby's return, Bob took two weeks off from work to help Betty set up a schedule of care for their son. A physical therapist and a visiting nurse each came to the house weekly. The medical personnel admired the work done in the Carters' home and recommended some minor adaptations to Robby's physical environment. Everyone worked together to improve the veteran's surroundings. However, throughout his first month home, Robby remained sullen and uncooperative.

A few days before Thanksgiving, Betty drove Robby to a follow-up appointment at the rehabilitation center in the city. While there, she noticed Robby perked up a bit when he met with a peer group of other physically challenged veterans. During the drive home, Betty asked Robby what he and the group had discussed.

"You wouldn't understand, Mom," replied Robby.

"But I want to. Try me," implored Betty. She was glad Robby was finally starting to talk after weeks of silence.

Robby let out a bitter laugh before he said, "How could you possibly understand? Your generation fought a good war. Dad and his friends were honored as heroes. My generation is fighting an unpopular one."

"But *you* are a hero, Rob. You received a Purple Heart."

"That means nothing to me, a cruddy decoration from a corrupt government. You have no idea how we vets have been treated by people and the press. Everyone questions what we did over there even though we were just following orders from our so-called superiors."

"All wars are hell, and I'm sorry you had to see that firsthand," sympathized Betty before turning positive and continuing, "But, you're alive, and you're back home. You must try to adapt and move forward."

Her plea was met with a cold stillness, so instead she tried, "We just need to find something that will spike your interest and give you a goal. There must be some kind of activity your father and I can help you pursue."

"Well..." started Robby cagily. "I was one of the best marksmen in my unit. I wouldn't mind going to a range for target practice. I can at least still hold a pistol and aim for a bull's-eye."

Betty was thrilled the two of them were making a connection. She would ask Bob to investigate purchasing their son a handgun and taking him to a local range.

"That would be great! I'll look for a Long Island gun range we can go to," gushed Betty. "You know, Rob, your dad and I and all your friends just want to help. Meeting us halfway is the key. You'll see, my love, things *will* get better."

"Sure, Mom," Robby quietly retorted and tuned Betty out for the remaining car ride home. She didn't notice, though, because all she thought of was her son's new pursuit; surely, a hobby would bring him out of his shell.

The day after Thanksgiving, Susan Marino, home for the holiday from her junior year at college, crossed the street from her house to the Carters'. She had telephoned Betty around noon to ask if it would be a good time to visit Robby. Betty, without checking with her son who was rooted in his room with rock music blaring, happily said it was a fine time to come over. She was afraid if she had asked Robby, he would refuse to see Susan. Hence, when the young woman arrived, Betty immediately ushered her into Robby's room and brightly announced to him, "Look who is here to see you, my love! Isn't this a nice surprise?"

Robby raised his head from his stereo where he had just removed a record album. He placed the album on the shelf next to the turntable, pushed his shaggy brown hair out of his light gray eyes, and then turned his chair to face the door.

"I'll just leave you two young folks alone," Betty said cheerfully before offering, "May I get you anything, Susan? Something to drink or perhaps a snack?"

"No, thank you, Mrs. Carter. I'm fine."

"Okay then! You two have a nice chat. If you need me, just call," Betty replied as she softly closed the door and proceeded to stand just outside of it, straining to listen.

"I'm sorry, Robby. I seem to have caught you off-guard," Betty heard Susan say. "But I did telephone, and your mother said it was cool to come...."

Betty then heard Robby's raised voice, "Mom, we won't be needing anything, so you can move away from the door and go back to the kitchen."

Betty made an inaudible mumbled reply from her side of the door and then noisily walked away. She then removed her shoes near the front door and, in stockinged feet, crept silently back to listen outside the door again.

Betty overheard Susan softly chuckling before offering, "Mothers! They can drive us crazy!"

"Not difficult to do when you actually have a crazy mom like mine," replied an acerbic Robby.

Betty felt hurt. Is that really what her son thought of her? She had lived the past twenty years of her life with the sole intention of making her son's life a blessed one. She knew they had their differences, like any mother and son. He had sometimes told her she had pushed him too hard to do things he thought were pointless, like pursuing college. Even so, he had always declined cordially; he had never called her crazy.

"She's not so bad," answered Susan. There was a change in the direction of her voice. Betty surmised Susan must have sat down on the only chair in the room and was now eye-level with Robby. "So, how are you, Robby? It's good to see you. I'm sorry I couldn't get here sooner..."

"But you were so busy with your awesome college and exciting life in general," a snide Robby finished for her.

"Aw, don't be like that, Robby," Susan chastised softly.

Betty was surprised her son didn't scold Susan over using his childhood nickname, as he did with most people who called him Robby.

Instead, he responded, "Be like what, Susan? Bummed out? Bitter? Well, I am, and you'd be too if you were me and could understand how I feel."

"I want to understand how you feel, and I think I might have a concept of how you do. I'm a psychology major at school. And this semester, I'm volunteering some hours at a veterans' hospital located upstate near my college. I've seen many men who feel the same...."

Robby quickly cut her off, snapping, "Don't psychoanalyze me, Susan. I had enough of that crap in the hospital I was in. I just want to be left alone."

"There is some super assistance if you would just get involved in a disabled vets' support group of some kind. I'm sure there's a local one you can join. I can look into it for you, if you'd like."

"I rapped with other guys in the hospital. All they want to talk about are wartime experiences. I'm sick of reliving it. I just want to forget all of it. But guess what? I can't forget because every time I try to stand up, I can't!" Robby cynically snickered. "So, the hell with all the supposed help. I'll figure it out all by myself."

"You were never a pessimist." From Betty's side of the bedroom door, she could clearly hear the sadness in the young woman's voice.

Susan continued. "You were always a righteous kind of guy, super pleasant and friendly. I know that guy is still in there, Robby. I hope you find yourself again."

"Yeah, that was me, the brotherly type, as you so aptly told me last summer when I asked you out. Isn't that right, Susan?" Robby asked sarcastically. Betty wasn't surprised he was still bitter over that past exchange. After his failed attempt with Susan, Robby had never dated anyone else. Betty couldn't help thinking how things could have been different now if Robby had had a girlfriend, or a wife, like Susan, to welcome him home.

Betty heard Susan, obviously trying to ignore Robby's negative attitude, sincerely reply, "You *are* like a brother to me. That's why I care. And everyone in this neighborhood cares. You have to help us help you."

Betty heard a creak in a chair and Susan's voice changed direction again as she rose to a standing position. She must have handed something to Robby because Betty could hear her say, "This card has my address and phone number at college. I'm leaving tomorrow to go back. I'll be home again at Christmastime for a longer visit. Between now and then, if you want to talk or write me a letter, you've got my info. Goodbye, Robby. I really hope you consider getting some support. If I've learned anything in my college studies, it's that there's help for every problem. All you need to do is ask."

Susan seemed to wait in vain for a response. When Betty then heard the visitor moving closer to the bedroom door, she quickly trotted back to the front door and slipped on her shoes. She turned just as Susan exited the bedroom, softly closing the door behind her.

"How did it go?" asked Betty expectantly. She had previously had such high hopes that Susan could be the person to lift her son's spirit. However, between the conversation she had overheard and the fretful look on the young woman's face, Betty knew that had been a pipe dream.

"It was fine, Mrs. Carter," replied a resigned Susan, attempting to give Betty a tiny smile. "I think he still needs some time for adjustment. Things will work out."

"That's exactly what your mother told me over a month ago," stated a bewildered Betty. "But things only seem to be getting worse..."

CHAPTER 21

Anna - 1970

Anna shivered as she prepared for her shift at the hospital. She raised her home's thermostat a smidge as she bustled about. It was the Monday morning before Christmas, and, although the day was clear and still, the temperature was frigid. Sal had left for his store an hour earlier, dropping Christina at her high school on his way. Anna was alone in the house, since Susan wasn't coming home from college until Wednesday, just two days before the holiday.

Since September, when Christina had started her senior year, Anna had worked full-time as a delivery room nurse. For the previous seven years, she had stuck to a part-time schedule so she could be home more for her daughters. However, with Susan in her third year of college and Christina in her last year of public school, Anna had felt she was free to pursue her career on a more permanent basis. She worked five rotating days a week and, for the most part, scored daytime shifts.

As she was sitting at her kitchen table preparing a sandwich for work, she looked through her large window and saw a bundled-up Betty quickly exiting her house directly across the street and getting into her car in the driveway. Anna also noticed Bob's car was gone and surmised he must have had an early shift. Betty had only recently started leaving Robby alone when running her local errands, as he'd insisted that he could exit the house on his own in case of an emergency. Formerly, Betty would only go out if Bob or a visiting adult was present. However, ever since Robby had proved he could maneuver his wheelchair easily, even taking himself on many long unaccompanied excursions on the neighborhood's sidewalks, Betty finally relented and stopped her constant hovering.

Anna was worried about the Carters. Susan had shared with her mother the conversation she'd had with Robby on the day after Thanksgiving. Her daughter had described his angry outbursts and overall depression. Anna knew from her weekly telephone conversations with her firstborn that Robby had not contacted Susan since then. Furthermore, Anna recalled a conversation she'd had with Betty two weeks ago.

Betty had confided, "Bob and I are so distressed, Anna. Robby is having horrible flashbacks and nightmares. He constantly wakes us in the middle of the night with his shouts. When Bob or I shake him awake, he doesn't remember yelling out."

"Oh, Betty, I am so sorry. What can be done for him?"

Betty had replied, "I'm convinced that with my love and devotion, over time, I can eventually help him to heal. It's just taking so much longer than I expected."

Anna had gently suggested, "Betty, Susan recommended Rob join a specialized support group. That could be a good idea so he can talk with other vets. Or what about a psychologist? Someone who can help him one-on-one with his issues. I'm sure the VA hospital can suggest a local therapist."

However, Betty had been adamant. "Anna, I appreciate your and Susan's advice, but I think Robby's time among strangers at that veteran's hospital only set up constant reminders of his horrific experience. I know that as his mother, I can find a way to help him forget and move forward."

Anna shook off her recollection. Finally ready for work, she slipped on her heavy winter coat and gloves before opening the front door to leave her house. As she stepped on to the front stoop, a movement across the street caught her eye. She noticed Robby wheeling himself down the Carters' front walkway. When he reached the sidewalk on his side of Strong Lane, he turned his chair right and kept his gaze straight ahead, despite Anna's wave of greeting to him. *What a brutally cold day to take one of his excursions!*

Although Robby was wearing his army-green military flak jacket with a black wool cap pulled low over his increasingly long hair (he had not let anyone cut it since he had returned home), he was not wearing any gloves. And Anna knew the jacket was only made of lightweight canvas. She briefly contemplated giving a shout out to him, to recommend he wear a heavier coat, but then quickly dismissed the idea of telling a grown man what to do. *Besides, I'm going to be late for the hospital if I don't leave immediately!*

As she unlocked her car door and started to get into the vehicle, she took one more glance at Robby's retreating back as he quickly wheeled past Norma's former house, now the Bordens' home, and approached the sidewalk in front of the corner town-owned property that housed the sump. Anna turned her attention back to her task at hand and started her cold car, immediately turning the knob for the heater. Then she realized she had forgotten her brown paper bag containing her lunch. *Oh, Lord; give me fortitude today!*

She left the car running, grabbed her house keys, and trotted back into the house. As she walked in, the telephone mounted on her kitchen wall started to ring. She picked it up, extending the long curly cord to the nearby table so she could claim her lunch bag. Sal was on the line asking her a question he'd forgotten to raise earlier that morning. She answered her husband quickly and told him she had to hang up if she had any hope of arriving on time for her shift. Then she replaced the receiver in the phone's holder and retraced her steps to head back to the car, relocking her front door on the way.

As she approached her car on the driveway for a second time, she noted there was no sign of Robby. Anna contemplated, *he must have given up and returned home, or he's already turned the far corner to the next block. Either way, I can't think of him any longer.*

Anna was then distracted from her thoughts when her eyes travelled to the Flynns' property next door. Jane was standing on her front step shaking out a throw rug. Anna gave her neighbor a big silent wave.

It was at that moment the two women heard an immense crack in the near distance, shattering the still morning air. The sound echoed around the chilly neighborhood, where it appeared only Anna and Jane were standing outside. Perplexed, Anna instantly thought the noise was too powerful to be a car backfiring.

"What the hell," shouted Jane over to Anna. "Was that a gunshot?"

And that's when Anna knew.

She dropped her key ring and lunch. She started to run, as fast as she could in her bulky winter coat, across the width of her driveway, then cut diagonally over Jane's front lawn toward the corner sump. As she passed her confused neighbor, Anna yelled, "Call the police, Jane, and tell them to send an ambulance, too!"

As she approached the sump next to the Bordens' home, Anna prayed that her gut-feeling was wrong. But she was not encouraged when she immediately noticed one of the double gates, in the rusty chain-linked fence surrounding the property, had been pushed open. For years, the Strong Lane residents had been calling the town's government offices to request these gates be secured with a lock in addition to the spring latch that held the two openings together. It was dangerous having the reservoir's deep pit, the size of a football field, accessible to curious children in the surrounding neighborhoods. Some teenagers had even recently made a habit of sliding down the sump's precipitous sides and gathering on the slopes to smoke cigarettes, undetected by the neighborhood adults.

Anna hurried through the gate and drew near the edge of the closest slope. She looked down and then let out a strangled cry of despair. She slipped and slid down the steep drop, pulling off her coat as she finally approached the overturned wheelchair settled in the frozen mud on the bottom of the sump. Robby's body was face down and sprawled out a few feet in front of the chair. The right side of his head was grossly disfigured. A pistol was lying not far from his body.

Anna wanted to sink to her knees in anguish, but she forced herself to move forward and reach for the young man's wrist. There was no pulse. She dropped her coat over his head, grateful she could not see his eyes, and stumbled back to the sloped side of the pit.

She sank down to a seated position, rested her elbows on her raised knees, and dropped her head into her hands. She could hear sirens approaching, and, within minutes, she detected raised voices at the top of the incline. Jane's shocked mantra of "Oh my God, oh my God," was the loudest of all.

Later, Anna couldn't remember exactly how she had climbed up the sump's steep wall. She thought a policeman might have helped her. She did recall at the top of the hill Jane putting her own coat around Anna's shaking shoulders and leading her to the inside of a police car. There, a young police officer questioned the two women. Jane answered most of the pertinent questions, giving Robby's name, address, and the necessary information on his parents.

Anna lamented, "I should have stopped him. I saw him wheeling himself down the street, and I didn't shout out to him."

Jane insisted, "Listen to me, Anna! There was no way you could have known what he was planning. None of us neighbors even knew he owned a gun!" This last part she directed at the police officer.

"I knew," a deflated Anna countered. "Betty told me."

When the brief inquiry was over, the officer escorted the two neighbors back to Anna's property. As the three approached her house, the policeman immediately noted Anna's car was still running, parked on the driveway where she had left it. After shutting the motor off, the officer handed the key to its owner. Then, he asked which house was the one owned by the parents of the deceased. Jane pointed to the Carters' home and noted that since neither car was on the driveway, no one was currently there.

"But Betty will return shortly," said a dazed Anna. "She probably only ran a quick errand. She'll panic when she sees the police cars and an ambulance. What should we do?"

"We'll have a squad car wait for her, ma'am. The department is sending another one right now, along with a police chaplain. In the meantime, with the information you ladies gave us about the family, we'll also try to contact the father through the Long Island Rail Road's main office," replied the officer. Then, looking at Jane, he added, "You should get your friend here inside." Turning to Anna, he noted, "That was quite a discovery you made, Mrs. Marino. You might go into shock, having seen all that blood and all...."

"For your information, young man, I'm a nurse. I've seen plenty of blood in my life, probably more than you. I'm not going into shock."

"Still, Anna, let me go inside with you and make you a cup of strong coffee," soothed Jane. "And thank you, officer. Let us know if there's anything we can do."

After Jane and Anna made their way inside, the policeman walked across the street to wait for the precinct's squad car. Within minutes, it arrived, and its occupants waited for Betty's return.

Meanwhile, Jane tried to convince a pale Anna to lie down.

"I'm fine, Jane," insisted Anna.

After telephoning the hospital to tell her supervisor she wouldn't be in, Anna sat stoically in a chair at her kitchen table with a clear view towards the Carters' house. Her clothes were dirty and wrinkled from her slide down the sump's slope, but she refused to change into a clean outfit. She calmly asked Jane to make a pot of coffee.

Thirty minutes later, as the two women were silently sipping from their mugs, they anxiously observed Betty's arrival home. In the distance, two police cars and the ambulance were still parked in front of the sump with warning lights flashing. When Betty started to exit her car, an officer and the police chaplain stepped out of the squad car in front of her house and approached the fearful woman.

Anna jumped out of her chair and exclaimed, "That's it, Jane! Let's get over there. We can't let her get this news all alone."

Without stopping to don a coat, Anna was out her kitchen door in a flash with Jane at her heels. The two reached Betty just as her knees seemed to buckle, the chaplain and officer preventing her from falling all the way to the ground.

After the two men had helped Betty into the Carters' house, Anna and Jane stayed with her until Bob arrived within the hour. By then, the cars and the ambulance down the block were gone. The police officer and the chaplain, still in attendance at the house, briefly filled Bob in and gave their condolences before departing.

Anna and Jane left Betty with Bob. As the two women walked back across the street, Sal pulled up his car in front of his house.

"What's Sal doing home this early?" questioned a weary Anna.

"I called him, Anna, while you were holding Betty," explained Jane. "I know you insisted you aren't in shock, but I'm very worried about you. I thought you would need your husband here with you."

Sal wordlessly exited his car, walked to Anna, and enveloped her in his arms. Anna sunk into his warmth, her extreme tension finally easing a bit. For the past two hours, she had solely concentrated on Betty. Yet now, in Sal's loving embrace, she felt the enormity of all she had personally experienced this dreadful morning.

Jane told the two of them, "I'll contact Ella and Wilma when they each return from work to tell them what happened on our street today." She visibly shivered before adding, "And we will all need to tell our children. That will be a tough thing to do."

"Yes, I know," acknowledged Anna sadly. "Thank you, Jane, for all you did today. I don't know what I would have done without you."

Jane just shrugged, gave Anna and Sal a sad smile, and turned to walk home.

"Come on, sugar-pie, let's get you inside," encouraged Sal, keeping his arm around her waist.

Together, they turned towards their front door, and Anna stared at the Christmas decorations gracing the outside of her home. She scowled, realizing for the first time that this heartbreak had occurred only days before the most joyous holiday of the year. As Sal held the storm door open for her, Anna glanced back over her right shoulder to look at the corner of Strong Lane that housed the now ominous sump. She trembled and quickly retreated inside.

CHAPTER 22

Ella - 1970

Just as the gray dusk rolled into a wintery night, Ella eased the car onto the driveway of her home. It had been a hectic day in the children's room at the Levittown Public Library. She had started her shift in charge of the morning's toddler story hour and concluded her workday directing an after-school holiday craft program. In between, she had cataloged a new shipment of juvenile books while answering dozens of questions from parents and children. Despite working in what most people would consider a hushed environment, she now craved complete silence. The only things she wanted to do were pull off her heels, put on her slippers, and peacefully sip a cup of coffee before her family came home.

However, just as Ella exited her car, she observed Jane trotting across the front lawn making a beeline for her. Ella took a deep breath of the cold night air and tried not to look annoyed at the interruption.

"Ella, I have some horrible news I need to share. May I come inside with you?"

"Yes, of course, Jane. What has happened? You're as white as snow," asked a concerned Ella, her desire for tranquility forgotten as she led Jane into her warm living room. "It's just me here. John won't be home for another two hours. Natalie went to the Marino house after school today, and Nan is sharing a ride home from college with Susan on Wednesday."

"Let's sit down. I can't relay this to you standing up. It's that bad, Ella," Jane said. Then she let the whole tragic story of the day's events tumble out. Ella listened in quiet horror, tears starting to pool in her eyes as she gripped Jane's shaking hands in disbelief. When Jane was finished with her exhausting recitation, the two women started to contemplate the unfathomable sorrow the Carters must be experiencing.

"Oh, Jane. I couldn't even imagine losing one of my girls. Betty must be a total wreck."

"While Anna and I were sitting with her, waiting for Bob to get home, she didn't murmur one word. She sat like a statue, only moving to shake her head to indicate she didn't want anything Anna offered. I can't describe to you the look on Betty's face. I've never seen such grief."

They were interrupted by the return of a distressed Natalie. She walked in sobbing, and Ella immediately wrapped the seventeen-year-old in a hug. She guided her daughter to the sofa.

"Oh, Mom," choked Natalie. "Mr. and Mrs. Marino told Christina and me what happened. Poor Robby; it's so horrible. He must have been unbelievably sad to do such a thing."

"Yes, Mrs. Flynn just finished telling me. We must pray for the entire Carter family. Mrs. Flynn tells me the Carters are completely shattered Their only child gone..." Ella trailed off.

"I'm still shaking from the whole ordeal," added Jane as she joined them on the couch. "And I can't imagine how Anna is holding up, since she is the one who discovered him. How did she seem to you, Natalie?"

"Mrs. Marino is doing okay. She broke down a little when she started telling us, but Mr. M finished the story."

"Yes, I'm dreading telling my boys," Jane said. "I was able to telephone Danny earlier to tell him. Matthew has after-school basketball practice, and Danny will pick him up on his way home from work. We'll tell him together. Mark is away on a ski trip with friends to celebrate the end of their first semester of college. He'll return tomorrow. And I guess I'll have to call Pam up in Canada. These are going to be tough conversations."

"I know, Jane, I know," sympathized Ella while rubbing Natalie's back. They were still for a moment before a thought occurred to Ella. "Do the Bordens know yet?"

"I told Anna I'd inform you and then call Wilma later when she returns from work. I didn't want Anna to have to relive the whole day by telling anyone on Strong Lane the news," said Jane.

"That was kind of you."

"Yeah, well..." Jane stood abruptly. Ella knew her restless friend was not one for quiet contemplation. "I'm going to get back now. Danny and my Matty will be home soon. I don't want them walking into an empty house."

"And I'm going to my room, Mom," said Natalie. "Good-bye, Mrs. Flynn."

"So long, Natalie. Take care."

As Ella walked with her neighbor through the kitchen, she said, "Thank you, Jane, for coming over in person to tell me." Then, quietly, she added, "I'll inform Norma. I think she should know. Do you agree?"

Jane just grimly nodded.

After a solemn dinner with John and Natalie, Ella prepared herself mentally to telephone Norma. She felt nervous anticipating a conversation with Norma about her old enemy. Over the years, it had been only on very rare occasions that Betty's name was even mentioned. Nevertheless, she picked up the telephone and dialed.

When Ella concluded her summary of the day's events, Norma gasped, "This is so heartbreaking, Ella. I don't know what to say."

"Say you'll come to the services, Norma, whenever they may be," encouraged Ella.

"I don't know, Ella. Betty probably wouldn't want me there. It's been such a long time since we've seen each other. I don't think it's right to intrude."

"Please think about it. If this tragedy proves anything, it's that life is too short."

"I'll have to talk to Gordon. Please keep me apprised of the arrangements, Ella. I'd very much appreciate it. Thank you for letting me know," replied a sympathetic Norma before concluding the conversation.

Two days later, Ella informed Norma that Robby's wake at the local funeral home would begin the Saturday evening after Christmas. The funeral would take place on the following Monday, exactly one week after his death. Ella also told Norma that she, Jane, and Anna had collectively agreed they and their husbands would attend the first night at the funeral home. To reduce the number of first-night attendees, which they anticipated would be considerable, the mothers had asked their children to wait and attend with them the Sunday afternoon session of the wake. Norma silently collected the information Ella offered but still didn't indicate her plans. She again expressed her appreciation for being kept in the loop.

Over the days leading up to Saturday, Ella surmised, from the comings and goings of visiting cars, the Carters had a good support system among Bob's many nearby relatives. She learned Bob's parents, who had recently retired to Florida, were staying at the Levittown house.

Although Ella and the other neighbors supplied the Carters with some casseroles, they gave the grieving family their solitude for the remainder of the week. Because Bob's mother had gratefully accepted the dish Ella had walked over, Ella had not personally seen Betty or Bob since before that fateful Monday. She was dreading Saturday night and feared the sight of Betty's devastation. Ella wondered, *Betty's life has consistently revolved around her Robby, the sun in her private universe. What will she do now?*

CHAPTER 23

Norma - 1970

O n Saturday night, just before eight o'clock, a woman wearing a fashionable black pantsuit and a man in a dark business suit silently walked through the low-lit parking lot of a funeral home. Among the dozens of parked vehicles, they noted the familiar ones of their friends, the cars' owners already inside the building. The subdued couple reached the front portico where a bright exterior lantern illuminated their faces before they entered the building.

The two gave their overcoats to the cloakroom attendant and quickly walked to the entrance of the room designated for Robby's wake. It was jam-packed with rows of folding chairs and a crowd of people. From the back, they could barely see the front where Betty and Bob sat in wing chairs. The bereaved parents were positioned opposite their son's closed, flag-draped coffin, a dozen flower arrangements surrounding the dark wood casket. A few of Bob's relatives were standing in front of Betty and Bob, talking with them, and blocking their view of the pair now approaching them from the left side of the room.

The Flynns, the Schmidts and the Marinos were standing in a cluster at the front of the right aisle. It was Jane who must have been the first to notice the newly arrived couple because as they reached the front, the group clearly heard her gasp and mutter, "Here we go, kids!"

The people who had been conversing with the Carters moved away. Betty, dressed in a black crepe dress with a small, veiled hat, was clutching a balled-up white handkerchief. She looked up in anticipation of the next mourners paying their respects.

"Norma," whispered a surprised Betty as she rose from her chair. Her pale face registered desolation as well as shock. "I can't believe it..."

"I'm so, so sorry for your loss, Bets..." began Norma, holding out her arms and bursting into tears. Betty started to weep too, and she walked straight into her old foe's embrace. The two stood in a tight silent hold for several seconds before Bob vacated his chair and indicated Norma should take his place next to Betty. Gordon came forward to give Bob a consolatory hug and led him to the group of male neighbors. Jane, Anna, and Ella quickly sat in the vacant folding chairs located directly behind Betty and Norma. The three sat forward at the edges of their seats with Betty and Norma sitting sideways so the five reunited friends would all be able to communicate.

Norma was surprised by how much Betty had aged. Her haunted gray eyes were those of an old woman, and Norma noticed the hair peeking out from under her hat was laced with white strands. Norma's heart felt broken for the unimaginable grief her former neighbor must be experiencing.

"I can't believe my beloved little boy is gone," Betty was saying as she wept into her already damp handkerchief. Norma held her free hand, and Anna reached forward to rub Betty's back.

"He was just so unhappy," Betty continued. "And I couldn't make it better for him. I tried, I really tried."

"We know you did, Betty," murmured Ella.

"All his note said was 'I can't do this any longer. I want to go to a better place. I'm sorry.' He didn't even say he loved us…" Betty trailed off and broke into fresh sobs.

"But he did love you. You and Bob were wonderful parents," stated Norma quietly.

"You know, it… it wasn't just his injury. He… he had these terrible dreams that he was back in the jungle in the dark," said Betty haltingly. "He was such… such a gentle boy. He shouldn't have been sent to…." Then she abruptly broke from her train of thought, turned to Norma, and whispered decisively, "We weren't wonderful parents. You all don't understand." She paused with a look of dread on her face.

"What don't we understand?" asked Jane.

"We are the ones who purchased the gun! Robby wanted to go to a range and do target practice. We not only bought the gun as an early Christmas gift, but all three of us went to the range… several times! He was so proud of his marksmanship, and I thought it was good he was finally interested in something. I never thought he would use it to… oh, my God!" And with this realization, she collapsed sideways onto Norma's shoulder.

Norma put her arm around the sobbing woman and drew her in. Uncertain what she should say or do, Norma looked pleadingly over Betty's head in the direction of the other three. Their eyes conveyed the same helpless despair. After a few moments, Betty's shaking body stilled, and her crying ceased.

"I'm just so completely knackered," Betty mumbled into Norma's damp shoulder. "I just want to die, too."

Anna crossed herself religiously and scolded, "Betty, don't ever say that."

Betty lifted her head and with passionless eyes gazed at the three sitting behind her. "How can I go forward without him? He was my whole life. I've got nothing in this world now."

"You still have Bob. And his parents and your mother still need you," comforted Ella.

"And you still have us," encouraged Jane.

"Nothing else matters..." groaned a slumping Betty.

Something must be done to get this woman back on track, thought Norma. *The Betty I used to know was always a fierce fighter; one who wouldn't take no for an answer. I know Betty has survived losses in her life before. As heartbreaking as this one is, Betty can pull through this too.* Norma took Betty gently by the shoulders and turned her to face herself.

"That's enough, Bets. We won't listen to this kind of talk any longer," Norma demanded. She looked Betty square in the eyes and quoted, "'When things get tough, pull yourself up by your bootstraps and keep going!'"

"Mum," said Betty calmly.

"Yes, your mother. A woman who lost both her sons as young men during a war. She made it through the grief, and so can you," said Norma with a small smile.

Betty sat up a little straighter. There was some light and cognizance returning to her gray eyes.

"Now, you come with me, Bets," encouraged Norma as she started to stand with her arm around Betty's waist, gently pulling the grieving woman up with her. "Let's go to the ladies' lounge. We'll get you some water and fresh tissues. Come on, girls. Clear a path for us."

Less than an hour later, with the evening session of the wake concluded, the Lewises, Schmidts, Marinos, and Flynns met in the lobby of a local diner for coffee and dessert. An exhausted Betty had gone home with her husband and his parents. Earlier, in the funeral home's lounge, the women had calmed Betty and encouraged her to return to the reception room for the last fifteen minutes of the session.

The diner was packed on this Saturday night after Christmas. Norma asked the establishment's greeter for a table to accommodate eight but was told none that size was available. However, he could seat them immediately if they agreed to two tables of four in two different dining sections. The group agreed to split into male and female tables.

As the four women slipped into a booth, Norma commented solemnly, "It's just like the old Coffee Klatch days."

"Except we're missing a member," mourned Ella.

"Yes, poor Bets," replied a melancholic Norma.

"We all loved Robby. He was the nicest kid on the block," Jane added.

"This war is a horrible thing, taking a young man like that. Even if he didn't die over there, the war still killed him," began the usually serene Anna angrily. "Susan is inconsolable. She felt like she didn't do enough for Robby when she saw him after Thanksgiving."

"She's too hard on herself," said Ella. "She's only a student of psychology. She's not a certified psychologist yet. The mind is still a mystery. We don't always know why others do what they do."

With that, a harried waitress appeared. "Do you ladies know what you want?"

"What kind of pies do you have today?" inquired Jane.

"Apple and cherry."

"Bring us two slices of each and four coffees. Is that okay with all of you?" asked Jane.

"That's fine, as long as the coffee is strong," said Norma, and the server scurried away. "Maybe we should have gone to a bar instead. I think we all could use a stiff drink. What a night!"

"We still have two sessions of the wake tomorrow, and the funeral on Monday. Monday is when we'll need the alcohol," said Jane.

"Sal is catering the cold-cut luncheon at the Carters' house after the funeral," added Anna.

"Good. All of you can come to my house after lunch for a drink. We'll have a send-off for poor Robby," offered Jane. "I don't think Betty and Bob will necessarily serve alcohol at the lunch, do you?"

"No, Jane. Irish wakes are your thing," replied Norma with a smirk.

"You don't have to come, Nor," a haughty Jane answered.

"Oh, I'll come! I'll need a drink to blot out my morose thoughts."

The coffees were brought to their table, and the four silently added their sugar and cream. Norma broke the lull, admitting, "I was ashamed of myself today, truly guilt-ridden over carrying on this feud with Betty for so long."

"Oh, Nor," Anna consoled wearily. "It's water under the bridge. It was so long ago."

"Yes, but I still feel guilty. Do you ladies realize the last time I actually saw Robby, he was only three years old?"

"But Betty has never really seen your girls either, Nor. You two stopped talking before the twins were born," pointed out Jane. "She could have tried one more time to make her peace with you when you brought your babies home from the hospital, before you moved away."

"She knew I wouldn't have accepted an olive branch from her if she offered it again. I refused to accept her first apology. I was too stubborn. And now over seventeen years have passed."

"Don't beat yourself up over it. What's done is done," observed Jane.

"I'd like to do something for Betty and Bob now, though," Norma contemplated.

"We all do," agreed Ella. "But what?"

"Whatever we do, it'll have to wait," began Anna. "I understand Betty and Bob are planning on leaving soon after the funeral to fly to England. They want to break the news to Betty's mother in person. Since she's seventy-five and hasn't been in good health as of late, they didn't want to tell her about Robby over the telephone."

"Maybe getting away will do them some good," said Ella.

"I hope so," replied Anna and then added, "Bob's mother also told me tonight that Betty refuses to go into Robby's bedroom. She has shut the door and won't let anyone open it. Bob had to sneak in when Betty was upstairs so he could get his son's military uniform from the closet to give to the undertaker."

"I bet the two of them will eventually sell the house," guessed Jane. "I don't see them living there in the future with Robby gone. There are just too many memories."

Norma, who had been deep in thought, lifted her head and interjected, "Well, if they do decide to sell, that's how I can help Bets. Six months ago, I completed a real estate course and received my broker's license. I've recently started working for a local sales office. Although I'll mostly be selling homes in the Huntington area, I can certainly broker a deal for Betty and Bob without charging them any commission."

"That would be an extremely helpful thing for you to do," said Ella.

Jane exclaimed, "So, you're a real estate agent, Nor. That's so cool! And look at all of us with our careers! Those women libbers burning their bras have nothing on us! The ladies on Strong Lane practically invented the feminist movement!" To punctuate her statement, she picked up her fork, stabbed a piece of pie, and shoved it into her mouth with a triumphant grin.

"I think the feminist movement is more than just women having jobs outside the home," Ella observed. "It also involves equal pay and benefits."

"And the right to use birth control and make decisions about our own bodies in a safe and legal way," added Norma, thinking of her past.

Each of them mulled over what had been said as they sipped their coffees and shared slices of pie.

"I wonder how different it will be for our daughters in the future," pondered Norma. "My style-conscious Joy has applied to the Fashion Institute in New York City. And Janet wants to follow in Gor's footsteps and become an engineer. I hope she can achieve her dream without too much male chauvinism in a field usually dominated by men."

"After her undergraduate work is complete, Susan wants to further her studies to become a licensed clinical psychologist. Because of Robby, she plans to specialize in disorders due to war neurosis," said Anna. "I hope she'll someday get the same pay as males in the psychology field."

"Pam's finishing her teaching certification in Canada, but that's a field of work women have done for decades. She's not really breaking down any barriers like Janet and Susan," noted Jane. "How about your girls, Ella?"

"Nan is very happy studying to become a librarian, but she thinks she'll want to work in a big university library someday, not a local public library as I do," replied Ella. "And Natalie has excellent foreign language skills, like John, and talks about studying international business, travelling, and making lots of money! But business is a difficult field for women to excel in, unless they're happy being secretaries, which Natalie wouldn't be. I'm hopeful our daughters' generation will be strong enough to make great progress for equal job status."

"And what about Christina, Anna? She'll be graduating this June from high school with Natalie," inquired Norma.

Anna laughed and explained, "My dramatic Christina wants to study acting in New York. She's had the lead in every high school play and musical for the last three years. Talk about a career where there's competition and heartbreak! I've tried to encourage her to have a backup plan and study something else in conjunction with the theater, but Sal supports her the whole way. He thinks she's destined to become a big star."

"She's very talented and has a marvelous voice," said Ella. "I've attended every production she's been in, and Sal's correct. Christina is a star."

"Thanks, Ella. I think so too, but that's just in small productions in Levittown. Her desire is Broadway, and that will be a long and challenging goal to achieve," worried Anna.

"As long as Christina sticks to the idea of Broadway and doesn't fly off to Hollywood, she'll have her family nearby to support her. She'll do fine," Jane offered generously. Then, with a sparkle in her eyes, she continued. "Speaking of families and since we could use some happy news to chew on over these next few sad days, I've got an announcement." She paused to make sure she had everyone's attention.

"Well, go on, Jane. You've got us all intrigued," demanded Norma.

"I'm going to be a grandmother!" shrieked Jane excitedly. When she realized people at the surrounding tables were looking over at her raised voice, Jane contained her excitement, lowered her tone, and continued, "I can't believe it! Pamela and Paul phoned us on Christmas Day with the news. My baby is going to have a baby. Isn't that a gas, girls?!"

CHAPTER 24

Betty - 1971

A week after their son's funeral, the Carters flew to England to see Betty's mother. The last time the couple had visited the country was a year ago, after the unexpected loss of Betty's father. At the time, they had traveled with Robby, just prior to the receipt of his draft notice.

Both still exhausted, Betty and Bob planned to return home from this trip within a week's time. However, with their discovery that the health of Mrs. James was on a steady decline, they stayed longer. When Betty realized the extent of her mother's frailty, she decided not to inform the confused woman of her only grandchild's death.

On the last day of January, Betty experienced another heartbreak when her mother passed away in her sleep. Betty mourned the loss of

Mum, a quiet, dignified parent who was a steadfast example of love and support during Betty's youth. *I wish I had inherited more of her admirable traits,* thought Betty sadly. *Instead, I got my combative personality from Dad.*

With her mother gone, Betty's ties with England were finally severed. Although she had visited over the past decades, she hadn't lived in the country of her birth for twenty-five years. During the month's stay in her former hometown, she realized she now considered herself an American. No longer would she feel like an outsider among her Levittown neighbors.

Bob helped Betty settle her mother's meager estate. While sorting through her mum's possessions, Betty had long and honest conversations with Bob about their future. It began with Bob asking, "Betty, honey, what do you think of selling our house and getting a clean start somewhere?"

"I'll be honest with you, Bob," said Betty, as she organized a box of her mother's clothes for charity. "I've been thinking of nothing else. I don't know if I can face living in Levittown without... Robby." She gulped and wondered, *Will I ever cease getting choked up when I try to say his name aloud?*

She sealed the carton she had been working on and asked, "But where can we go, Bob?"

Bob picked up the box and carried it over to the door, adding it to the others they had already completed. "What about joining my parents in Florida? They're living in one of those senior citizen communities, but we can buy our own house nearby. My father says we can get more for our money down south. We'd probably make a nice profit on our Levitt home."

"I don't know," Betty said with uncertainty. "Other than your parents, we wouldn't know anyone. And what would you do about your job?"

"I've been with the railroad for twenty-five years. I can take an early retirement and collect my pension..."

"An early retirement?" reiterated Betty incredulously. "Bob, you're only turning forty-seven this year."

"I'd get another job down in Florida, honey. Maybe sell insurance like my father did as a career before he retired. A change would be good for me. Besides, I'm tired of being on my feet all day as a conductor."

Betty thought sadly, *Bob's not admitting it, but he doesn't want to return to a job our son had also been doing. As our house holds constant reminders of Robby for me, I'm sure for Bob, the LIRR triggers memories of Robby's time working there.*

Betty said, "By moving out of state, we'd be leaving your sisters and their families. And what about our friends? I'd miss Anna terribly."

"I'd miss Sal too... and my sisters' families. But they can all visit. And there's always letters and phone calls to stay in touch with them. Just think about it, honey..."

Betty and Bob finally returned to Strong Lane in mid-February. They arrived home with a definite verdict on their future. They would sell their house and join Bob's parents in Florida. Despite the regret of leaving her friends, Betty was looking forward to buying a new home and starting over.

Betty wanted to make a point of telling Ella, Jane, and Anna personally about the decision to relocate. She did not want to have such important conversations on the telephone, nor did she want to share her news in a group setting. Therefore, on a Sunday when everyone was at home, Betty knocked on each door, purposely leaving Anna's house for last.

Ella, in her serious way, congratulated Betty on her and Bob's decision and offered these words of encouragement: "After I lost my family in Germany, starting over in a new locale was the best way for me to move forward with my life. It will be for you also, Betty. We never forget those we've loved, but we must remind ourselves we're still part of humanity. I hope you find your purpose again in Florida."

Jane also thought the move was a good idea. She told Betty, "I predicted you two would sell the house; I told the girls so! But truthfully, Betty, I'd do the same exact thing. There's nothing holding you here, except all our friendships. Strong Lane will miss you and Bob tremendously, but a fresh start is the only way to get on with life. I admire you for taking the plunge."

At Anna's kitchen table, Betty told her best friend her news, concluding, "I'll miss you, Anna, most of all. We've been through a lot together."

"Yes, Betty, it's been a great stretch of twenty plus years," said Anna with a smile. "Sal will miss Bob, too. We'll stay in touch, though."

"You two must come visit us, especially when the winter here has you cold and bothered," Betty urged.

"We'll do that," agreed Anna. "Sal and I will be glad to take a Florida vacation!"

"Anna," hesitated Betty. "I have something else I've wanted to say to you for the past two months since… you know… Robby…"

Anna reached across the table and took Betty's hands in her own. "You don't have to say anything, Betty."

"No, I have to tell you," Betty insisted with gratitude in her eyes. She pushed ahead before she choked up. "I want you to know how it has been a comfort to me that it was you who was with my Robby at the end. I know when you found him, he was... already gone. But you were with him when his soul left this earth. I'm thankful and grateful that someone, especially a person as loving as you, was with him at his last."

Tears started to well in Anna's eyes before she spoke. "That day was one of the saddest in my life, and I've always felt guilty I couldn't prevent Robby's death from happening. But now I feel a burden lifted, as if there was a reason I was there on that awful morning. Thank you, Betty, for giving me peace."

A few days after Betty had shared the relocation news with her neighbors, she received a telephone call from Norma. Betty had not seen her since Robby's funeral. Although she was grateful for their mutual reconciliation, Betty still felt awkward speaking one-on-one.

"Good morning, Betty. I'm glad to find you at home. My heartfelt condolences on the loss of your beloved mother." Betty detected an unusual uneasiness in Norma's tone, one that matched her own apprehension.

"Thank you, Nor. Bob and I received your card and the basket of fruit. It was so very thoughtful of you and Gordon," Betty stiffly replied.

"You're both welcome; it was nothing. We just wanted you to know we were thinking of you."

Betty wondered: *how does Norma really feel about me after all these years of not speaking? I must admit, Norma was magnanimous at the services for Robby. And I'm profoundly grateful she was able to help me during my breakdown at the wake. But where do the two of us go from here?*

"Listen, Bets, I know you have lots to do, and I don't want to hold you up," Norma continued in a nervous rush. "But I learned of your plans to move, and I wanted to offer you and Bob my assistance. I recently got my real estate license. I would be happy to list your house for sale... without charging any commission. I want to make the process as easy as possible. Will you let me help you?"

"I don't know what to say, Nor," a surprised Betty responded. "You'd do that for me?"

"Yes, I certainly would," Norma reassured her with obvious relief in her voice. "Why don't we set up a day and time soon? I can come over to survey your house from a realtor's perspective and then determine the best listing price for you. Darn it, Bets, I'll even help you start packing! What do you say?"

"That would be lovely, Nor. I'll accept both of those offers. Thank you very much."

Consequently, it was on a cold, windy day in March of 1971 when Norma Lewis stepped into Betty Carter's home for the first time in almost two decades. There were cardboard moving boxes of assorted sizes already scattered throughout the cramped living room. Betty met her at the front door where Norma gave her a warm embrace and again expressed her condolences over her mother's death.

"Yes, it's been a brutal year for me," began Betty, taking Norma's coat. "I don't know if you heard, Nor, but I lost my father in January of 1970. Then Robby in December and now my mum this past January."

"I learned about your father from Anna, and I'm sorry for that loss too," replied Norma. "It's been a lot for you and Bob to bear."

"Thank you," said Betty. As she returned from the coat closet, she crossed her arms and hugged her midsection. She was lost in thought for a moment before quietly adding, "You know, if it doesn't sound too crazy, I try to picture the three of them together and happy in the great beyond. My parents taking care of their only grandchild. Or maybe Robby taking care of them in their old age. Perhaps the baby I lost is there with them, too. And my older brothers. Oh, I don't know... I probably sound like a lunatic."

"Not at all," reassured Norma in a soothing voice. "You've certainly had a lot of loss in your life so far." She reached out to lay a comforting hand on Betty's arm. Betty uncrossed her arms and started to relax.

"For the past month, Bob has convinced me to go with him to a grief support group at our church. I was reluctant at first. I think talking with strangers about my feelings is a bunch of rubbish. But I must tell you, I think it has helped me to discover Bob and I are not the only ones out there with profound grief. It was one of the group participants who turned me on to the idea of thinking about those we loss all together in a better place."

"If it gives you peace, I think it's a wonderful way to think," sympathized Norma.

"Have you lost anyone from your immediate family, Nor?"

"Other than my two sets of grandparents, no, I haven't. My parents still live in Garden City. They're retired, active, and in good health. My brother and his family are in Connecticut."

"You're lucky. It's sad to be the only one left."

"But you have Bob, who loves you, and his parents, who have always treated you like a daughter. There is a wonderful new start waiting for you in Florida with them."

"I suppose that's true..."

"And, Bets," continued Norma with heartfelt compassion, "when you're feeling sad, you should instead try to remember all the happy times you shared with the departed people in your life."

"Yes, I'll do that," agreed Betty, brightening. "I have to say, it's wonderful sharing my feelings with you, Nor. I wish... I wish..." She hesitated, not quite sure if she wanted to admit her thoughts.

"What do you wish?"

Betty had never wanted to expose her insecurities to anyone, especially Norma. *But now, with my former world shattered, it seems trivial to worry about such things. Why not express my emotions,* thought Betty. *I'll be leaving Long Island anyway and may never see Norma again. Too many years have passed not to be honest.*

"I wish we could have had more of this kind of conversation when we first met," announced Betty. "I must admit, my jealousies put me into a blue funk when it came to anything having to do with you. You seemed to have it all, Nor. Since I didn't grow up here, I always felt like a struggling outsider."

"Oh, Bets. *I* was the one who felt like an outsider. You four all had children, and I couldn't have any. And I wouldn't confide in any of you the real reason I couldn't."

"Until I discovered your secret." Betty sighed, then continued with profound sincerity, "As I told you after I confronted Gordon, I am truly sorry for my spitefulness."

"I know you are. And I was no saint either," admitted a contrite Norma. "I was so catty with you. You and your questions used to put me on the defense all the time."

"And I used to think you were a secretive and selfish person," began Betty and then, as she noticed Norma's eyes start to narrow, quickly continued with her reasoning. "BUT, upon reflection, you were *un*selfishly there for me on two of the saddest occasions in my life. Despite your feelings for me and my treatment of you, you supported me through my miscarriage and Robby's death."

Norma's face relaxed again as she replied, "I'm sure you would have done the same for me if the situations were reversed. And I must tell you, once you exposed my past, I did feel free of all the anxieties I had kept bundled up inside of me for too many years. So, *I wish* I had admitted that to you then and forgave you. We wouldn't have had all these wasted years between us."

Betty smiled. It felt so good to have this out in the open, even at this eleventh hour when she was preparing to move to another state.

"You know, Nor, I realized recently that we had something in our past we could have bonded over. I'm talking about the time after my miscarriage and before you adopted your girls."

"What's that, Bets?"

"We could have bonded over the feeling of helplessness that comes with infertility. I never could conceive again." Betty saw the understanding in Norma's face.

"Yes, sadly, we had that in common," agreed Norma.

"Also," Betty continued, "I've always wondered if we might have connected even earlier, that is if I hadn't had my miscarriage. My second baby was due in January, the same month you were expecting your adopted one. I raised my Robby with Anna's Susan, and because of that, she and I are close friends. The two of us might have raised children together too."

"True, that would have been nice. But we can't live in the past. Let's just try to move forward."

"Yes, I agree." Betty took a deep breath and then changed the subject. "I appreciate you coming today to lend a hand packing and go over the real estate listing." She gestured to the boxes in the room and added, "As you can see, I started to box up the easy things like kitchen gadgets and such."

"Great. Give me a box and tell me what I can do for you."

Betty hesitated and started to gnaw on the side of her thumb, a habit she had acquired only recently.

"There is something you can do for me, Nor." Betty paused again before finally blurting out, "I can't bring myself to go through Robby's things in his room."

"Oh, Bets," Norma responded, wringing her hands. "I empathize with you. It would be an impossible task for me to go through the belongings of either of my daughters."

Betty continued, "Bob said he would box it all up, so I don't have to go in there, but I don't want to bring *everything* to Florida. We'll be staying with Bob's parents for a short time, while we search for a home of our own. As much as I'd like to bring all my son's things with me, I won't have the room, and, truthfully, I know from the support group, that I shouldn't hold on to too much."

Betty sighed and gallantly finished her plea. "So, I figured you're the best person to help me, since you didn't know Robby for most of his life. You can be more detached and rational about what I should keep and what I should dispose of. Will you help me?"

"Of course," promised Norma. "We'll create a lovely memory box, or two, of items from all phases of Robby's life, so, on dark days, you can look back with a smile."

"Oh, thank you, Nor. That would be wonderful. I'd really appreciate it," Betty replied gratefully.

"No problem, Bets. What are friends for?"

EPILOGUE
1997

For the last time, Ella carefully locked the front door of One Strong Lane. Nan would be driving her to Levittown's Fiftieth Anniversary Parade. Before making her way to her daughter's car, she took one last long look at the homes surrounding her.

The block had changed drastically over the decades. The trees, once just saplings, had all grown tall and sturdy. The houses, no longer cookie-cutter duplicates, were all unique with added dormers and extensions. Even Norma Lewis's former home, which had retained most of its originality for almost forty years, was now a large saltbox colonial. Ten years ago, when Wilma and Roger Borden had passed away within a year of each other, Two Strong Lane had been purchased by a young family who immediately expanded the small Cape Cod.

Ella slowly pulled open the passenger door and got into her seat. Since the car had been backed onto the driveway, Ella's direct view through the windshield was of the corner sump, its firmly locked chain-linked fence harboring the heartbreaking memories of a life lost in 1970. Ella was the only neighbor remaining on the street who was aware of the tragedy of Robby Carter.

"I'll miss visiting this old neighborhood, Mom," began Nan. "You know, it's funny. People never believe me when they ask where I was born. I tell them at home in Levittown, and they think I'm making it up. Of course, everyone from my generation was born in modern hospitals. They can't quite wrap their head around a home birth."

"Yes, it's unusual in this country, although it wasn't so uncommon in Germany between the wars. I was a home birth back in 1928," stated Ella as she pulled her seatbelt across her body and locked it in place. "Your birth was my happiest day in this house. And the death of your father was my saddest. This one house witnessed both a birth and a death..." Ella trailed off, lost in her thoughts.

Six months ago, in April, John Schmidt had passed away in his sleep from a ruptured cerebral aneurysm. Ella and her family were still shocked by the sudden loss. Before tragedy struck, John had been relatively healthy for a man of seventy-five and had been enjoying a decade of retirement with his beloved wife.

Nan reached for her mother's hand and said, "I'm grateful you and Dad had some golden years to share. And I'm so glad you both made that trip to Germany three years ago."

"I am too. It's a very special memory when I think back to the two of us revisiting Berlin and its surrounding areas. The city had changed so much, yet I could still feel my parents' and brothers' presence as I walked some familiar streets. And, of course, it's the country where I met your wonderful father, and my life began again," Ella added wistfully.

Nan started the car's engine, and they drove in silence for a while.

"Mom, do you think you and your friends will get together after the parade?"

"Yes, we spoke of going to the local diner to have lunch and catch-up. You're welcome to join us, Nan, or did your possible plans finally work out?"

"Yup, they did. I'm going to go to Sally Marsden's house party after the parade. Since she still lives around here, she's gathering a bunch of old high school friends. It'll be a fun reunion for me. I'll give you her phone number, Mom, so you can contact me when you're ready for me to pick you up from the diner," said Nan. She pulled her car into one of the last available parking spaces in the large bank parking lot located near the Levittown Public Library.

"We'll try to view the parade on the turnpike from in front of the bank. Then afterwards, I'll walk with you down to the library to meet up with the old neighbors. How does that sound?"

"Perfect," replied Ella as she exited the car. The two made their way through the throng of residents, both current and past, all of whom were maneuvering for good viewing positions on either side of the six-lane thoroughfare of Hempstead Turnpike. The main access road was shut to traffic and would serve as the parade route for the celebration.

"I hope the weather holds out," observed Ella as she glanced at the gray clouds threatening possible rain. She was chilly despite her wool pants and corduroy jacket.

The beginning of the parade came abreast of the front spot they had been able to secure. Ella marveled at the lengthy procession. There were antique cars, many from the 1940s and 1950s, reminiscent of when the town was young and new. Perched on the flatbed of a decorated truck was a scaled-down three-dimensional model of the exterior of an original Levitt Cape Cod house. Homeowners who had been the first to settle Levittown in 1947 were waving and smiling from their seats on a red trolley-style bus. Public school marching bands played lively musical numbers. And finally, riding in modern convertibles, there were the local politicians, resolute not to lose an opportunity to glad-hand with voters at the conclusion of the parade.

"That was something!" exclaimed Nan when it was all over. "I wish Nat had come out to join us."

"I think she would have liked to come, but she only flew in from Europe late yesterday. It would have been too much for her to catch a train from Manhattan early this morning."

Through the years, Ella's second daughter, Natalie, had worked her way up the corporate ladder in the field of international banking. At forty-four, Natalie was the only female vice-president at a major German bank in New York, the same city where she resided with her stockbroker husband.

Ella and Nan walked the short distance to the front of the Levittown Public Library. As Ella glanced at the building's facade, happy memories of her years there as a librarian came tumbling back. She had enjoyed her tenure as a public employee and had stopped working ten years ago when John had retired from his position at the United Nations. During their last decade together, the couple had travelled extensively throughout the United States and had made that memorable trip to Germany.

The area around the library was crowded with dispersed parade viewers, many, like Ella, waiting to rendezvous with friends or relatives. Again, Ella wondered which members of the former coffee klatch would show up today. Suddenly, she heard her name being shouted in the noisy horde of bodies. Not surprisingly, she heard Jane Flynn before she saw her.

An energetic Jane made her way to Ella's side and enveloped her in a heartfelt embrace. At seventy-two, the trim, petite Jane was still a force to be reckoned with. Her short hair, blow-dried into soft waves, was still reddish blonde, thanks to monthly visits to her salon. She was dressed casually in blue jeans, a colorful heavy-knit oversized sweater, and comfortable shoes.

Following Jane was the still glamorous Norma Lewis sporting a sleek look. Her expertly dyed chestnut hair was shaped in a shorter version of the popular Rachel haircut, the bouncy face-framing style introduced on the television show *Friends*. With her youthful hairdo and figure, Norma, at seventy, looked like a much younger woman. She wore a white turtle-neck sweater tucked into a pair of high-waisted navy trousers with low-heeled ankle boots. A plaid wool blazer in the popular fall colors of navy and plum completed her outfit.

"You came together!" said a surprised Ella as she enthusiastically hugged her two friends.

"Yes," replied Jane. "Since the hubbies didn't want to come – I believe Danny's exact words were 'Why do I want to stand outside on a cold day like this for something no one will show up for' – Nor and I thought we'd save the gas and carpool. Danny was wrong! This crowd is crazy, although I'm glad it was a good turnout for the old town's fiftieth!"

"I hope we can secure a table at the diner," wondered Ella.

"My car is parked right around the corner. Let's get going so we can beat the mob there," Norma declared before adding, "Will you be joining us, Nan?"

"No, thank you, Mrs. Lewis," answered Nan. "I have a reunion of my own to attend."

"That's fantastic, Nan. I'm sure you don't want to hang out with us old ladies," Jane said with good humor "But before we take off, tell me, how are Ben and the kids?"

"Everyone is well, Mrs. Flynn. Thank you for asking. My son, Jeremy, just started college in Boston. So that's one kid down, and two to go!"

"How old are your girls now? And do you still work at the university library in Stony Brook?" asked Norma.

"My daughters are fifteen and twelve. And, yes, I still work at the same library. It's amazing to think, but I've been employed there for almost twenty-five years!" Nan hastily answered before saying, "It's been wonderful seeing you both, but I've got to get going. Call me, Mom, when you are ready to go home."

"I will, dear." After her daughter left, Ella asked her friends what she had been wondering all morning, "Will Betty be joining us?"

"No, I'm sorry to say she won't be," replied Norma. "I spoke to her on the phone last night. I'll explain when we get to the diner."

"I can't say I'm surprised," Ella stated with disappointment as the three headed to Norma's car.

"Neither was I when Nor told me this morning," chimed in Jane.

When the three were finally secured in a comfortable booth at the diner, Norma explained Betty's absence.

"She and Bob did fly up from Florida, as promised. They stayed a few days and visited Bob's sister and husband in Queens. They planned on heading out here for the parade and flying back home tonight. In fact, Gordon had said he would have come with me today to see the two of them and not leave Bob with all of us women. But once he discovered the Carters had cancelled and that Danny had refused to come, he stayed home."

Before she could finish her story, the server came to take their order. After he left, Norma continued, "Where was I? Oh yes… so yesterday morning, Bob got a call that a pipe broke in their coffee shop and apparently there was some flood damage. They changed their flight to late yesterday afternoon. When Bets called me from Florida last night, she sent her apologies and said she had really wanted to see you girls."

The coffee shop. Ella had anticipated that might be the excuse, as it had been other times. Their business was like a child to Betty and Bob, monopolizing most of their attention over the years.

Shortly after the Carters had relocated to Florida, Betty had accepted a position as a baker at a small coffee shop owned by an elderly couple. Jane had been right when she suggested years ago that Betty should use her skills for a career. Betty had found she enjoyed the job and discovered keeping busy sustained her. When the owners had retired, Betty and Bob bought the coffee shop and took over its management. They renamed the breakfast and lunch establishment *Robby's Place.*

"I haven't seen her since 1976," an annoyed Ella said. "She didn't accept the invitation to either of my daughters' weddings or to your girls' weddings, Norma. She promises and then makes excuses, usually attributed to the supervision of their shop and how they can't get away. I will admit, it bothers me that she doesn't come to see us. Occasionally speaking on the telephone is not enough."

"I haven't seen Betty in over twenty years, too," confirmed Jane. "I still send Christmas cards, and she sometimes gives me a call after she receives one so we can catch up a bit. But honestly, she's basically estranged from us."

"That's because you two haven't vacationed in Florida," pointed out Norma. "Gor and I go almost every winter, and, if we are in Bets' area, we make a stop at *Robby's*. The two of them are very happy running that little place. Betty told me she tries to live in the present and not think too much of the past. Being busy and committed to their business has really worked wonders on her. I must admit, she looks good. She lost weight, and finally changed her old hairstyle."

"I'm glad she found some peace," said Ella begrudgingly. "I just wish it was important to her to keep one of her promises and come see us for a coffee klatch reunion."

"Maybe the three of us should do a road trip and go down south for a conciliation vacation?" suggested Norma with a bemused grin.

"Hey, that rhymes! I'd be cool with a girls' trip," said Jane before observing, "I was just thinking… it *is* sort of weird, Nor, that you, *of all people*, are the closest to Betty now, considering your ancient feud. But now she's telephoning you; you're visiting her…"

"Yes, well, I guess I took Anna's place in Betty's book as her person on Long Island to keep her up to date," Norma replied. "Truthfully, gals… and please note she has not said this to me directly… I think the reason she keeps refusing our invitations to return here is because she's a bit afraid of stirring up her old emotions. She's worked very hard at moving forward in her life. I was actually surprised she originally agreed to meet today because, deep down, I don't think she wants to get together with the three of us without Anna."

And with that one name mentioned, it was as if the air was sucked out of the room. The three grew quiet for a moment, as each of them remembered Anna in their own way.

In early autumn of 1976, their treasured friend and former neighbor had passed away from advanced pancreatic cancer. The disease's alarming speed, from the springtime diagnosis to its swift aftermath, had devastated her family and friends.

Jane suddenly grabbed her pocketbook and extracted a small photograph. She turned it to face Norma and Ella and slid it across the table.

"Remember this day, girls?" prompted a subdued Jane. "I came across this recently and had to bring it today to share."

There, in the slightly faded 3 ½ inch by 4 ½ inch amateur color-film shot, was an image of the original five Strong Lane neighbors. The photograph had been taken in the Marinos' living room, where a thin Anna was sitting up in a hospital bed with a platter, containing a cake with candles, on her lap. Betty was sitting next to her, and both women had birthday crowns perched on their heads. Jane, Norma, and Ella, each wearing a cone-shaped party hat, stood behind the bed's headboard. All five had brave smiles on their faces, but the photograph also revealed hints of sorrow registered in each of the women's eyes.

"Anna's and Betty's combined fiftieth birthday celebration," stated Ella in a whisper.

"Yes, the last time we five were together, just two months before we lost Anna. I'm so glad Betty and I each flew back to New York for that day," a reflective Jane recalled. "Of course, we saw Betty again at the funeral. And that was the last time Ella and I saw her in person. Maybe you're right, Nor, when you said seeing us all together is too brutal for her. Betty was so close to Anna. I know the Marinos vacationed in Florida with the Carters several times before Anna became ill."

Norma sighed, "Anna was a true angel. I can understand why God wanted her back."

The three continued to gaze at the photograph before Ella finally cleared her throat and said, "Has anyone heard from Sal lately? He mailed me a condolence card when John passed and apologized for not attending the service, but he had a stomach bug at the time and wasn't well enough to travel. That's the last I've heard from him."

Jane put the photograph away and said, "Last I knew of him was when he retired from the family food business, sold the house on Strong Lane, and moved in with Susan and her family up in Westchester. But that was like six or seven years ago, wasn't it?"

"Betty tells me he has his own little in-law suite in Susan's house," supplied Norma. "With both Susan and her husband employed as psychologists, they do very well. Betty and Bob visited Sal there once. Betty says Sal just adores that grandson of his! The boy is twelve now, and he and his grandpa are as thick as thieves; they really enjoy each other."

"That's so nice to hear. I'm truly glad for Sal," said Ella.

"Do you know if Sal and Bob are still close?" asked Jane.

"Yes," Norma responded. "Sal still goes down to Florida regularly and stays in the Carters' guest room. He sounds like he stays busy. Betty says he frequently travels into the city to see his Christina, too."

Just then, the server approached, balancing his tray on one hand while with the other he distributed the lunch plates to the three friends. He refilled their coffee mugs and water glasses before retreating.

After he left, Ella brightly inquired, "So, how is Huntington these days, ladies?"

"For Danny and me, it's still a work in progress," began Jane, rolling her expressive eyes. "We are, though, getting very close to completing our house's unlimited projects. It's been a long haul since my husband started the renovations, but I'm proud to say our old home is almost ready for occupation. I can't wait to move into it completely, hopefully before Christmas. Living in the little one-bedroom guesthouse on the property is okay for one occupant, but the two of us sharing the space is getting on both of our last nerves! If both of us hadn't quit smoking when we first moved to Toronto, we'd each be going through two packs a day with the anxiety of it all!"

Two years ago, Jane and Danny had returned to Long Island from Canada. In 1971, shortly after Betty and Bob left Strong Lane, the Flynns had also sold their Levittown home and moved to the Toronto area with their younger son, Matthew. There, they joined Pamela's family and their older son, Mark, who had found a job as a carpenter there, and a way to avoid the Vietnam draft. Once the family had reunited in Canada, Danny had fulfilled his dream and, with Mark, formed Flynn and Son Construction.

Eventually, Jane's youngest child, Matthew, had returned to the United States for medical school. After graduation and marriage, he established himself as a physician in a small primary care group located in Huntington. In mid-1995, when Jane discovered Matthew and his wife were expecting, she convinced Danny they needed to move back to Long Island. After helping raise their five Canadian grandchildren among Pamela's and Mark's families, Jane wanted to be a part of this new grandchild's life in Huntington. Consequently, Norma had provided Jane and Danny with her professional assistance in finding a large residence. They wanted their home to accommodate the extended Flynn family from Canada during future visits to Long Island. Jane and Danny had purchased a 1920 dwelling on an acre of land with a small guest house at the rear of the property. The vintage home desperately needed loving care and Danny's renovation expertise. Norma had also recommended a young local contractor to assist Danny with the home's restoration.

Now Norma replied to Jane's comment about the small guesthouse by saying, "I told you, Jane, when you moved to Huntington, you and Danny could have stayed with Gor and me. We have the room."

"And I told you I appreciated the offer, but it wouldn't have been good for our friendship if we had to live under the same roof, especially for almost two years!" said Jane. "I'm glad we had our secondary cottage to live in. It's a cute little place, and thankfully it was more up to date than the big house. And now the house is almost done, and everything is so new and beautiful. I know each of you have seen it in different stages of repair, but I can't wait until you girls see it completed!"

"Living through construction projects is definitely not easy," agreed Norma. "That's why Gor and I moved again within Huntington, when our old house started to need major renovations. It was the biggest perk of being a real estate agent in the area; I was able to see the houses new to the market before the general public. But after we moved five years ago to this last house, Gor proclaimed that would be our very last move."

"Do you think you can finally stay put and stop driving Gordon crazy?" teased Jane.

"Yes, I can," chuckled Norma. "Especially since I retired from the real estate office this past June, and I don't get tempted by new listings. Yes, after forty plus years in Huntington and three different addresses in the town, I'm happy where I am. This ranch house with winter water views of the bay is perfect for Gor and me at this stage of our lives. Its location isn't that far from my twins, and now, it's only three miles from you, Jane."

"Has it really been over forty years since you, Gordon and the girls moved from Levittown to Huntington?" reflected an amazed Ella as she dipped a fork into her chicken salad platter.

"It's hard to believe, but it's true," said Norma, sprinkling a small portion of dressing over her mixed vegetable salad. "My girls were just infants back then and now look at them, women of forty-four. It's truly amazing how fast time flies."

Jane and Ella knew Norma's twins were each contentedly settled within an hour's commute of their parents' home. Janet Lewis, a mechanical engineer, lived in New York City with her husband. The pair, much like Ella's daughter Natalie and her husband, were childless by choice. In fact, the two Manhattan couples were great friends and socialized on a regular basis. In contrast, Joy Lewis was the happy mother of four children. In 1983, Joy and her husband, a dentist, had bought, and subsequently renovated, Norma's parents' house in Garden City. It was bittersweet for Norma to visit her daughter's family in the home where she herself had been raised decades ago. However, after Mr. and Mrs. Wolf had both passed in the early 1980s, Norma had been happy the property had stayed in the family. Joy's family of six brought new life to the old house.

Jane took a huge bite from her corned beef sandwich and returned it to its plate. Wiping the mustard from the corner of her mouth with a paper napkin, she chewed thoughtfully before swallowing and reminiscing, "I lived in Levittown for almost twenty-five years, and over twenty in Toronto. And now we are back here on Long Island. Danny and I have made a lot of friends living in two different countries over these decades, but there's nothing like our oldest friends." And she reached both her hands across the table to pat a hand of each of the two women sitting across from her.

"Are you saying we're *old*, Jane Flynn?" scolded Norma with a hint of a smile before taking a sip of her coffee.

"Certainly not old," replied Jane. "Although we're no longer the young newlywed ninnies we were when we all moved to Strong Lane!"

The three of them laughingly agreed before Jane continued, "When I say my oldest friends, I mean my dearest friends."

"I agree, my darlings," acknowledged Norma before changing the subject. "Do tell us about the new apartment you're moving into, Ella. It's near Nan and her family, right?"

"Yes, it's about a twenty-minute drive west from her home in Stony Brook." Ella smiled and added, "Now that I think of it, I would guess the garden apartment complex is located about midway between you two in Huntington and Nan's house. I'll be able to visit all of you easily. The only drawback is my apartment is not located in a town with a railroad station for my city trips to visit Natalie. I'll need to drive about fifteen minutes to the nearest train."

"How do you feel about moving from your own home to an apartment?" asked Jane.

"I suppose it will be easier to maintain," contemplated Ella. "However, I'll miss my garden. Once I retired, I started planting all kinds of flowers and even some vegetables. I really enjoyed it. Although this is called a 'garden apartment,' it ironically does not allow residents a patch to cultivate."

"Oh, that's a shame..." trailed off a pensive Jane. She had a furrowed brow as Norma and Ella continued chatting.

"Ella," interrupted Jane with a gleam in her eyes. "How attached are you to the idea of staying in that garden apartment?"

"I signed a six-month lease," answered a puzzled Ella. "I didn't want to commit to anything long term until I had an idea of what it would be like to live in an apartment, after almost fifty years in a private house. Why do you ask, Jane?"

"Uh-oh! Watch out, Ella," exclaimed Norma. "Look at that sparkle in her eyes. Our Jane has one of her ideas again!"

Jane ignored her and spoke directly to Ella. "Ella dear, how would you like to live in my guesthouse after Danny and I finally move into our big house? We're located on an acre of land so we can carve out a little garden for you at the back of the property where the cottage is located. Heck, I don't have a green thumb, so you can plant flowers all over the place! And Huntington has a main station branch of the Long Island Rail Road for your visits to Natalie in New York City, and...." Jane explained in a continuous excited rush.

"Hold on, Jane," said an overwhelmed Ella holding up the palm of her hand in a signal to stop. "What would Danny think of this idea? Shouldn't you discuss it with him first?"

"Danny and I *have* discussed what we want to do with the guest-house," insisted Jane. "We agreed that Danny would refurbish a few things in it, give it a fresh coat of paint and then… rent it out! Why not rent it to someone like you, Ella, whom we love and trust! Danny will adore the idea! And I guarantee you the rent we charge will be a lot less than that garden apartment."

"Won't you need the guest cottage when Pam's and Mark's families visit from Canada?" interjected Norma.

"No, we won't. We never intended to use the cottage for the kids and their families. Our house has five bedrooms and three bathrooms; plenty of space. And if for some reason we need more, Matthew and his wife live close by and have room for the overflow."

Jane finally took a breath then enthusiastically added, "Don't you see, Ella? It will be just perfect! In Huntington, you'll still be fairly close to Nan's house, probably less than a forty-minute car ride. Or if you don't want to drive to her, you can hop on the Huntington train and travel east to her Stony Brook train station. And besides, who do you know in that apartment complex? Over the last two years, Nor has introduced me to all her friends in Huntington. We now have quite a nice group of retirees who do a lot of fun things together. Nor and I will incorporate you right into the mix. We'll have a blast!"

"It sounds good, but I still don't know. I would have to speak with Nan and Natalie. What do you think, Norma?" questioned a dazed Ella.

"Well, Ella, I'm not sure I'm the one to ask," an amused Norma commented. "I'm a selfish person, so, of course, I'd love to have you living close to me... and this crazy one," rolling her green eyes and pointing a finger at Jane.

Norma then grew serious and offered, "Look, Ella, you already have the apartment rented for the next six months. And, Jane, you said you have another month or two before you vacate the guesthouse, and then Danny will need a little time to do the cottage's smartening up. Maybe, Ella, you should live a month or two at the garden apartment complex and see what you think of it before making the decision to move to Huntington."

"I suppose so," replied Ella deep in thought. "Yet, it will be difficult to start over among strangers at the apartment complex. With you two, I will have at least a pair of built-in friends in Huntington."

"Just say yes, Ella," pleaded Jane.

"Jane, I want you to speak again with Danny and tell him of your idea before we make any final decision. And there are many details still to work out as well," stated Ella, attempting to appear business-minded.

Deep down, though, she knew the small cottage on the Flynns' property could be something to make her happy during this next stage of her life.

"Oh, Ella, you'll see. It'll all work out. I know it will," proclaimed Jane grinning like a Cheshire cat. Then, she thought for a minute before she gasped out the words, "Just think of it… the three of us will be together again in the same town. It will be as if coffee klatch never ended!"

ACKNOWLEDGMENTS

During the 1960's and 1970's, I was raised on Long Island in a Levittown neighborhood where, like my novel, everyone knew the names of everyone else. I vividly recall coming home from elementary school and finding my mother wrapping up an afternoon coffee klatch. Back then, I was only concerned with the leftover treats and not with the stories the women of the block could tell. Since then, I have wondered what it was like for those first homeowners when they moved into their new homes on the barren potato fields of Long Island. Where did they come from? How did they cope? Always an avid reader of historical fiction, I have devoured plenty of novels about women's roles during the second world war, but not many stories concentrated on women immediately after the war.

When my husband and I became empty nesters, I finally had the time to attempt to write something to represent these suburban pioneers. Fueled by memories of my parents' original Levitt cape cod and the places on Long Island that I frequented as a child, I started to sketch an outline with fabricated characters and a plot revolving around their insulated fictitious neighborhood. Since I'm not an author by trade, I read everything I could about the process of writing a manuscript and turned to many people for encouragement and guidance. Consequently, I have numerous thank-yous.

As early as 2016 when my book was just an idea, I wrote an email to a local New York author whose two novels I had enjoyed. Like me, Helen Simonson had a late start to writing, and I took inspiration from this shared trait. I questioned how an unknown writer gets published and what my process should be. Helen encouraged me to "put aside questions of publication and devote substantial time to doing the work of writing. Write just for yourself." And I did. Thank you, Helen.

Seven years later, after I completed my manuscript, I give many thanks to another local author, but this time in my new neighborhood in Pennsylvania. Barbara Rubin graciously shared with me her time and publishing knowledge after seeing her own memoir come to print.

The bulk of my gratitude goes to my extraordinary freelance book editor, Anne Brewer. First through a thorough developmental edit and then a careful line edit, Anne helped me tighten my original (and much longer) manuscript and offered her superb advice to extract the best version of my story. Although we are from different generations, Anne immediately understood my five ladies and gave wonderful suggestions to make them stronger characters. I am forever indebted to you, Anne.

Gratitude and love go out to my first reader, my sister Linda. Since you are three years older than me, I counted on your memories of our town and the details of the original Levitt houses that were part of our shared childhood. It was fun reminiscing with you.

Special thanks to my wonderful family (both siblings and in-laws) and my treasured friends who have all furnished support and encouragement during this process… and didn't look at me as if I were crazy when I mentioned, "I'm writing a book."

Finally, a huge thank you and all my love to the three men in my life and my daughter-in-law. To Kevin, Sean and Carolyn: I love the support and laughter you each supply. And to my husband, Steve: I could not imagine traveling through my life without you.

ABOUT THE AUTHOR

Lorrie McCabe grew up in Levittown, New York. After raising a family in another Long Island community, she and her husband retired recently to Bucks County, Pennsylvania. This novel represents her first attempt at writing something larger than an undergraduate capstone project.